THE GAMING HOUSE
Volume Four in the continuing story
of the people of
THE ISLAND

At first she was irritated by O'Ferrall, annoyed at his high-handed arrogance, his air of being a flamboyant adventurer.

Then caution and sanity whispered that it would be better to sell Ravensdowne to him as he wanted, rather than leave it to the raging winds and storms of the Island. She could not stay there any longer. Pregnant widows were vulnerable, especially when they were beautiful – and envied . . .

When the deal was done he took his leave, standing by his carriage, smiling, big. And suddenly she was glad – glad he would be living in the isolated house, glad he would be near her – even if he was an adventurer . . .

Also by Alexandra Manners

The Island Books

ECHOING YESTERDAY
KARRAN KINRADE
THE RED BIRD

and published by Corgi Books

The Gaming House

Volume Four in *The Island* series

Alexandra Manners

CORGI BOOKS

THE GAMING HOUSE

A CORGI BOOK 0 552 12384 6

First publication in Great Britain

PRINTING HISTORY

Corgi edition published 1984

This book is set in Plantin 10/11

Corgi Books are published by Transworld Publishers Ltd.,
Century House, 61-63 Uxbridge Road, Ealing, London W5 5SA

Made and printed in Great Britain by
Hunt Barnárd Printing Ltd., Aylesbury, Bucks.

For GRAHAM HADLEY whose fertile and sadistic imagination matches my own and who has brightened many a Monday morning. Thanks.

PART ONE

Changes

The red kite was flying above the rocks, a huge crimson bird, swooping and plunging. Karran could see it out of the corner of her eye, reminding her of Gideon. But she mustn't think of him. She must get on with her new life as a widow: there'd been enough gossip about herself and Gideon Collister. He'd gone away at her own request to still those wagging tongues.

Catching sight of herself in the dusky mirror, she couldn't restrain a smile. It was a good thing she hadn't had time to go into Port St Mary or Castletown lately. There'd have been enough talk to last the good ladies a year. Karran Howard pregnant and her poor husband dead for months! A parting gift, she'd say, if anyone mentioned the fact outright. A parting gift. Make a joke out of it even though her heart was silently breaking.

Only one letter from Gideon and that full of his sister. Her feyness, her beauty, her dependence on him after the death of the aunt who'd brought her up as if she were the child's mother. Mary Collister wasn't like anyone else made of blood and guts. She was a wraith, a moonbeam, far too exquisitely sensitive to withstand the smallest blow and Gideon was now her strength and protector.

The sight of the black mourning gown depressed Karran. Gideon had liked her in black, had said that she looked like a Spanish lady. She hadn't told him about the coming child. Each time she'd thought of doing so, the pen had grown clumsy in her hand. She'd imagined Mary's delicate, predatory fingers on Gideon's sleeve, the huge, childlike eyes swimming with tears.

Gideon certainly had suffered deeply when he and Mary had been separated so long ago. It had been obvious in the way he spoke of his childhood. The insensitivity of the father, blaming his children for the loss of his wife who'd died at Mary's birth, the possessive aunt who'd coveted the pretty little girl left motherless, Gideon's own loneliness at boarding school and afterwards.

Now Mary had inherited her aunt's wealth and Gideon needn't return to Castletown. He'd be well able to afford a partnership in another firm of solicitors in Glasgow. Mary Collister would wish it and consider it money well spent.

Karran wondered if she'd read too much between the lines. Of course she hadn't. Gideon could have written more often. It wasn't difficult to sense the undertones of apology and regret in his only missive. Each time she'd read it, her heart had plunged to depths of guilt and despair. Still traumatized by John Howard's as yet unexplained death, and the discovery that she was to have a baby, Karran had brooded over the long, unsatisfactory epistle that seemed, on each re-reading, to reinforce the suggestion of Gideon's defection.

Each week she promised herself that she'd answer it, but always balked at the last moment. Every month made the thought of writing harder. He'd send another letter. It would be easier to reply to that.

She'd been almost glad as time passed by and there was still no word from him. Writing to Gideon meant telling him that she carried a child that would almost certainly be his. There'd be the implication that he must do something about a situation that could well be unpalatable to someone of his nature. In retrospect, Karran recognized the fact that Gideon was at his best and most charming while free as that kite in the sky. She shrank from trapping him with unwelcome responsibility. If he loved her well enough, he'd come.

But he hadn't.

The light tap on the door brought Karran back to the present.

'Come in,' she called.

A bonneted head looked into the room. 'You wouldn't rather I went away again?'

'Charlotte! Why should I?'

'I did knock five minutes ago.'

'I'm sorry. I didn't hear.'

'Mrs Quinn told me to come up.'

'Yes, I gave her those instructions. I like to have some warning when it's anyone else.'

Charlotte Costain closed the door and pulled off her bonnet to reveal a head of shining brown hair. Hazel eyes lent character to a small, dark-skinned face that was filled with concern.

'You can't stay in purdah forever, my dear.'

'I know that. Actually, in my present mood, I'd love to drive to Castletown and flaunt myself around the waterside.'

'I'll go with you!' Charlotte's eyes danced.

'Don't encourage me.'

'You wouldn't be the first widow to have a posthumous child.'

'My dear, everyone will imagine they know whose child it is.'

'John's,' Charlotte said promptly and sat down. 'If they're at all decent.'

'After all that chit-chat about Gideon?'

'He put paid to all that by leaving. After a good many hints in the right quarter that there were laws of libel and slander. It was the only thing he could do.'

'Oh, no one will go so far as to actually incriminate themselves after that. He is an advocate, after all. But there's no power on earth that will stop anyone thinking. Looking, condemning—'

'I won't condemn.'

'No, my dear.' Karran lifted her head. 'Thank God for that.'

9

'There's nothing to condemn.'

'Isn't there?'

'You couldn't help John's later instability. There was an unfortunate accident. He suffered brain damage. You weren't to blame for the storm and that falling branch. And I refuse to listen to any more about your own culpability. *Are* you capable of summoning up thunderbolts? Are you, Karran?'

'Put like that—'

'What other way is there?'

'My grandmother had – powers.'

'Hogwash!' Charlotte pronounced forthrightly.

'What did you say?'

Charlotte repeated her prognostication.

Karran laughed suddenly. 'I'm glad you came. Why did you come, incidentally? I wasn't expecting you till Friday.'

'Papa asked me to speak to you,' Charlotte said carefully.

'Oh, why?'

'Remember you said you'd probably sell Ravensdowne as it was difficult to keep staff nowadays?'

'Yes.'

'Well – Cormorant Cottage is for sale. If you want it.'

'So – Gideon's letting it go. I thought he might.' Karran's heart was beating hurtfully. She felt almost suffocated by its strong irregularity. 'He's staying with Mary?'

'Well, it's for the best, isn't it,' Charlotte went on, purposefully practical. 'He can't come back yet to embarrass you. And he's responsible for that sister of his. I never thought to see him responsible for anything or anyone, but he's adopted that yoke with astonishing alacrity. I could despise him for not having accepted another responsibiity with the same enthusiasm!' she finished, hotly.

'He doesn't know,' Karran told her flatly, 'that I'm pregnant. I couldn't bring myself to put pen to paper.'

'Oh, Karran. Shouldn't you tell him?'

'It's obviously never crossed his mind and he seems

content where he is.'

'How can you decide how he'd react?'

'Shackle him? Unwilling? No, my dear. I've had one communication that spoke volumes. He loves it where he is, adores Mary's adulation. Recapturing that lost, regretted childhood to which she, alone, can take him.'

'He'll have to return to normality eventually,' Charlotte pointed out uncomfortably.

'I shan't detach him from that nirvana. Don't you recall how you were cheated? I remember how it felt. We were never children. It's sad to grow up too soon. Let Gideon have his taste of enchantment when it's offered. He'll want more one of these days and so will she. At least, I hope she will, for his sake.'

'But – if he's broken his links with Man?'

'If he has, then nothing has gone deep enough.'

'Something has,' Charlotte observed wickedly.

'Why, Mrs Costain, who'd have suspected you'd be so crude!' Karran's face was pink and she clasped her hands over the small bulge under her gown.

'Anything to bring you back to reality! Your grand-mother's powers! Gideon's ensnarement into a world of fantasy. We're real, you and I, and you deserve better than a man who'd reject you for a parcel of moonbeams. The cottage was only let and still belongs to Papa who's now got so many irons in the fire that he'd like it off his hands. And Bart does love it so. He often talks about it to Rosemary.'

Charlotte's voice changed as she mentioned her daughter's name.

'Have you – heard from Abel?'

'Only once recently. From an accommodation address in Liverpool. He complained peevishly that my jewellery hadn't fetched as much as he'd hoped for, and could I send him more money. The effrontery!'

'And will you?'

'No,' Charlotte said shortly. 'Relent once and I'd never be free of him. I ignored it as I shall any future demands.'

11

'You've made up your mind? You won't have him back?'

'Once bitten, my love. Abel's destroyed any ideas of a second attempt. Anyway, no one's thought fit to bring up the subject.'

'They might if you weren't still legally wed.'

Charlotte's mouth twisted. 'The snares we make for ourselves. It's pathetic!'

'I shouldn't have mentioned him.'

'Why not? I touched on your Achilles heel.'

'I know, we'll have a glass of wine to cheer ourselves. Friends do have the right to probe. Real friends, that is. You're the only person I can talk to about what really matters.'

'Then wine it shall be. Wine and honesty. It's always worked for us.'

The wine ran glinting into the crystal glasses.

'You know George Seyler's in love with you,' Karran said. 'It's a shame you can't make that possible. He'd be just the right husband for you. And it would please your father. He gets on well with George.'

'Papa got on well with Gideon but that didn't make him the right man for you. You need someone strong Karran! You've always picked the dependent ones, needing *your* strength.'

'You could be right.'

'I know I am. Don't let anyone else batten on to you. Promise.'

'How can I make promises like that? In any case, who's going to want to take on a woman in my situation? Be realistic, my dear.'

'I didn't mean at this moment.'

'Just as well. In any case—'

'You've still got Gideon in your blood.'

'It's unfortunate that I'm the faithful type. It takes years for me to switch allegiance.'

'About – Abel.'

'Yes?' Karran studied Charlotte with black eyes grown suddenly serious.

'He'd turn nasty if he knew I wanted my freedom so badly. Better to let sleeping dogs lie. He'll never forgive me for giving him his marching orders.'

'Poor Charlotte. You are in a cleft stick.'

'Both of us. In cleft sticks.'

'Sounds very uncomfortable.' Karren laughed unexpectedly.

'And as Mama is always reminding me, I've no one to blame but myself.'

'Erin! How is she?'

'Much as usual.'

'Oh, dear. That sounds ominous.' Karran smiled secretly. 'But you're lucky having a father like Barney, aren't you. I wonder what I should say to him?'

'About Cormorant Cottage? Why not yes?'

'It's too small. There's Bart, myself and this little unknown quantity.' Karran stroked her stomach reflectively. 'And I'd want to take my loyal Mrs Quinn. Molly Quayle too, if she'd come. She's widowed now and can please herself. She looked after it perfectly while Gideon was there. Such a willing worker. I could manage beautifully with them and one of the girls to help Mrs Quinn. But that's three extra.'

'You could add to the cottage. There's enough ground,' Charlotte suggested.

'I never thought of that. But wouldn't it spoil the symmetry?'

'It needn't. A wing to each side. An outbuilding at the back. It's a lovely position.'

Karran swung her foot so that the soft black leather reflected the glow of the fire. 'I'm terribly tempted. I'm as fond of the place as Bart. It's full of memories, of course. I won't pretend that it isn't.'

'It's a solution, though. Ravensdowne's too large without a man to cope and a large staff—'

13

'Which I can't find at present. All these people leaving—'

'Everyone wanting the excitements of Douglas now that it's beginning to grow.'

'Can't blame them,' Karran said, shrugging. 'It's where the opportunities are. Some of the servants of course, have gone because of all the talk about John's death. I realize that.'

'So, shall I tell Papa you're interested?'

'Yes. I'll advertise the impending sale of Ravensdowne in all the newspapers possible, especially on the mainland. That's how the house was sold last time, to John. Liverpool in particular, I think.'

'I should include Ireland. Cumberland. Scotland. You can see them all from Snaefell.'

'Oh, I shall.'

'Will you miss it?'

'Ravensdowne?' Karran pulled her shawl more closely round elegant shoulders. 'Of course I shall, but I won't sell the bit that was left to me by Laurence. I've never given up the idea of rebuilding there, but I haven't time to do it from scratch. I must have something ready for the baby's birth. But with two children I may need that other piece of land in the future.'

'Why not just admit that you're sentimental about it?'

'Why not? But I'm learning to think like a businesswoman, too. Land's collateral. Anyway I'm certain Laurence meant that land for Bart. He was his father after all.'

'You've got your aunt's at Peel, too, ' aven't you?'

'Yes, but there's a long-term tenant there. It won't come back to me for quite some time yet. Still, three corners of the island, all mine. All with their own value and attraction. Not bad for a farm child with hardly a rag to her back a few years ago.'

'In all the time I've known you, I've never heard you so businesslike. You were the least materialistic person.'

'I was fortunate to have John Howard's protection when

Bart arrived, after Laurence died. But it's different with this new child. I'm on my own. I have to think about my responsibilities. Free of the necessity to worry about this big house, I'll have some time to think of the future and it'll be a comfort knowing that there's more money to tide me over for a bit. Bart needs an education. Adding to the cottage will cost me dearly, I expect, but should I ever want to resell, I won't lose by it.'

'You are changed. Quite—' Charlotte hesitated.

'Businesslike? You've already said that. But I have to be from now on. You have Barney standing at your shoulder. I have no one.'

'Do you think I want that? I'd often give anything for independence.'

'Would you really, Charlotte? Don't you secretly find your father's championship the greatest of comforts?'

'In one way. But Mama constrains me.'

'I do see that Erin could constitute a problem, but Barney can deal with her, can't he?'

'Up to a point.'

'There's always someone to keep an eye on Rosemary. You do have that sort of freedom.'

Charlotte sighed. 'Yes – it's just that there's always somebody – watching.'

'We should change places. Here am I feeling vulnerable, not on my own account, I've always been able to take care of Karran Kinrade! Because of my children. They've no doting grandparents. Not even a father. That's the kind of security that money alone can't give you.'

'Abel's gone.'

'But Rosemary knew him. Her father has reality. I never knew mine. Nor will Bart or this little stranger.'

'You can't know that!' Charlotte objected strongly. 'Gideon might come to his senses at any time. He's bound to remember what you had together. Want it again.'

'But will I?'

'Don't you know?'

Karran shook her head. 'Part of me would certainly

respond if the door suddenly opened and he was standing there. But I can't speak for the rest. The truth of the matter is that Gideon's hurt me.' She looked away and a tightness affected her voice. 'Hurt me very much, Charlotte.'

'Karran—'

'No. Don't say anything. I have to get over him and your sympathy isn't going to help me to do that. Not that I don't appreciate it. But we are never going to speak of Gideon again. I don't expect to see him in the future. And I won't talk about Abel. We've said all there is to say on both subjects.'

Charlotte stood up and reached for her bonnet. 'I expect Papa will come and see you himself.'

'Send Rosemary with him. Bart would be delighted.'

'Yes, I will. And – you'll be all right?' Charlotte tucked a piece of hair under her hat-brim.

'I expect so.'

They embraced, drew apart, walked downstairs together talking about their children, of anything but the lack in both their lives.

'You're taking that child where?' Erin Kerruish's voice was angry.

'You heard me, my dear. Ravensdowne.'

'That woman and her son are bad influences.'

'Rubbish, my dear,' Barney replied calmly. 'Miss Philips! Haven't you got Rosie ready yet!'

Miss Philips's voice floated reedily from the direction of the hall. 'Almost.'

'I'm leaving *now*.'

'Very well, Mr Kerruish.'

'So you are going to override my objections,' Erin said, breathing hard.

'My dear.' Barney smiled. 'You remind me of a dragon. A handsome Irish dragon, all fire and emeralds.'

'You needn't think a bit of soft talk will change my mind. It's a bad idea to get too close to Karran Howard.'

'Charlotte has been close to her for years. You can't have missed that.'

'I've not approved.'

'They don't need our approval, Erin. Both grown women, long ago. Anyway, this is business. I've had a good price offered for the cottage, provided the sale goes through quickly, and ·I'm taking the papers to be approved.'

'You don't have to take my grandchild.'

'Our grandchild. Now listen to me, my dear Erin, and listen very hard. We're not going to squabble over Rosie. I won't have that.'

'What's Karran's hurry, anyway? All this haste to possess something that's too small for her.'

'She means to enlarge the place. The wheels are already in motion.'

'So he's definitely not coming back.' Satisfaction permeated Erin's tones. 'No one's been certain.'

'Collister? No.'

'He really said so?'

'Definitely.'

'And she's saddling herself with building operations here. Well, I always did think Gideon would be as hard to pin down as a bit of quicksilver.'

'That's your trouble, Erin, you think too much. It's none of our business what they choose to do. I admire Karran Howard and always will.'

Erin stared at her husband with a certain disquiet that didn't pass unnoticed.

'And you needn't read anything untoward into that observation,' Barney told her more gently. 'I'm a one-woman man as you very well know, and if you don't know that after all this time, then I must have failed somewhere. Ah, here's Miss Rosie herself. What was the delay?'

'My gloves fell down behind the hall stand, Grandpapa.'

Barney looked at the little, smiling face and muttered. 'Gloves! The puny, unimportant matters women like to fetter themselves with. You aren't cold are you, child?'

17

'No.'

Bemusedly Barney shook his head. 'We'll be off, then. I can't prevail on you to change your mind?' He looked hard at Erin, amusement gone.

'No, you can't. I've more than enough to do today to waste precious time gallivanting.' Erin flounced out of the comfortable, well-furnished room to leave an impression of pulsating discord.

'Grandma's cross.'

'Aye, Rosie. She'll get over it. Come, my little lass, the trap's waiting and it's a fine day.'

It was a beautiful day, the sky a high arc of pure blue, the streets of Castletown shining after yesterday's rain. That same downpour had freshened the grass that had taken on a miraculous greenness. A not unpleasant breeze shivered the grasses and the hedgerow weeds and set them dancing.

Rosemary Costain stared out over the passing scenery with the same absorption she maintained for everything she saw, whether or not it was of any real interest.

Barney noted her promise of beauty, the dark red of her curling hair. Wryly, he conceded that those indiscreetly loud comments that sometimes reached his ears as they travelled together were fully justified. Beauty and the Beast, folk called them. He'd never had any illusions about his own lack of looks. That hadn't mattered too much. And he wasn't such a bad old beast. The thought made him laugh and Rosemary dragged her mind from its almost mechanical recording of country scenes to ask him why he was so cheerful.

'You can see why, surely? The world's so full of exciting things. There's more to it than saying to yourself that's a flower or that's a wall. The flower's the result of a seed blown to that particular spot, fed by the sun and rain and bursting out in a kind of defiant triumph. See what I did against all odds, it says, and the wall grew too, from a mass of irregular stones put together to make a pattern. Something that'll last, something of great use. To keep in animals and to keep out the gales. To mark a man's territory.'

Rosemary couldn't restrain a yawn. Barney laughed ruefully. 'Stony ground, I see. Well, perhaps you're just too young as yet, my love.' He hoped, without conviction, that Rosie's immaturity was the reason for her boredom, and not a basic lack of imagination. Unimaginative folk were inclined to dullness, and it would be a sin if God had made the child so exceptionally good-looking and then given her nothing else to bring those looks alive.

'Tell me about the Shen-ven,' Rosemary suggested, and now her charming face held all the interest Barney could wish. He told her about the fairy in the red cloak who flitted about the stones on the Ridge of Carraghan, and the goose that went with her to hiss at any who came too close. 'Good watchmen, geese, Rosie. Always have been.'

'I think the goose is really a prince.'

'So long as you remember that princes and fays are only tales for distraction, little lass. There's a real world beyond that, one you must learn to live in and cope with.'

'And the Moddey-Doo,' Rosemary begged, ignoring the warning. She had only recently heard the tale of poor Eleanor Cobham, accused by Queen Margaret in the fifteenth century of being a witch and imprisoned in Peel Castle. Somehow she had freed herself but during her flight through the bare glens, the moon gibbering through the black branches of the trees that bordered the watercourses, Eleanor lost her reason and lived for ten years, mad and lonely in a cave by Garwick.

'And when she died she turned into a dog. A great dog who frightened people. So she must have been a witch after all, Grandpa.'

'I've yet to meet anyone who's seen the Moddey-Doo.'

'I know someone!'

'And who's that, child?'

Rosemary retreated into a knowing silence that she broke only when the trap approached the drive into the grounds of Ravensdown. 'They say Mrs Howard's a witch,

19

like her grandmother before her. That she can ill-wish folk—'

'Who says?' Barney was angry now.

'I – forget.'

'Lies are wrong, Rosie.'

'People do say it,' she persisted.

'But you haven't forgotten who. Don't let me catch you repeating such nonsense again, my girl.'

'No, Grandpa.'

The dark tunnel of the drive enclosed them in green mystery until, turning a bend, it was as though a giant hand had torn a hole in the dimness and let the light pour through. Barney's spirits rose at the sight of that strong white glow: it seemed a good omen. Perhaps his life was on an upsurge. Erin might learn tolerance. Charlotte could find happiness.

The trap burst out of the green obscurity into the brilliance that surrounded the big house on the cliff. The sea lapped around the rocks below and the black cormorants preened long, sinuous necks and spread their wings to shed the sea-water like diamonds.

Pigs might fly, Barney thought ruefully. Erin wouldn't change. Charlotte's intricate nature wouldn't allow content. A blink of sunlight changed nothing. And he'd been preaching to Rosie about facing up to reality! Even a cynic like himself could be diverted by a touch of magic.

Mrs Quinn let them in, ushering the visitors into the morning-room where a fire burned cheerfully. Barney straddled the hearth, warming his backside under raised coat-tails. The clock ticked inexorably. Never before had Barney been conscious of the passing of time. He shook himself free of the unwelcome realization that he was growing old.

The sight of Rosemary wandering round the room, touching ornaments and writing equipment, reminded him of the day Erin had visited him in Castletown with her youngest child, Sebastian. While Erin had told him about her husband's imprisonment for smuggling, the boy had toddled about, enjoying just what Barney's granddaughter was finding so compulsive, the pleasure of laying hands on another person's treasures.

'Don't do that, Rosie! Those are Mrs Howard's things. Come away from the inkwell.'

Karran came into the room, unseen until he heard the silken rustle of her skirts. 'How good of you to come so quickly.' She had a lovely voice, he thought.

Studying her, he saw why the matter of the cottage was so urgent.

'I see you understand. But you'll keep my secret, won't you, just a bit longer. The servants are quite loyal, thank God. They won't gossip.'

'I wouldn't have said anything. It's not my place or my way.'

'Do I sense a reproof? Then let me make amends. You don't want anything so tediously feminine as tea. Is it too early for a measure of whisky?'

He shook his head, recognizing at last the real reason for Erin's dislike of Karran. Karran exuded quality. Both had started their lives in impoverished circumstances, but Karran's inborn strength of character stamped her with an integrity that made her a lady in spite of her frailties.

Erin remained what she'd always been. Not all her aping of those she secretly considered her betters could make her what she so ardently wished. It was very sad. Barney thought he'd never loved Erin more than in that moment of discovery.

Karran produced the whisky, and, looking round for Rosemary, found that the little girl was no longer there. No prizes for guessing that she was with Bart.

Barney drank his measure and spread out the papers appertaining to the transfer of property. Karran sat down at the desk and studied them. Barney watched her, admiring her carriage and the elegance of her white neck, made paler still by the high-collared black gown with the pearl brooch to relieve its severity. There were small pearls in her ear-lobes. Most women would have worn sharply-faceted jet as a sop to their consciences, but Karran was honest enough to cast off overmuch convention and please herself.

She smoothed the papers when she'd finished reading. There was a ring with a single pearl on the third finger of her right hand, and its pale lustre echoed the colour of her skin. 'This seems perfectly satisfactory. I'll get the builders to start the first wing immediately and the extension to the rear. They've promised to engage some extra labour. I'll leave the original much as it is. Did – did Gideon say what's to happen to his belongings? Does he want them sent on?'

'He didn't mention the furniture. He took away some bric-a-brac, china and the like.'

'Some of his pieces are quite valuable.'

'I'll ask him if he wants them sold or put in store.'

'I – I'd take them for a fair price. But I'd prefer it if you didn't tell him that I'm the buyer. He's bound to find out sometime but I'd rather it wasn't now.'

'Very well.' Barney said, and, aware of Karran's increased pallor, felt quite angry with Gideon. The man was a fool to put small value on such an asset. He was behaving like a bull in a china-shop, oblivious of this woman's wounded feelings.

'We'll seal the bargain,' Karran said, lifting her head proudly, like a dark swan. 'It's a great load off my mind.'

'Where's my little baggage?' Barney asked, suddenly missing Rosemary.

'She knows where to find Bart. She's been here with Charlotte.'

'Oh, yes, Charlotte.' Barney thought that Karran must know more of the inner workings of his daughter's mind than anyone alive. *He* couldn't fathom her!

'To Charlotte.' Karran raised her glass.

'Not – to Cormorant Cottage?'

'To them both.'

The glasses clinked companionably and the sun found its way inside the window, spilling its gold across the papers on the desk.

'Don't let all those old harpies embitter you. I'd not like to see you spoiled, Karran.'

'So, they are still talking. As if I didn't know!'

'They don't matter, not in the long run.' Barney was growing expansive.

'It isn't for myself that I mind. It's for Bart and – the other.'

'A pity John didn't live to see his child.' He raised his glass again.

'How staunch you Kerruishes are. And it's encouraging to know that the next generation may be even more friendly. There's a great bond between our children. I hope it lasts.'

'Folks change,' Barney was impelled to say. 'Sometimes I think Rosie has a deal too much of Abel in her. Quite a lot of Erin as well. She seems – unstable. One minute she's incapable of imagination, the next she has too much of it, the wrong kind.'

'How odd. That's almost how I'd have described my son if you'd asked me. He seems his grandfather to the life from all I've found out about Luke Karran.'

'Well, there's little wrong with you, my dear.' Barney drained the glass and clapped Karran on the shoulder. A pity that such a beautiful and desirable woman must spend the next years occupied with a couple of children. But he was no longer angry with Gideon. There was nothing else Gideon could have done to preserve Karran's good name. Yet, he should have left her some hope.

'Nothing wrong!' Karran laughed. 'You can't mean it.'

'You've too kind a heart.'

'No. I'm weak in certain respects. I have to admit it.' She was unbending too.

'You're a woman. I've always thought there's nothing much amiss with a female who behaves like one. Doesn't hold back on the important things between man and woman.'

'Well, no one could accuse me of that. Yet I've been

indiscreet, and indiscretion leaves rather undesirable legacies for others. That's my only regret.'

'Karran—'

'But I've learnt my lesson. No more.' She toyed with the pearl brooch at her throat.

'So you'll put on armour and devote your life to good works?'

'Something like that. More whisky?'

'No thanks, I've Rosie to get back home safely. But I'm willing to bet that you'll never be able to keep that resolve.'

'Oh, yes, I will.'

'Twenty guineas?' Barney suggested, grinning.

'Really! You're incorrigible. I'm glad your wife can't hear you.'

'So am I! But I know I'm right. I trust you to let me know if I've won.'

'I wonder why I can talk so easily to you and Charlotte and find it so difficult with others?'

'It's my fatal charm.'

'And whisky in the morning, I suspect.'

'Probably. Now, where's my granddaughter? Rosie. Rosie!'

Rosemary and Bart were at the bottom of the old orchard. The trees were crouched and took on strange shapes, the bark hidden under an encrustation of sage green lichen. They made satisfactory serpents and dragons and more than once, a backdrop for Atlantis after Bart had discovered a mention of the submerged city in a book in the library.

Rosemary had been jealous of Bart's ability to read. 'Why can't I?' she'd demanded.

'Mama says I'm very quick.'

'I want to be quick too.'

'My mother reads to me.'

'So does mine.' She'd been petulant.

'You're younger,' Bart had pointed out.

'Yes. That must be why.' Rosemary was satisfied that there really was a good reason for her lack. But every now and again that resentment revisited her and she felt the need to show herself to be as good as he.

'I can read now,' she boasted today under the most Caliban-like of the ancient apple-trees.

Bart stared, suitably impressed. 'That *was* quick!'

'It was a book about plants and country things.' And Rosemary reeled off, almost verbatim, her grandfather's dissertation on flowers and stone-walling.

'That's very good,' Bart told her. 'There are new worlds in books. Once you've started to read, you need never be lonely. You just open the pages and you go wherever you want. I'd like to hear you reading out loud—'

'I'll show you how a flower grows,' Rosemary said hastily and performed a strange, compelling dance under the lichened branches, her small body weaving to and fro like the blown seed, then pressed flat against the stony ground, rising slowly, reproducing the movements of the gradually unfolding leaves and lengthening stem, smiling as she reached full height so that her face indeed echoed the triumphant perfection of the flower.

Bart watched her lazily, only half-convinced that she'd spoken the truth, yet captivated by her grace and invention.

Rosemary, in spite of the pleasure she took in her ability to mime, felt a little sick and cheated. *She* wanted new worlds. One day Bart might escape her because of her own stupidity. She couldn't allow that to happen. Bart was hers.

'We'd better go back,' she said, sensing his doubts. 'Grandpa will be looking for me. Grandmama said we mustn't be late for lunch.'

'When are you coming with your mother?'

'Friday. It's always Friday. You can't have forgotten!'

'Every day seems the same when we aren't at school,' Bart explained. 'This isn't like Castletown.'

'It'll be quieter still when you go to the cottage.'

'I like it there. This house reminds me of John Howard.'

'Didn't you like him?' Rosemary trod on a rotten stick.

It fell apart slimily.

'You know I didn't.'

'You've got your hate mask on.' She rubbed the side of her boot on some grass to clean it.

'I did hate him. And now it seems as if he's still here. Watching me.'

Rosemary shivered. 'Like – a ghost?'

'It *is* his ghost. First there's a smell of candle-wax, then the bedclothes rustle—'

'Don't! I shan't sleep!' Her voice rose shrilly.

'He wants his medicine. He holds out his hand—'

'Mama says there aren't such things as ghosts.' Rosemary tried to crush her panic.

'Your mother doesn't know everything. There's a place at the Chasms where I know someone died. No one told me. But when I walk past it I feel that someone wants me to go off the path. There's a sort of whispering and sometimes it's just as if a hand touched my hair—'

'You're pretending, just to scare me!'

Bart shook his head, and, in the green dimness under the hunched, dead orchard trees, Rosemary thought his black eyes looked like the holes people said existed under the gorse and heather on the cliff-top on the way to Spanish Head. The Chasms were awful places. You died if you stayed there.

She began to run back the way they'd come, tendrils of mahogany-coloured hair snagged on the crumbling twigs. But she remembered what Bart said about Mr Howard's medicine. Grandmama had told them that John Howard had given himself too much of his draught because he was unhappy living with Bart's mother. Perhaps he hadn't taken it himself. Maybe someone helped.

How strange Bart was at times. She'd never want to walk to Spanish Head again in case an invisible hand touched *her* hair. Legends were exciting but things that happened to real people could be equally terrible. Dimly, Rosemary perceived what her grandfather had meant. Howard's ghost was infinitely more dreadful than the

Moddey Doo or the Shen-ven.

Breathless and distressed, she let herself into the house and returned quietly to the morning-room. Grandpa was touching Mrs Howard's shoulder and laughing. There was a sharp smell of yellowish spirits. They were talking about money and something that Grandmama mustn't know.

Mrs Howard smiled when Grandpa said something about his fatal charm. Fatal things killed, Rosemary thought and shuddered again.

'Ready for going home,' Grandpa asked eventually, noticing her presence.

Her hand was taken inside his large warm comforting one. 'I'm ready,' she said, and quite suddenly and thankfully, felt safe again. Almost safe—

PART TWO

The Buyer

'It's another of them,' Mrs Quinn told Karran almost apologetically. 'He's in the study.'

'Which one is it?' Karran picked up the hairbrush and drew it reflectively over the front and sides of her thick hair. She was wearing the high-waisted dress that allowed gentle folds to part-conceal her condition. It really was quite flattering till she stood sideways.

'A Mr O'Ferrall.'

'Let me guess. Could it be the gentleman from Dublin?'

'Why, yes. How did you know?'

Karran giggled involuntarily. 'Perhaps his name had something to do with it?'

'Very skittish we are today,' Mrs Quinn said in a governessy tone that almost threatened tears before the day was out.

'I'd go mad if I couldn't laugh now and again. All shapes and sizes they've been. Every age-group you could mention. Any colour under the sun. And they've all fallen in love with the place but it's too expensive or too isolated, too difficult to run. It's hysteria, my dear Quinn.'

'Aye. You've borne up well but I can see your patience is wearing thin. Being as you are doesn't help. You must lie down after he's gone. Put your feet up.'

'I've got to sell it this time! That building's coming on marvellously fast at Black Rocks but I have to pay for it soon. All that Irish labour. It would be fitting if the visitor from Dublin were to pay for it, don't you think? Find Bart

28

and clean him up for me just in case he breaches the citadel. He's very curious about this procession of men. He won't be the only one. Perhaps the "ladies" imagine I've started up a high-class brothel.' Karran laughed again with a touch of desperation.

'Don't ever let me hear you talk like that again!' Mrs Quinn put her arms akimbo and glared at her mistress, red-cheeked.

'I told you. I'm at the end of my tether. I'll go to the study.'

Mrs Quinn tutted a couple of times and bustled kitchenwards. She was a tower of strength, Karran thought, going in the opposite direction. Quietly she slid into the study. It looked empty at first sight but a further scrutiny revealed a motionless figure in the window embrasure.

Karran's heart-beats quickened. Something about the long, lounging body encased in dark clothing of expensive cut reminded her of Gideon Collister. She pressed a hand against her heart.

For a long minute she watched him, wishing for yet fearing the moment that he turned towards her. When he did, the face was unfamiliar, well-bred but containing the beginnings of impatience, then a dawning interest.

'*You* are Mrs Howard?'

'I am.'

'Then you know I'm O'Ferrall.' It was as though he'd announced he was the King. She had a compulsion to giggle.

'I do,' she replied gravely, stifling the impulse.

They took stock of one another. He was attractive, Karran decided, but she'd need to keep her wits about her. It was difficult to deduce what he thought, now that the faintly interested expression had reverted to one of studied stillness. He'd probably make a good poker player.

'You must have received my references,' O'Ferrall ventured coolly.

'Yes, indeed I did.'

'So you'll know my money's as good as my word.'

She couldn't resist the opening. 'And just how good is your word?'

'It's never been doubted. Not so far.' A flicker of irritation passed over his face.

Karran composed her own features. Demurely she said, 'A woman must keep a cool head in business matters. You may be well known in Dublin circles, Mr O'Ferrall, but I have been visited by so many strangers that I've had to learn caution. Most had no references whatsoever and looked quite put out when I pointed out this fact. Some had smudged papers signed by arthritic spiders. Very unsatisfactory.'

'You couldn't truthfully suggest that mine were so lacking?'

He toyed with the knob of his elegant cane, avoiding her amused eyes.

Karran tried to regain her sense of caution. Even if the Irishman did have an inflated sense of his own importance, she must ward against antagonizing him. She didn't for a moment doubt that was exactly what he appeared. Yet some devil of impishness had entered her and she would find it hard to remain as level-headed as would be judicious.

Mr O'Ferrall was obviously not unaware of her continued diversion. 'You know, Mrs Howard, you really should treat the matter with greater seriousness. It's not a dozen eggs you're trying to sell.'

'I'm perfectly aware of that. I suppose this is the reaction one could expect after the rigours of the last weeks, since Ravensdowne went on the market.'

'Deuced if I know how to take you.'

'Suppose you look on me merely as a widow who must sell her home.'

'I wasn't expecting anyone so young,' Mr O'Ferrall said frankly.

'And all your prepared speeches are to be wasted. What a pity.'

He tapped the top of his boot with the silver-headed cane. 'This interview isn't going at all as planned.' Obviously he was beginning to look on her as an irresponsible child.

'Perhaps we should start again.' Karran motioned towards one of the leather chairs that flanked the hearth. 'Do sit down, Mr O'Ferrall. Would you care for some refreshment? Wine?'

'Oh, no you don't! Get me at a disadvantage and I'll get the worst of the bargaining. We'll keep the wine for later.' He smiled thinly. 'I prefer to keep a clear head.'

Karren sat in the opposite chair. 'Mr O'Ferrall, I've seen a great variety of would-be buyers for Ravensdowne, most of whom took me to be a naïve countrywoman, helpless and alone in the world. Let me assure you now that it's a fallacy. I have an asset and I've taken advice on its worth. Have I made myself plain?'

'Indeed, you have.' Mr O'Ferrall's cool eyes had descended to the gathers under Karran's waistband. She could read the speculation in them.

'You must have seen sufficient on your way here to form some sort of opinion of the grounds and exterior of the house.'

'Sufficient.'

'And you'd have to agree that you'd not find a better setting anywhere?'

'Agreed.'

'Then, knowing that I don't intend to drop my price very readily, you do still wish to see the interior?'

'I didn't come all this way to be put off so easily.'

'I speak plainly because I've at least two others—'

'Fighting for the place?' Mr O'Ferrall smiled blandly. 'The devil you have!'

'They've both made good offers. There's a good deal of land. It's worth far more than the house.'

'Don't expect me to outbid them. I too have made enquiries. I also have a figure in my head beyond which I've no intention of going. I've other properties on my list.

Oh, I admit the outlook seawards is little short of miraculous but for my purposes that hardly matters.'

'Indeed? And what purposes had you in mind?' She was curious.

'Nothing I'd wish to reveal at this stage,' Mr O'Ferrall said smoothly.

Damned adventurer, Karran thought, then wondered why she'd formed such an impression with so little foundation. He wasn't really flamboyant. Arrogant, there could be little doubt of that, and set on having his own way. And he'd seen through her faintly desperate mention of the fictitious rivals for the ownership of Ravensdowne. Not that she must allow him to know he was right. She began to wish she'd not been so flippant.

'I'll have my factor accompany you—'

'Have no fears, Mrs Howard. The silver will be perfectly safe.'

'I'll treat that as a joke,' she said coldly. 'You've probably noticed I'm not equipped for too much wandering upstairs and downstairs. Brand knows all the history of the place. All its advantages and disadvantages. Nothing will be kept from you. My husband was a careful man and maintained the property in good order.'

'We shall see for ourselves,' Mr O'Ferrall said maddeningly. The royal prerogative irked.

Karren rang the bell for Brand and watched the two men leave. She wanted to sell the house but did she want to part with it to the infuriatingly self-opinionated Irishman? Sanity whispered that it would be better to see O'Ferrall installed here than for the big house to lie empty and unproductive, dampness spoiling the hangings and expensive wallcoverings. Pregnant widows were particularly vulnerable and islands were chancy places, at the mercy of wind and weather. Not everyone could stand the loneliness, the sensation of being cut off from the bustling vitality of the mainland. Why did O'Ferrall want the place? The sane reason would be business. Or perhaps he'd become engaged to an heiress over in Douglas and it was his fiancée who had delusions of grandeur. There weren't that many available mansions on Man. Most passed on from generation to generation. But surely he'd have brought his fiancée with him?

Karren went on walking the floor and fidgeting until she heard the unmistakable sounds of returning footsteps. Brand left the visitor at the door. Karran sat down again, composing herself.

'Come in, Mr O'Ferrall.'

The tall figure lowered itself into the buttoned chair opposite. Karran was suddenly nervous. She waited for him to speak.

'As you said, it's well-maintained.'

'Oh, I already knew that! Is it adequate for your purpose?'

'Well—'

'Come, Mr O'Ferrall, don't let's be coy. You're astute and I'm no fool. Is it what you want?'

'It could be.'

'At your price, you mean. And what is that?'

The figure he mentioned was lower by five hundred guineas than that of the valuation.

'I'm sorry. I'd never agree to that. I have a child – children dependent on me. My husband didn't leave as much as everyone thinks.'

'It can't be easy being in your position.' Again he studied her. 'Wouldn't you be well advised to think about my offer? You have an advocate to advise you.'

'I'll think about it.' Karran stood up. She felt tired now and disinclined to haggle. Let him have time to realize what he could be missing if he dragged his feet too long. It was reasonably certain that he approved of the house inside and out.

'Is that what you said to the others?' O'Ferrall asked slyly.

'Others?' She dragged her mind back to what he was saying.

He laughed. 'Never mind. I'll be in touch. If I decide to

33

go on with the matter, that is.'

'You must please yourself.' She'd been stupid. Men like the Irishman didn't like to be made fun of, however discreetly.

'Oh, I shall, Mrs Howard. I usually do.'

Her eyes kindled and she knew that he was aware of her repressed anger. Did it really matter if he dropped the business altogether? Of course it did! There were no other buyers and soon she must pay for all that quite satisfactory labour at Black Rocks. She was getting tired of the burden she carried and must conserve her energies for the removal and for the birth of her child.

She had a fleeting and most disturbing image of a slender, dark young woman with Gideon's eyes, standing where O'Ferrall had been.

'Are you all right, Mrs Howard?' O'Ferrall's voice was kinder now, yet still with undertones of repressed irritation. The image of the girl had gone. He remained. Karran felt faint.

'Of course I am.' But how she longed to obey Mrs Quinn, to lie on her own bed with the breeze lifting the curtains, the sound of the gulls as they skimmed past the window. Who was that ghost from the past? Or was she the future?

Raising tired eyes to meet his, she surprised a look of unwilling respect.

'You'd best not be too long in thinking things over,' she warned, smiling with an effort. 'You could find the house whisked away from under your nose! I've a feeling you wouldn't care for that. I should want at least five hundred guineas more than you mentioned.'

Mr O'Ferrall laughed abruptly.

'You may laugh! I'm perfectly serious.'

'I doubt whether you'll be seeing me again if that's the case.'

'There are as good fish in the sea as came out of it,' Karran said composedly. 'As I told you, I'm not without other prospects, whatever you care to believe.'

'But can they pay now? Think of all the delays there might be, not to mention the pressing bill with the builder you must settle before long.'

Her eyes flew open, black as a shock of winter water. 'You *have* been busy.'

'It's as well to know all the facts about someone with whom you have business dealings.'

'So it seems,' she remarked distantly, recognizing his irony. 'Well, good day to you, Mr O'Ferrall. You know my terms. If you don't wish to meet them I'll not expect to hear from you again.' Karran tugged the bell-pull viciously. Her head had begun to ache.

'Anyone else would have used the same caution.' He rubbed salt in the wound as he smiled.

'Indeed?' She shrugged. 'It's really of little consequence. Oh, there you are, Brand. Will you show this gentleman out, please?'

'Another two hundred and fifty,' Mr O'Ferrall offered shamelessly.

Karran's heart leapt. He *was* keen. She'd get the full amount sooner or later.

'See Mr O'Ferrall out,' she told Brand remotely.

A brief look of fury drove the coolness from O'Ferrall's eyes.

'Good day,' she said and smiled in her turn.

'Good day,' he murmured and bowed with chilly politeness.

The room seemed very empty after he'd gone but Karran was curiously rejuvenated. She'd swear he was ready to take the bait. But why did he want the house? It seemed unfair that he knew so much of her affairs and that she knew nothing about his own.

She was swept with a giant lethargy. Even if he didn't offer the full amount she was too tired to battle further. No one else was going to reply to those advertisements and she wanted the matter settled. She'd have preferred someone likeable to have purchased the place but time was passing too quickly. Her new life beckoned. O'Ferrall had won.

There was a light tap at the door.

'Who is it?'

'Brand, Ma'am. Mr O'Ferrall left this.' He handed her a folded sheet of paper. 'Insisted he must see you again but I said you were tired and would be resting. So he wrote a note in the morning-room.'

She opened the paper.

'Mrs Howard,

    I've no time for fancy games so I'm agreeing to your ridiculous price. I've heard of the immovable object and the irresistible force, you see! Perhaps, in recompense, you'd come and dine with me later, when you are not so fully occupied?

Yours,

O'Ferrall.'

'Will that be all, Ma'am?'

'Yes, thank you.'

Karran went to the window and stared down at the gravelled drive. The infuriating man was standing by the small carriage looking up at her, his head on one side in an attitude of enquiry, lips faintly smiling.

She made him wait for her final nod of acceptance.

He'd returned later, bringing with him a pleasant young person called Tom Allen. O'Ferrall called Allen his right-hand man and together they came on tours of inspection. Tom Allen would take measurements and sometimes he'd raise his red head and smile engagingly at Karran, or exchange conversation with Bart who liked to be present on these occasions.

Karren became certain that her son couldn't wait to shake the dust of Ravensdowne from his well-shaped and growing feet.

The first wing of Cormorant Cottage was completed just before the baby arrived. Karran was pleased with the large sitting-room that ran the full length of the ground floor, the sea visible from both front and side. Above it were the two new bedrooms, not large and grand like the ones at Ravensdowne, but cosy and easily warmed and certainly roomier than the ones in the original building. Mrs Quinn and Molly Quayle would have two of those and Lizzie, the maid, the smaller of the attics. Two doors knocked out of the outside walls allowed full access.

There would be a good deal more space once the other wing was ready for occupation. The long ground-floor room would become a dining-room, above it a bathroom and a guest room. In the meantime they'd eat in the parlour that used to be Gideon's. Karran had kept the extending table and the purplish press, the corner cupboard and chairs. In place of the Chinese elephants she arranged a pair of antique vases and a small French clock from the big house, but still she regretted the departure of the original ornaments which had cast their lifelike shadows against the white wall. Just as she missed the man who'd owned them.

'You'll have to change the name of the place, Ma'am,' the builder told her when he inspected the walls of the new portion of the house. 'It won't be a cottage any more.'

'It certainly won't. Is everything dry enough for painting?'

'Perfectly. Keep the fires going, though, and no papering yet, mind.'

'Oh, I like paint. A self-colour makes the rooms look bigger. You see the portraits better. I never cared for fussiness.'

Brand took charge of a family of decorators from Castletown, standing over them so that they had no chance to shirk, while young Brand kept an eye on the workmen busy with the extension at the rear. The painting of the wainscots and ceilings was finished in a week, the walls and doors in another two. The white, eau-de-nil and sand colours were very pleasing. New curtains had already been made by a woman in Port St Mary and the figured brocade lent richness to the rooms' simplicity.

'The sun and sea'll get at those,' Mrs Quinn said darkly as she helped to hang them.

Karran laughed. 'You think I'm doing the wrong thing, don't you?'

'I think you may regret it, Ma'am.' Mrs Quinn tied a bundle of forest green folds back with a silken rope and stood back to survey the effect.

'What else could I do? Mr Howard never discussed his finances and people, including myself, assumed that there was a bottomless well. After his death I discovered this to be untrue. These curtains are my only extravagance.'

'You'll miss Ravensdowne more than you think. There's drawbacks here. Winter—'

'It's a bit further to the village but we'll manage. We're closer to Castletown than we were. Bart will like that. And there's the carrier.'

'It's not going to be very peaceful for you and the baby, though. All that to-ing and fro-ing, banging and hammering.'

'But think how convenient everything will be once the conversion's finished.'

'You can't call it Cormorant Cottage after all that.'

'That's what Mr Bayley said. Well, what's wrong with Cormorant House?'

'Doesn't sound – right. Names of places and ships shouldn't be changed. It's bad luck.'

Karran looked at the housekeeper searchingly. 'You do want to come, don't you?'

'Of course!' Mrs Quinn sounded indignant. 'I go where you go and that's a fact. But I know you'll get hankerings.'

'I'll just have to subdue those. I think this is the last of the curtains. You've done them very well. There's an art in the hanging.'

'H'mm.' But Mrs Quinn looked pleased in spite of her obvious misgivings.

'The two Brands are supervising the removal from Ravensdowne of some of the more essential furniture tomorrow. Mr O'Ferrall will keep the rest.'

'Well, I hope that includes a bed, Ma'am. After all the liberties you've been taking, I fully expected you to be requiring one long before this.'

'There's time yet.' Karran patted her stomach, undismayed.

But there wasn't. Almost as soon as the bed was set up, Karran was seized by pains and an anxious Mrs Quinn was airing the mattress and sheets so that her mistress might give birth without getting rheumatic fever into the bargain.

'Should have happened sooner,' she told the builder who volunteered to ride for the doctor. Karran had kept up the fiction lately that the child was overdue though it was no one else's business.

Lying in torment, she saw the red kite in the sky and was riven afresh by the pain of Gideon's defection. It was fitting that the child should be born here where it had been conceived with such memorable passion.

'Gideon,' she whispered, remembering the day he'd given the kite to Bart. Surely that was the day this child began its being? Perhaps he'd not written again because of her own silence, interpreting that as indifference.

Closing her eyes she concentrated on the business of effecting its safe delivery, aware of the arrival of Dr Gresham and of Mrs Quinn's departure to ensure that plenty of hot water was available, glad that Bart was occupied away from the precincts of the house.

It was not so traumatic a birth as her son's had been.

'You have a daughter,' Dr Gresham said as he lifted the child and held her up to show Karran.

She was dimly aware of the narrow body, of damp, dark hair that clung to the contours of a well-shaped head, a tiny starfish hand that seemed to move towards her. Beyond the figures of the doctor and infant, gulls swooped past the window uttering sad cries. A black depression swept over her. She'd never felt so abandoned.

The baby was placed in a drawer, the cot not yet having been delivered. Brand would be fetching it, and some of the layette, later.

'She's a bonny little thing,' Mrs Quinn said after the doctor had gone. 'What will you call her, ma'am?'

'I'm not sure.' Tears had begun to gather in Karran's eyes. She was aware of her own weakness and fought against it.

'Little Miss Howard,' Mrs Quinn said, and tucked in a corner of the sheet that covered the child. 'That'll have to do for the present.'

Bart was allowed in briefly before Karran settled down to sleep. He stared at the quiet bundle in the drawer without speaking.

'Well?' Mrs Quinn prompted. 'What do you think of your sister?'

'I like Rosemary better. I can talk to her.'

'She won't always be so small.'

'She'll always be a long way behind. She'll never catch up.'

'That sounds very logical to me,' Karran told him tiredly and smiled at last.

'You'll have to look after her, then,' Mrs Quinn said. 'You're the man of the house now that poor Mr Howard's gone.'

'Am I really?' Bart sounded more interested. 'Am I the man of the house, Mama?'

'Yes.'

'So you see, Master Bart, you've to look after both of them.'

'Will I always be?'

'I expect so,' Karran replied.

'Your mother's going to rest now. She's tired.' Mrs Quinn took Bart away to be fed and distracted in the old part of the house.

Alone with the baby girl, Karran thought of Bart's expression as he'd looked down at his half-sister. It was not a look that she welcomed. She'd seen it before when John was alive, resentful and a little frightening. Bart had detested John as much as John had disliked Bart towards

40

the end, when he was ill and hatefully changed.

She wondered when her life would run its course free of animosity and warped emotions, but could see no end to her problems. Chiding herself for the weakness, she hoped with all her heart that it was merely transient.

The child moved in its exhausted sleep and gave a little sigh.

'You feel it, too,' Karran whispered. Leaning over the tiny girl's temporary bed she tried to discern the small features, but there was little to be seen but the curve of a pale cheek, the smoky darkness of hair and eyelash.

She tried to push away the feeling of bitterness that Gideon seemed not to care. Surely someone must have informed him of her condition? It was unrealistic of her to imagine that such a secret could be kept indefinitely. But he'd made it so plain before he went that he'd take action against any spiteful gossip about their relationship that it would take courage for anyone to write, telling him that Mrs Howard was with child. He could construe that as a veiled accusation. If he did find out, would he come?

Don't be a fool, she told herself angrily. Forget him. The child had a name and an identity. She'd be John Howard's daughter and no one could prove otherwise. But it hurt! How it hurt. Yet it could be entirely her own fault for not having replied. He might have taken that neglect as a severing of relations.

If he'd really loved her he'd have tried again! If—

Charlotte arrived with flowers that brightened some of the gloom of a wet day. Leaning over the cot which had arrived the day before, she inspected the tiny face against the lace-trimmed pillow. 'She's lovely.'

'She'll be tallish and slender,' Karran said.

'You seem very sure.'

'She's quite long. Narrow. Not the usual baby shape.'

'So far she doesn't look like anyone in particular.'

'Lucky, isn't it!'

'You're not – bitter?'

'A little, perhaps.'

41

'How has Bart accepted the new arrival?'

Karran grimaced and moved into a more comfortable position. 'He hasn't. I know Bart. Being naturally secretive, he can hide a great deal, but his expression spoke volumes.'

'That's a pity.'

'I feel I can never leave them together.'

'He's with Rosemary at present. She's desperate to catch up with her reading at the moment. He's so much better than she is. All of us, including Papa, must teach her endlessly. She's been able to write her name for some time but she got stuck after that. So many other pleasurable distractions! Now, she's so keen to improve. Amazing what a bit of competition will achieve.'

'She's very intelligent.'

'I wonder sometimes if it's the right sort of intelligence. She's got Abel's and Mama's blood in her, both of them devious. However, we won't dwell on that. What's your darling's name?'

'I was going to call the baby John. It was the least I could do. Now, I can't decide. There's nothing really like John for a girl. Is there?'

'Oh, I don't know. Jane, Josephine, Joanne—'

'There's her great-grandmother. Johanne. If anyone could protect her from Bart, she could.'

Charlotte sat up. 'The one with the powers?'

Karran nodded.

'But she's *his* great-grandmother too!'

'That's why it might be a good idea. Apparently Johanne and Luke were thick as thieves. If Bart is a small replica of Luke—'

'Karran! Call the baby Johanne by all means, but forget all about that old witchcraft nonsense, for goodness sake.'

'I've decided. She'll be Johanne Howard. It's near enough to be a tribute to the old John I loved, and it's a family name. A dark tribute, I suspect, but *she* could keep the children apart. Stop them from destroying one another.'

'What strange talk, Karran. You're only emotional from

the effects of childbirth. That's all. Most women have a husband to prop them up at such times—'

'And I don't. I expect you're right.'

'What about our usual panacea? Or isn't it advisable?'

'Yes. Let's have a small sherry. I feel distinctly in need of it.'

Charlotte fetched two modest glasses and the decanter.

'To Johanne.'

'Johanne. God bless her.'

The rain drove against the window, suddenly strong and hostile.

'Oh, dear!' Charlotte said. 'Perhaps your intuition's better than my scepticism. And the child now has her eyes wide open, as though she's listening.'

'So long as she doesn't cry just yet.'

Johanne didn't, just lay and stared at the lacy hangings on the carved cot, occasionally raising a small hand as though to fight off the world.

'And what of O'Ferrall? The new lord of Ravensdowne?'

'I haven't seen him recently. There have been letters, of course, and papers to be signed. He's a law unto himself.'

'Good-looking, I heard.'

'The Irish race is handsome. You should know that. It's all in the bone structure. But looks aren't everything. Your father's a living reminder of that. I'd rather know him and have him as a friend than a thousand O'Ferralls.'

'I wonder why he chose Perwick? Why not Douglas or Castletown?'

'He didn't say, just intimated that the house was suitable. It was obvious he didn't want to let it go without a fight.'

'Yet you said he weakened eventually.'

'I was – unexpectedly firm.'

'I wish I'd seen you! This house is going to look rather well once it isn't so lop-sided. They've been very clever, co-ordinating the line of the roof and putting upper windows in the old part to match the new.'

'Mama.' A small voice broke into the conversation.

43

'Good gracious! Rosemary! What is it, my dear?'

'Can I see the baby?'

'Only if you are clean. Let me see your hands,' Charlotte demanded.

'She'll do,' Karran said. 'I think one can go to extremes in order to keep infants healthy.'

'Don't touch her, then. Well, what do you think?'

'She's not very pretty, is she?'

'New babies aren't.'

'Wasn't I?' Rosemary looked put out.

'Not particularly.'

'But I am now, aren't I. Everyone says so.'

'You vain little minx! Pride goes before a fall.'

'She won't be as pretty as I am.'

'You mustn't be so pleased with yourself.' Charlotte looked vexed. 'Looks aren't everything, you know!'

'We seem to have been over this ground before today,' Karran said, laughing. 'I think Miss Costain has been casting her eyes over a possible rival and, quite rightly, dismissing the incipient threat.'

'She's a conceited miss.'

'She doesn't look like Mr Howard,' Rosemary continued unabashed.

'Babies don't always look like their father, or their mothers come to that. They can be a mixture, or resemble their grandparents, uncles, cousins.'

'Grandma thinks—'

'We don't wish to know what she thinks!' Charlotte almost shouted. 'Go away and play with Bart for a bit longer. Really that child has far too big an opinion of herself these days. Everyone we meet drools over her. It's not good for her character.' She watched the girl depart with a certain displeasure.

'She's only a child.'

'I still don't want her to be spoiled. She won't always be a child.'

'There's something about real beauty that draws. Real good looks.'

44

'Not, though, in the case of Mr Nick O'Ferrall. Eh?'

'He's a cold fish. Calculating. Nowhere near as nice as Tom Allen.'

'I'm glad you're sounding positive about something. You look more alive. Not so worrisomely broody.'

'The approach of autumn always makes me broody.'

'Me, too, if the truth were told.' Charlotte stood up and looked again at the quiet infant. 'I still think you should have told Gideon. I think he'd have come back.'

'There were good reasons why it was better he should stay away. I couldn't have it both ways.'

'No. I suppose not. I'll be back soon. It'll be easier with the children at school again.'

'It was good to see you. Give Barney my regards.'

It was quiet after Charlotte had gone. The sky was a deep violet colour crossed by a rainbow. Karran was reminded of the day she'd lost John. The sky had looked the same the day they rode on the cliff-top. Then, the crash of thunder, the lightning, John struck to the ground. It was a stranger who survived that terrible accident, unhappy and frightening. And then Gideon had become part of her life. The result of their snatched meetings lay beside her now. She'd never been able to hide her mistakes.

Who cares, Karran asked herself?

But she did care.

Erin Kerruish had taken her granddaughter out, ostensibly to buy her a new muff for the approaching autumn and winter. The harbour was full of boats, their reflections shivering in the green, sullen water.

'Did you see the new baby?' Erin was consumed with curiosity.

'Yes, Grandmama.'

'What – was it like?'

'Thin. It's hair was black. Its eyes were a funny sort of blue. How do ladies know they are having babies?'

Erin considered. 'They get a little bit fat. Then later

they get fatter still as the baby grows.'

'Mrs Howard was a little bit fat the day Grandpa had his arm round her.'

Erin stopped dead. The motion of the boats accentuated her sudden feeling of sickness. A gull screamed discordantly. 'Which – day was that?'

'When he took me to Ravensdowne that time. He sent me to play with Bart but Bart wasn't in a very good humour so I went to look for Grandpa. They didn't hear me because they were laughing about something.'

'And – he had his arm round Mrs Howard?'

'Yes. He had some whiskers—'

'What do you mean, whiskers?'

'Yellow stuff in a glass. They both had.'

'Whisky,' Erin corrected mechanically. Although she'd been warm enough when they left the house, she now felt deathly cold. 'Why – were they amused?'

'There was something you weren't to know. Something she didn't want you to hear about.'

'Did Grandpa say anything else?'

'Something about his charm. Oh, and he said there was nothing wrong about a female who behaved like one.'

'Had you been outside with Bart for very long?' Even Erin's tongue seemed coated with ice. A band seemed to tighten around her head.

'Oh yes. We were in the orchard. I was dancing and he was watching.'

'And when Grandpa and Mrs Howard saw you they stopped laughing and – touching?'

'Yes. He said you'd be cross if we were late for lunch. Oh, and something about twenty guineas.'

The spars of the boats seemed to reel against the sky. Erin couldn't move.

A whore like Karran had to have a man dancing attendance. And Gideon Collister had seen the sense of staying away once he'd gone to his sister's. Karran must know he'd gone for good. But Barney—!

She began to move jerkily, like a rusted mechanism. A

hot current of hatred had begun to move under the icy shock. Erin wanted to kill Karran. Kill—

'Grandmama, we've passed the corner to the shop.'

'So we have.' Even to herself, Erin's voice sounded hoarse and unnatural.

'Have you got a cold, Grandmama?'

'I think I must have.' They began to retrace their steps.

'This is where we should have turned.' Rosemary, her thoughts obviously centred on the muff she'd been promised, tugged at Erin's hand.

Erin realized that she must go through with the meaningless ritual of shopping. Barney had told her he'd no interest in Karran as a woman, only as a buyer of that wretched cottage at Black Rocks. I'm a one-woman man he'd said, laughing. Erin wanted to cry out loud with the force of the pain that beset her. It wasn't the first time she'd faced losing Barney Kerruish, but it was the first time she'd feared losing him to another woman. Karran was young, beautiful and, hatefully, free as the air that tossed the boats and down whose currents the gulls drifted with outspread wings, crying like lost children.

The shadow of Rushen Castle engulfed them coldly. Rosemary, as though aware of the haunted atmosphere, clung more closely to Erin's unfeeling fingers. This was where Jesse had died early one morning, hanged as a smuggler. Erin was wearing a piece of jewellery he'd bought her with the proceeds of one of his sorties. The ghost of her former husband was, briefly, tangible.

Karran's mother, Jesse's niece, had never forgiven Erin for demanding the trinkets that had led to Jesse's downfall.

It was a long time since Erin had thought of Jesse, lusty and handsome, father of Elizabeth and Sebastian. Boyce wasn't his, not that he was ever sure of that. Boyce had blue blood in his, Irish-landowning blood. His worthless snivelling father had a title, not that she'd ever been able to boast about it. Barney wouldn't have stood for that.

Erin had a terrible picture of Karran Howard and Barney in the kind of closeness he and she had enjoyed, and the boiling anger threatened to break out of the rigid bounds she'd set up to control it. She tried to hate Barney but couldn't. All of her fury was directed towards the woman who'd laughed and said Erin Kerruish mustn't know what they'd been doing. Salacious images came and went, remorselessly.

The bell behind the shop door pinged and Erin found herself in the dim emporium with mantles, hats and muffs arranged on stands, the mingled smells of fur, new materials and chrysanthemums assailing her nostrils. Today, the shapes of the hats didn't excite her. What did hats matter? Only one thing mattered. Her relationship with her husband.

'That's the one I like, Grandmama,' Rosemary insisted.

Erin managed to behave in character in spite of the leaden weight of misery.

'That thing! It's far too rabbity! Your grandfather'd expect you to wear something better than that, my girl!'

Rosemary removed her reluctant gaze from the white fur creation. It seemed she knew Erin far too well to protest overmuch, but she looked sulky. A succession of muffs was produced but she enthused over none of them. 'They're all brown and I wanted the white one.'

'The fur will rub off too easily, then you'll be able to see the brownish underpart. That won't look nice, a piebald muff! Everyone will jeer at you. Then you'll find out how *they* feel! You often laugh at ill-dressed children, and grown-ups, come to that. Yes, perhaps you *should* have the white. It might do you good. I'd make you wear it until it looked positively diseased.'

The assistant was looking at Erin strangely. She must pull herself together, Erin decided belatedly.

'You should behave, Rosemary, when you know I feel unwell. I usually do know best about clothes and accessories. I saw a picture of the Empress of Russia wearing one like that, with a little round Cossack hat to match. I do believe there is a hat like that one, isn't there, Miss Ainslie?'

'Yes, Ma'am. It's the only one in stock. There it is, lovely, isn't it.'

Rosemary's eyes grew large and intent as they always did over mention of any kind of royalty. She agreed to try on the round fur hat and slipped her small hands inside the muff, then walked up and down in front of the cheval mirror, her head held high and her back straight.

'A truly beautiful child,' Miss Ainslie murmured, sotto voce.

'And a difficult one at times.'

'You were right about the quality, Mrs Kerruish. She'll outgrow this and leave it good as new.'

With difficulty, Erin dragged her granddaughter away from the long glass before which she'd been acting out her fantasy of being a Tsar's daughter. Rosie was no longer any man's daughter, Erin thought wryly as she watched hat and muff boxed and put down to Barney's account. Rosie hadn't said much about Abel's disappearance from their lives, yet she was bound to have her own thoughts. She was better off without him! No one could dispute the fact. Anyone who went off with another woman when he was married, with family responsibilities, wasn't worth a tinker's curse. To find out that Barney—!

The fresh air struck Erin's face like a blow. The hot anger had dulled to a grinding ache of loss. Her original intention of flinging her knowledge in Barney's face no longer seemed the best course of action. If he was as much under Karran's thumb as Rosie's innocent reporting suggested, those tactics could be worse than useless.

Only once had Erin estranged her husband to the point of total separation. She'd denied him the son he'd wanted so badly, had gone on doing so until she knew there never would be another child. She'd got him back but that was long ago when she'd been at the height of her beauty. This was her punishment.

Woman and girl walked in silence. The life of the town went on around them, boys shouting and scuffling up a narrow lane, a dog barking at the seabirds, women with shawled heads gossiping at shop doorways, babies fretting.

Erin had never felt old, not really, bone-achingly, wearily old, but she did now. She recalled Barney's violent anger when she'd repeated the tales she'd heard about Gideon Collister and Karran. He'd barred some of her friends from the house because of their hostility towards young Mrs Howard. Erin no longer wondered at his vehemence. He was caught in the same silken snare and she wanted to die. How could she face Barney and pretend that everything was normal?

But she wouldn't need to, not today. Barney was off to Foxdale for his weekly inspection of the mine, the accounts and requisitions. He wouldn't be back until tomorrow evening. Her body slackened with a relief she had never thought to feel over one of her husband's absences.

'Grandmama's not well,' Rosemary announced as they entered the house.

Miss Philips, the children's governess-cum-slave, said, 'You'll want me to supervise the children's tea then. Master Timothy and Miss Virginia have returned from music lessons. Mrs Costain is out this afternoon and won't return till six.'

Timothy and Virginia were Elizabeth's children, left behind when their mother had gone off with the overseer at Foxdale mines. Pale, dull children, Erin had always considered them with unreasoning resentment, totally unlike her own vibrant red-haired, green-eyed brood. Quite overshadowed by their cousin Rosemary.

She couldn't have the three children with her at tea today as she usually did when Barney was absent. Oh, Barney! My love—

'Yes. They can stay in the nursery. I'll lie down for a while.'

Stretched out on the big double bed in her bedchamber, Erin was unable entirely to shut out the family's presence. Rosie's voice was inevitably the loudest. Tim and Virginia were mouselike, quiet and obedient. Unremarkable.

Try as she would to exorcise him, Barney came back,

time after time, to Erin's mind, wooing her with the memories of his kindness and patience. To think that all that was gone, that he'd deceived her so successfully.

Anger and pain fought conflicting battles.

It was pain that won, leaving her to cry soundlessly into a pillow that smelt faintly of some bitter-sweet herb.

Erin slept long and heavily, awakening to a fine morning but with a leaden weight inside her breast. What could be so shatteringly wrong?

Opening her eyes, she reached as always for the other side of the bed. There was no companionable warmth, no compatible flesh covered with a nightshirt, no sound of breathing. She'd always hated the Foxdale trips but Barney had pointed out the necessity of ensuring the profitable running of their grandchildren's inheritance. Timothy was too young to run his own mine and Elizabeth had abandoned her babies. Barney said that animals fought more wholeheartedly for their young and it was easy to see his revulsion for his heartless step-daughter.

Erin struggled unwillingly into an upright position and reached automatically for her corset. If only Barney knew! There'd been a point in her own life when she'd been heartsick of poverty and a parcel of children. She'd have run away without another thought. But Clemence had come to look after them almost with a mother's love.

And now Clemence's daughter Karran had designs on Barney. Clemence had always brought bad luck. Luke Karran had lusted after her and died as a result. His child had flourished, been adopted by John Howard who'd later married her. Men were fools and women were trouble. Didn't *she* understand and herself one of the damned female tribe?

She tugged the bell-rope for Bessie to come and lace her in. Bessie always did it when Barney wasn't there. When he was he liked to perform the task himself. Sometimes the sight of her in the provocative French garment was too much for him and they'd end up on the bed. She'd never envisaged him being seduced from her side. But now she was old and the world was full of young girls, offering second chances. Hadn't she herself had Dermot O'Neill and Jesse Kinrade? Yet, youth and good looks were nothing compared with Barney's kind of loyalty and need.

What loyalty? It had been an illusion. Erin wept angry tears into the Spode wash basin and dried her face too roughly on the new towel. What did it matter if she ruined her skin? Her husband was no longer interested in her. He'd not notice.

The sense of outrage mounted all through a breakfast that consisted mainly of cups of coffee. They'd be talking in the kitchen about Mrs Kerruish's lack of appetite, not that they'd been too surprised since she'd retreated to bed early yesterday, indisposed.

Erin's fighting spirit reasserted itself. When had she run from problems? Never, and she didn't intend to start now. Barney was away and there was no one to stop her from going to Black Rocks and confronting that black-haired bitch with a penchant for other women's men. She'd frighten the daylight out of Mrs Karran Howard, just see if she didn't!

She took care to make up her face carefully and wear her most fashionable bonnet and cape. Deep green always suited her best. Her reflected self looked attractive and resourceful, if a little puffy under the eyes, but be damned to them.

Erin was halfway to Black Rocks in the trap when she realized she didn't know what she was going to say. But she was sure of her ground. Rosie had no need to lie.

Erin arrived in treacherous sunlight spanned by the hint of a rainbow. The lop-sided house was unquiet with the sound of hammer-blows. Erin's lip curled. Anyone with half an eye could see that it was foolish to have expected such an arrangement to work. Yet, if she covered up the view of the unfinished side with her hand, the rest did seem to blend with a certain odd harmony.

Erin lowered her hand and began to descend from the

trap. She'd left the vehicle some distance away from the house, not wishing to be seen too early in the proceedings. Now that she was nearly at the door she was not so sure of being admitted. She'd had a glimpse of Brand, the factor from Ravensdowne. He'd not allow any antagonistic visitor within a mile of his mistress and that Quinn person was a better watchdog than a gaggle of geese.

It occurred to Erin to look up at the chimneys. There was sure to be a fire in Karran's chamber. But most of the chimney-pots on the left-hand side were smoking. It wasn't so easy to go barnstorming into someone's house after all. Then she remembered being told that Karran's labour had begun just as the bed had arrived at the new wing. She'd have earmarked the bedroom at the front overlooking the panorama of the bay.

There was a door at the side. Quietly, Erin opened it and peered into what must be intended as a drawing-room. Green hangings were looped back to either side of the elegant windows and there was a strong smell of fresh paint. A few small items of furniture stood in the corners. It seemed that the rest hadn't yet arrived.

She crossed the parquet floor and opened the inner door which gave on to a narrow staircase. From somewhere above her, someone was crooning a little Manx lullaby.

Erin began to climb the steps, the sound of her footfalls masked by the dull noises of hammering. Karran's door was open and from the gap Erin could see her reflected in the cheval mirror, her dark hair spilled over the pillow with its wide lace edgings. There was lace on her nightgown too, and the negligée that was flung across the foot of the wide bed. Nothing to see but whiteness and darkness—

Erin moved in order to see the infant's cot and a board creaked under her weight.

Karran's eyes met hers in the depths of the mirror. It had obviously been placed there so that Karran could see whoever came upstairs. She sat up quickly and pushed back the bedclothes, intending to get up.

Erin was in the room, advancing towards the bed. 'I shouldn't bother to rise. What I have to say won't take long.'

'Why have you come? What can you possibly want with me?' Karran was amazed.

Colour suffused Erin's cheeks. Her voice became strident. 'Can't you be guessing? Wouldn't you know I'd not care for you taking *my* man as well as those others?'

Karran's face became terribly white. 'You – must be mad,' she whispered.

She's Luke Karran to the life, Erin thought, momentarily shaken, then flung off the superstitious fear.

'I know you and Barney have been familiar.'

'How can you know something that never happened! He's a friend, that's all.'

'A friend! A man you drink with in the mornings and your belly swollen with another man's child! A middle-aged man with wife and family who *embraces* you. It's disgusting.'

Karran swung her legs over the side of the bed. 'Someone's lying to you, trying to stir up trouble. The only time I offered Barney a drink was when I approved the papers appertaining to this house. As for embraces, it's slander—'

'Well, you can't send for your precious advocate, Gideon, *this* time, to scotch the truth! He's scuttled away to safety just in time with his tail between his legs.'

'Who has told you this story?' Karran, swaying, tried to reach for the lace-trimmed robe at the bed's foot. Erin, beside herself, pushed her back again. Karran sprawled for a moment on the edge of the bed then slid to the floor.

Erin's harsh breathing was the only sound: the room seemed charged with menace.

Painfully, Karran pulled herself to a sitting position. She was so pale that Erin experienced a brief pang of fear. But Karran had brought this ugly scene on her own head. 'You deserve to be punished for your looseness. I even know what your favours, if anyone could call them that,

54

are worth. Twenty guineas! I doubt if the Queen's favours are worth that much.'

To her surprise, Karran began to laugh. 'You've been listening to some garbled account from Rosemary. She's the only one it could have been. A child!'

'Rosie takes in everything and it might pay you to remember that in future. She's no intellectual but her mind stores up all she hears and sees as a squirrel does nuts. She could tell me what she had for breakfast a year ago today.'

'She couldn't have understood. Adult conversations have nuances that go over a child's head. Surely you realize that?'

'Fancy words! You're no better than I am for all your airs and graces. D'you think I don't recall you at that stall of Jesse's, selling cheese and butter?'

'That was my mother,' Karran said quietly.

'No matter, you were there later.' Erin sounded uncertain.

'Rosemary was too literal. She must have been if you imagined that Barney and I—'

'I wouldn't put anything past you, Karran Kinrade!'

'Believe me, I had no more idea of seducing your husband than he had of bedding me – It's – unthinkable. I've *never* thought of him in that way, I swear.'

'That's what you say. But you left your mark on my daughter Elizabeth's husband. It was *you* Clive remembered at the last. There was a letter he left you, I heard. A christening mug for your son. And,' Erin stared in to the cot behind Karran's head, 'there's Gideon Collister's daughter. Bart's father was shot by the lawmen from Cumberland. John Howard died under dubious circumstances. So did his first wife. A lot of people think she was put out of the way so's he could have you. What do you say about that, my fine lady?'

Karran struggled to her knees. 'Nothing at all. I know the truth behind all these rumours. My conscience is clear. Barney and I had a drink of whisky because he preferred that to anything else I offered. He wanted to be rid of his cottage and I needed it because John had left me little but a living legacy. If I remember rightly, Barney patted my shoulder once because he'd worried about being left with a comparatively useless property which I'd taken off his hands. He's a man of business, after all. It pays to be pleasant.

'He's also Charlotte's father, and your daughter and I have been friends for a long time. I'd have welcomed you too, but you were bound up in perpetuating a useless feud. What our parents did has nothing to do with us. It was another generation. It's all in the past and that's where it should stay!'

'Why should he offer you money?'

'It was a bet that I refused to take up. Something perfectly trivial – a joke. It had nothing to do with an illicit relationship. Don't you trust your husband more than that?'

Erin watched silently as her erstwhile enemy climbed to her feet and got back on to the wide, rumpled bed, her body trembling. Karran had been curiously convincing.

'Everyone knows that Kerruish is devoted only to his wife. Why sour the future because a child remembers a few perfectly harmless words? She couldn't possibly understand their implication. Don't make yourself needlessly unhappy. You have an exceptional husband. It would be a mistake to antagonize him, please believe me. You are the most fortunate of persons. Keep what you have.'

Erin stood there, unable to decide whether she had, indeed, been misled by a small girl, envious of Karran's undoubted attraction, pale and drawn though she now appeared. Rosie's recital had been the facts as she'd seen and heard them. But, between adults, there were undoubtedly the – nuances? – that permeated the conversation of grown-ups.

A great load was sliding off her shoulders, not that she'd ever admit it to that girl on the bed. Karran was too distinctive by half, while she – Time was closing in, inexorably.

There was a heavy tread on the stair. The squeaky board cried out like a tortured cat.

'Oh!' Mrs Quinn sounded vexed. 'However did you find your way up?'

'Mrs Kerruish came to visit me and little Johanne. She was just about to leave. Isn't that so, Erin?' Karran sank back among the lacy pillows, exhausted.

'That's right,' Erin said. 'I was just going.'

'Goodbye, Erin.'

'Goodbye.' Erin turned away, filled with conflicting emotions. The meeting hadn't gone as she'd intended. But she thought Karran had told the truth. The girl could have taunted her, filled her with doubts, but she hadn't.

Mrs Quinn followed Erin downstairs, a disapproving bodyguard. It was odd how Karran managed to inspire such loyalty. Erin felt foolish.

'Just come to the front door next time,' Mrs Quinn said, her red polished cheek like a wooden doll's. Her voice was grudging, her eyes cold.

Erin said nothing, but later, as the trap bowled along towards the dark stone ramparts of Castle Rushen, she had to hold back the tears that threatened. She'd never be absolutely certain that Karran had spoken the truth and that seemed almost worse than knowing that she'd lied.

It took Karren longer to recover from Johanne's birth than she'd expected. Part of this was probably due to the unpleasant shock of Erin's unexpected visit. She'd been upset after that and her disturbance was reflected in the infant's change from tranquillity to fretful crying. The child seemed always hungry, forever seeking sustenance that Karran seemed unable fully to provide.

The days became colder and the skies were dull. Karran grew thinner.

'You never want to do anything with me,' Bart said

jealously. 'Not now you've got *her*!'

'Don't be silly. Should I neglect Johanne? A helpless baby? That would make me a monster.'

'There's nothing to do.'

'It's windy weather. You could fly your kite.'

'I don't want to.'

'Don't want! What way is that for the head of a household to talk?'

Bart was silent. Then he got up and went to the window. His profile looked bleak as the day outside. 'There's someone coming.'

'Oh, I don't want to see anyone. Not today.' Karran rose and pulled the Paisley shawl closer round her shoulders. 'Who is it? Can you see?'

'It looks a bit like Mr Collister.'

'Gideon?' For a moment Karran was perfectly still, then she ran to join Bart at his vantage point. The dark figure on the black horse did look like him, poignantly, disruptingly so. All the old, sweet feelings of weakness and need overcame her. He *did* care. He did feel responsible. Karran grew dizzy with relief.

'No, it isn't him,' Bart said calmly. 'It's the new man at Ravensdowne.'

'Mr – O'Ferrall?'

'Yes. There isn't any other new man, is there. Tom Allen only works for him.'

'I suppose I must go down, then. Not that I relish the encounter.'

'I should go with you, if I'm in charge,' Bart said arrogantly.

'I suppose you should. Do I look a fright?'

'Does it matter?'

'I don't imagine it does.' Karran laughed ruefully.

'Let's go down to the parlour, then.'

The lack of furniture in the new, large room had necessitated their present use of Gideon's old parlour, but Karran had discovered how warm and welcoming the small room became with a decent fire roaring up the chimney to offset the autumnal melancholy.

Mr O'Ferrall was shown in by a reluctant Mrs Quinn, who, judging by her expression, would dearly have loved to send the Irishman away, and who insisted that Bart went back with her to the kitchen.

'Mama said—'

'Never mind that. She shouldn't be disturbed just now.'

'Am I likely to disturb you?' Mr O'Ferrall enquired softly as the door closed behind them. The flickering flames cast his features into patterns of light and shade.

'It all depends on why you've come.'

'First of all,' O'Ferrall disposed himself in a chair once Karran was seated, 'I wish to congratulate you on your new child.'

'Thank you.'

'Always an anxious time,' O'Farrall murmured and ran his hand over the silver knob on his cane. That familiar habit.

'Do you speak from personal experience?'

Amused eyes sparkled, then were lost in shadow sockets. 'I've never been caught. Not yet. Entangled, perhaps, but the mesh was never close enough.'

'Indeed,' Karran said coldly, and yawned.

'Do I bore you?'

'Somewhat, I'm afraid. I've always found that those who protest most are those who've had so little success that they must fabricate their triumphs.'

'Why, Mrs Howard, that's downright unfriendly.'

She could swear he was laughing at her under all that injured innocence.

'What else did you come to see me about?' she asked crisply.

'I must rob you of Brand and his son a little earlier than expected. But don't look so put out! I'll see that they move your furniture first. All I wanted to ascertain was whether you felt able to cope with its arrival.'

'Yes, of course. I'm grateful. There is just the matter of the bed and the rosewood table for the uncompleted wing.

Would you have room for those if they were dismantled? It wouldn't be for very long. They've promised the outside walls and roof before winter sets in and the inside work should be completed soon after that.'

O'Ferrall frowned, then he said, 'I daresay some space could be found.'

'I'm much obliged. Mr O'Ferrall, you never did say why you wanted the house.'

'Neither I did.' The shifting firelight showed Karran his lips, curved in a smile as faint and elusive as on the day he awaited her agreement of his offer.

'Well?'

'My dear lady, perhaps I'm not disposed to let out my secrets.'

'They'll be known soon enough if you're on the point of taking up residence.'

'I daresay you're right. Well, since you've asked, I don't see why you shouldn't be the first to know. I'm to emulate my countryman Buck Whaley, and open a gaming-house. Don't look so shocked! It'll be very discreet. It's far enough away from anywhere else to ensure that it can cause no annoyance.'

'But – where are your customers to come from?'

'Well, you alone know how many rooms are available as bedchambers. I'll have the rich sailing practically to my own door. Staying in the house for a week, two weeks, a month. A year if they're happy! I've a ship of my own to sail between here and the mainland. Many of my visitors will have their own yachts.'

'My dear Mr O'Ferrall! There's all too much of the year when that's not so simple! The weather can be fiendish. Man can quite quickly become stormbound.'

'There are sufficient suitable people living here to fill in such unwelcome gaps. I've made enquiries. The house would become a hotel where one can play games of chance. And, remember, Buck Whaley no longer owns Fort Anne.'

'You'll acquire a bad name with some. Not everyone looks kindly on gamblers, however you intend to describe yourself. I know how it feels to have a dubious reputation.'

'My shoulders are broad. Now, how about that invitation to dine with me? You've not referred to it.' He stared at her challengingly.

'If I accepted, that really *would* put paid to any claim on your part to respectability.'

'I've no great yearning for such a state.' He shrugged.

'But I have – my children. They are halfway already to being damned along with their mother.'

'My dear woman, would it be so world-shattering for a widow with many months of mourning behind her to dine with the purchaser of her previous home? Aren't you placing a little too much importance on the event?'

'Perhaps. I'm not sure— This isn't London where such licence might pass.'

'Oh, come, we are our own people, are we not? No ties. No need to make explanations. We're adults, Mrs Howard. Unattached. Where's the harm?'

'Where were you proposing we should dine?'

'At Ravensdowne. The food would be excellent. I have a chef—'

'Just you and I?' Karran demanded sharply.

'Why, yes.' Again that barely-discernible smile.

'You must see how impossible that would be, Mr O'Ferrall. Here the accent is all on blameless family life—'

'That sounds as dull as ditchwater. Sometimes one longs for a return to the times of Charles the Second. A reprobate of course, but interesting. Life was vastly more entertaining in the days of Old Rowley.'

'Not everyone would agree with that.' But she thought privately that O'Ferrall did look as though he belonged to some more exciting era.

'Don't you enjoy colour, good food, pleasant surroundings and stimulating conversation?'

'Yes, but where am I to find them?'

'I do think you are laughing at me,' O'Ferrall complained.

'Weren't you finding me amusing just a little while ago?'

61

'If you don't agree, I may have your four-poster and dining-room put out in the garden to fend for themselves.'

'Now you're being ridiculous. Mr O'Ferrall—'

'Nick.'

'Mr O'Ferrall, I couldn't agree. Not yet.'

'Does that mean you might, later on?'

'For one thing, it wouldn't be at all easy to leave so young a baby even for a few hours. For another, I don't care for the idea of going back to John's house, the place where we spent our married life together, quite so soon.'

'I see.' O'Ferrall rose, picking up his cane and gloves. 'How has your son settled down.'

'Not very well. If we'd been alone, if I wasn't always so occupied, it might be different. He resents Johanne. I had wondered if I should get a pony. My mare's just too big for him to cope with on his own, though he's ridden her while I've been out on her and in charge. Now I've lost the Brands to you, he could even later on ride to school by himself on good days. At present he'd have to go with the carrier.'

'An excellent idea,' O'Ferrall agreed. 'You've changed,' he went on disconcertingly. 'You look hag-ridden.'

'I don't know that I care what you think!' He was presumptuous!

'That's more like the handsome, spirited woman I remember.'

'One could describe a mare in similar terms.'

He smiled disarmingly. 'I knew you'd have to smile sooner or later.'

'How satisfying to know you are right!' But Karm n went on smiling for some reason. She didn't altogether care for Mr O'Ferrall but he'd been a diversion on a depressing afternoon. He'd also been accommodating over the storing of the two large pieces of furniture, and had troubled to ask about Bart's reaction to the precipitate move and the advent of a rival.

Even after he'd gone she found herself thinking about O'Ferrall and his astonishing plans for Ravensdowne.

Where they so far-fetched? Buck Whaley had been quite successful, if notorious. But he'd chosen Douglas as his base and he'd found no lack of fashionable young men to patronize his own establishment. There'd been some legend, something about Irish soil, but the story refused to return to her mind. All she could remember was laughing at Whaley's audacity and wit. These same attributes could well be laid at O'Ferrall's door.

Bart was nowhere to be found. He must have gone off into the woods in a sulk. He'd probably walk until he was tired. She hoped he wouldn't go as far as Stark's land. Stark was notoriously erratic. There'd been bad trouble at the farm a year ago. Stark and his shotgun.

Uneasily Karran went outside and called for her son.

Pigeons flew out of the woods but Bart never came.

It was deliciously eerie among the trees. There was a dank smell of water and the damp velvet of moss brushed Bart's ankle as his foot slid into a patch of bog. The light beyond the plantation was almost violet. His senses responded both to the beauty and the threat of the wildness that surrounded him. He forgot his detestation of Mrs Quinn for reducing him to puny child level when he'd wanted so much to be a man and to support Mama.

Bart wasn't sure how far he'd travelled, first running in a torment of angry frustration, then more slowly as the peace gradually enfolded him. The wood-pigeons had startled him with a sharp clatter of wings, but once he'd reduced his pace to a walk they'd only made their soft cooing noises. Caroo croo – croo croo. He discovered how they'd suddenly stop on a single croo while he waited, listening for the second. It was like someone throwing one shoe down on the floor of the room above yours. Your ears ached with the intensity of trying not to miss the thud of the other. It could become quite ghostly as the silence stretched out.

Sometimes he reached for something to hold on to as he crossed and recrossed the wandering waterway, a jutting branch or a large stone draped with slimy green that made him gasp at its cold, wet touch. The sensation of being a pioneer gave him a heady pleasure. What did it matter that his feet were wet and his hair dragged into disorder by the skinny twigs it was impossible to avoid altogether, that his hands were grazed? It was a long time since he'd enjoyed himself so much. Not since the day Gideon Collister had given him the red kite that was like a huge, exciting bird, free to roam the heavens. But nowhere else! On land it was still and dead but he, himself, was free, triumphing over that occupancy of the skies.

He could not quite remember when he first became aware of something coming through the woods, shifting the stones and rustling the leaves. Bart stood listening. It must be something large. Were there any such sizeable animals on the island? His mind flew to the giant elk that had been taken out of a Manx bog and displayed in Cumberland for a good deal of profit. Whatever it was didn't move like a human. It almost – flew.

Bart's superstitious mind returned to all the fascinating stories that he and Rosemary Costain had listened to in the past. The Buggane, the Fynoderee, the Lhondoo and the Ushag-Reaicht, the Tall Man of Ballacurry, Teeval, the sea-princess, the Moddey-Doo, the little red bird that Mama sang about to his baby sister. The little red bird – Tehi, Tegi, Manannen, the Night Man— He never cared to dwell on the Night Man.

Pale with terror, Bart shrank into the darkness between two lichened and distorted tree trunks and waited.

Something appeared in the dim, purple-grey distance, a fleeting band of anaemic light settling momentarily on a glimpse of palest yellow and waxen white. Bart covered his face and peeped through the cracks of his fingers.

Sticks cracked and branches were thrust aside. Quite suddenly something hurled across the small clearing, short, nerve-tinglingly fast. Although it must have been a figment of his imagination, Bart thought he'd seen a boy with wings.

The boy stopped and became mortal, even pathetic. His slight body was propped between crutches that hadn't been visible at first sight as they'd merged into the woodland background. The boy set the crutches aside and knelt to examine a plant. The pigeons began their soft seductive caroo – carooing and the child raised a remarkably blond head to listen. He had blue eyes that gave him an angelic appearance and his features were refined.

Bart had seen this boy before. It had only been a fleeting glimpse but he'd remembered the encounter because Mama had been dreadfully upset that day. The boy had run in front of the horse and trap in which they had been travelling and had only narrowly escaped being killed or at least seriously hurt. Perhaps the boy had been careless on another occasion.

Bart's eyes, travelling downwards in search of the boy's need for the rough wooden supports, saw that where one foot should be, there was only a stump of ankle protected inside a hand-stitched leather bag. For a moment he was revolted, then fascinated, lost in a cruel, legendary world where lurked something that snapped off foolishly neglected limbs. The Moddey-Doo? The Tarroo-Ushtey? The Buggane, perhaps, who'd had an encounter with Finn McCool of Ireland. The disabled boy became infused with a curious magic.

Bart must have made some sound for the boy sprang up, snatching at his crutches, and stood at the gap behind which he crouched, in two bounds. Bart was half-disconcerted, half-filled with admiration for the boy's incredible agility.

'Who're you?' the boy asked roughly. 'This is Stark land.'

'I didn't know.' Bart stood up, glad that he was taller than the country lad. The fact made him feel less foolish.

'Well, you know now.'

'You manage very well,' Bart was constrained to say.

'Manage?'

'On those crutches.'

'Granpa made them.' The boy looked at them with satisfaction. 'He'll make them bigger next time.'

'Was it – awful?'

'Losing my foot?' The child shivered momentarily, then flung up his head so that the fair hair bounced. 'Don't rightly remember too much about it. One minute I was going along this path. The next – something – something got hold of my foot. Something with strong, shining teeth—'

In the silence that ensued, Bart saw, in dreadful procession, all of his childhood fears brought to predatory life.

'What – was it?' he whispered at last.

'They never told me, Granpa and my uncles. It was so fierce, it held on to me and wouldn't let go. Just bit – and bit—'

'Don't think of it if you don't want to,' Bart said hastily, not wishing to dwell on something that could snap off anything as strongly attached as one's foot. Then he found himself staring into the grey-purple gloom as though IT might be waiting – listening—

'Didn't you – see?'

The angelic boy shook his head. 'It was getting dark. Dusky time.'

'Why were you out so late?'

'Can't quite recall that either. I just remember running from some fear, running, my breath getting short, not really seeing anything, just knowing I'd got to get away. Then – snap!'

'Aren't – aren't you scared to come out now? In case – ?'

'Granpa and my uncles say there's no need to worry now. I s'pect they killed it. They whispered a lot afterwards. I think they buried it. There's lots o' places on the moor if it wasn't easy enough in the woods. I'm sure that's what they did. Strong, my uncles are. Fierce! T'wouldn't be easy to get away from them. They'd not like one of their own being hurt.'

Bart thought he'd be able to breath more easily,

knowing that the dread attacker was no more. But it wasn't so easy to kill off the subject of legends. A band tightened round his chest. He'd read something about uncles in stories. Uncles were usually wicked, like step-mothers and step-fathers. He couldn't bear it if his beautiful Mama married another step-father. They never liked children. Gideon might have been different, but he'd gone away for good.

'Scared, are you?' the fair boy asked and laughed.

'Of course not! Your crutches sounded like an invading army, that's all. Anyone would have wanted to make sure.'

'I thought I'd hate them. I hated everything while I lay in bed, hurting, not able to do the things I usually did. But my crutches make me feel so free. Even more than before. I can push myself forward—'

'Don't you ever fall?'

'Not now. I did at first. D'you want to try them?'

Bart concealed his returning revulsion. It was one thing to admire another's acceptance of his fate, but did he really want to participate?

'Scaredy-cat!'

'I'm not! Give me the wretched things! I'll show you.' Angrily, Bart tucked the crude contraptions under his arms, then hesitated.

''Fraid you'll make a fool of yourself?' the young voice mocked with merciless accuracy.

'Not really.' Bart assumed an air of nonchalance. He'd never felt so clumsy and ill at ease.

'Slow, aren't you!'

'You must have been once. You said *you* fell at first,' Bart pointed out and shuffled uneasily between the too-short props.

The fair child screamed with laughter. The gay sound reverberated through the woods and was struck back by the interlaced branches in ghostly echoes.

Spurred by a fatal desire to match the other's enviable ease of movement, Bart launched himself forward and landed with a bone-jangling thud on the pungently uncomfortable floor of the plantation. The boy went on laughing.

'Shut up!' Bart shouted angrily, scrambling to his feet and turning in the direction from which he'd come.

'Aren't you going to give my crutches back?' the boy asked. 'I'll have to crawl for them if you don't.'

Bart hesitated. He hated being an object of derision, yet he couldn't ignore the truth of the child's predicament. 'Oh, all right,' he muttered and picked up the offending articles. He stamped across the clearing. 'There you are.'

The boy's face was suddenly pinched and white. It was as though he'd come to the end of his strength. He felt about him, then sank on to a tree stump, all his gaiety quenched.

'Are you all right?' Bart asked.

'Only tired. I gets tired. For while I feel that I could fly for ever, like a hawk. Then something trickles out of me and I can't go no more.'

'Are you far from home?'

The boy nodded, close to exhaustion.

'I'll help you, then. You put your arm round my shoulders and hop on your good foot. I'll carry these.'

'You won't go too fast?'

Bart shook his head. 'It's all right. I'm bigger than you and very strong.' It pleased him that he could show off his own assets after such humiliation.

They set off slowly. The boy was quite light and the crutches were more trouble to Bart, being fairly heavy and inclined to stick out awkwardly when the track narrowed and sharp twigs hedged them in.

It grew appreciably darker. Still, they stumbled on. Bart began to think of Mama becoming steadily more anxious. A small flicker of triumph grew into a burning satisfaction. If she was worrying about him she couldn't think too much about Johanne! The baby would take second place. He hugged, tightly, the feeling of self-importance. Just for today, there would be no fond glances in the direction of the cradle. Everything appertaining to the child's comfort would be hurried as Mama stared with growing disquiet at the clock or went outside to call his name.

The boy stopped. 'Can't walk no more.'

'Could you use your crutches now?'

The fair head was shaken. 'It's sore under my arms now and I know I'm too weary for any more travelling.'

'You shouldn't have gone so far.'

'Well, it's too late for that, isn't it!' The boy was recovering a little of his spirit. 'I didn't *know* I was going to be like that, did I. I just wanted to feel – whole.'

'Next time you must remember you've got to get back. Look, I'll give you a ride on my back for a bit but I can't carry these as well. I'll hang them on this big branch. They should be easy to find in daylight.'

'You can be my horse.' A trace of the former excitement entered the tired voice.

Perched on Bart's back, the boy didn't feel heavy at first. The moon was full and its cold blue light penetrated the now sparse woodland, showing him sufficient of the meandering track not to lose his way. Little by little, Bart's shoulders and arms began to ache and his feet to drag. He gritted his teeth.

'My name's Ben,' the boy volunteered.

'What's your other name?'

'Don't have one.'

'That's silly! Everyone has. What's your father called?'

'Haven't got one. He went away before I was born. Don't know his name. Never saw him.'

It was strange how that fact established a bond between Ben and himself, Bart thought. His own father had died, then Mama had wed John Howard of Ravensdowne. Bart didn't care to think too much about Howard, not here in the moonlit dark and the world a blue fantasy.

For the second time that day something was coming through the thinning trees. Whatever it was made a good deal more racket than Ben had earlier.

Bart stiffened.

'Don't stop now. It's them looking for me!' Small knees

nudged Bart's sides.

'Them?'

'The uncles, Reuben, Will and the others.'

How many were there? Rough male voices were shouting now. 'Ben? Ben!'

'I'm here! Here!' Ben bawled, clinging more tightly to his rescuer's neck.

Any thought Bart might have had of leaving his Old Man of the Sea to fend for himself while he plunged back into the comparatively safe anonymity of the overgrown track, vanished. Four huge brawny figures, outlined by silver light, surrounded them. Ben was whirled away to sit on one pair of broad shoulders while Bart was grabbed between two large hands and turned to face what little illumination there was.

'Who's this?'

'Don't know,' Ben said. 'He carried me when I got tired.' Then he launched into the full story of his meeting with Bart. 'Left my crutches dangling by the path way back, quarter of a mile.'

Bart was made to give his name. Not one of the four giants told him he shouldn't have been on Stark's land. His racing heartbeats slowed.

'I must go home now.'

'Can't leave you here, not this late. One of us'll take you down on old Bess. Mustn't have a fine woman like your mother upset 'cos you've been helping out our Ben.'

Bart would have preferred to run ten miles in the dark rather than be forced up on to a cart-horse with one of Ben's fearsome uncles, but he could hardly say anything quite so anti-social under the circumstances.

'Fine figure of a woman, Mrs Howard,' the largest uncle said in a way that Bart resented. There was an unpleasant, gloating quality in the man's voice that made him think of Mama caught prisoner in Howard's arms. Closed doors behind which happened things that he knew, instinctively, were distasteful.

Bart, in his turn, was swung on to manure-smelling

70

shoulders and the phalanx of uncles proceeded briskly towards a dimness lit by the far-off eye of a lamplit window.

The four men chaffed the crippled boy noisily, seeming to forget Bart's presence for the time being, while Ben revelled in the good-natured attention he'd aroused. There was obviously a bond of affection between him and these wild men.

Inexorably, the dwelling with the lit window grew closer and closer. The door was thrown open and an old man and a buxom woman came out, the woman running towards them over the moonlit ground, her large bosoms swinging inside the roughly-made gown.

Mama would never have let herself get so fat, Bart decided as he was set down in the clearing. Stout, floppy, noisy creature! How had she ever had a child like Ben? Then she was crying out Ben's name with a passionate insistence that filled Bart with emotions he couldn't, at first, define. She reached her son and grabbed him to her capacious breast, almost slobbering over the boy who tried to draw away with pale fastidiousness.

He was jealous! Bart knew this almost immediately. He'd like Mama to rush towards *him* with such affection but she never would. She'd stand a way off, just staring at him with dark, coolly appraising eyes, more judge than mother. She had been loving long ago, before they went to Ravensdowne. Then he'd turned to Rosemary Costain. There was no way to explain the bond between himself and Charlotte Costain's daughter. Mama had receded into unknown territory. He'd never get her back.

'Who's this?' the fat woman asked suspiciously, when she'd done with drooling over her lost boy and smoothing his fair head, to his obvious annoyance.

'Mrs Howard's lad. Found Ben not able to get back home and carried him a good long way,' the largest uncle told her.

'Mrs Howard, eh? Friend of those Costains, isn't she!'

'Is she, lad? Is your mother their friend?'

71

'Only Mrs Costain,' Bart replied carefully, scenting trouble.

'Don't care for anyone 'o that name,' the woman insisted, and the moonlight showed Bart a face that had once been darkly handsome but was now twisted with detestation.

'Nothing to do with this lad, though. Not much older than our young 'un. Can't rightly blame *him*, Kate.'

'Such talk don't right anything, our Reuben!'

'There's only one person who has to answer for any wrong done to Ben. And it's – that person who'll suffer. When the time comes.'

'How so when he's scuttled away like the coward he always was?'

'I've ways of finding out if ever he sets foot on Man. It'll be the last time.'

'What if he never comes back?'

Reuben shrugged huge shoulders. 'Can't do nothing, then, sister.'

The old man had been listening to these exchanges with ill-concealed impatience.

'Keep all that talk for the proper place! Which isn't out 'ere with strangers all ears. Get Ben inside to his bed. 'E looks asleep on his feet. And as for you, Master Howard! Listen to me well! You've not been touched this time because you meant well, aiding my grandson. But it's plain you were on my land and not the right o' way, and I'll 'ave none of it. You've been warned. See 'im on 'is way, Reuben.'

The scene had a grotesque unreality; the vengeful old man with his pale, carved features, the overblown, gypsyish woman, the frail white-haired boy and the great dark silhouettes of the Stark uncles, all combined to leave an indelible imprint on Bart's receptive mind.

The moon slid slowly behind cloud and they were left in starlight, nothing clearly seen. Everyone moved away. The house door banged shut. Reuben reappeared, behind him the shadow of an enormous horse. He mounted swiftly,

72

then reached down to pluck Bart from the dimness and placed the boy before him, one large arm constricting his waist. The smell of him was stronger than ever, the odour of stale sweat and privies added to the aura of manure that had previously predominated.

All the way down the track Bart fought the inclination to retch. Illogically, he blamed Johanne for his present predicament. If she hadn't been born, he'd never have wanted to run way as he once had from mad John Howard and his dreadful sister Martha. It was all Johanne's fault. He'd pay her back, never fear.

And then they were on the shore road and the waves were crashing over Black Rocks. Mama was waiting in lantern-light, her face schooled to impassivity.

Bart's heart sank like a stone.

PART THREE

The Return

Christmas saw the house outwardly complete and sufficient decorating having taken place for Karran to agree to the arrival of the bed and the table for the new wing. The furniture was brought in pieces on two great sledges, over the snow that arrived early.

Because the snow was hard-packed, the journey wasn't as difficult as it might have been. The long runners glided over the icy crust and the horses' breath smoked in the clear, crisp air. Karran, watching the approach from her bedroom window and hearing the sounds of hooves and voices, went outside, the baby in her arms. Delighting in the sight of the horses, the sledges, and the warmly-wrapped drivers, she was at first unaware that one of them was Nick O'Ferrall. Then the scarf slipped from his face and he was smiling at the pleasant picture she made, her hair loose, the purplish gown failing in its intention to suggest half-mourning.

'How good of you to bring them yourself.'

'The Brands were otherwise occupied and I'm one of those people who enjoys winter. A throwback from childhood.'

'Will you take a glass of punch? Mrs Quinn will see that the others are given refreshment.'

'I will, indeed. Where do you want these things set up? My men will see to that before leaving,' Nick O'Ferrall said. 'You couldn't manage.'

'Over there. Table downstairs. Bed upstairs front.'

'Did you hear that?' O'Ferrall demanded.

'Aye, sir.'

'Take care of them. I want nothing damaged! Now, Mrs Howard, where's that punch you mentioned?'

Karran led the way to the old parlour where a fire of logs burned brightly. Laying the child in a crib, she ladled mulled wine into pewter goblets.

O'Ferrall peered into the cot. 'Your daughter looks more human.'

'She seems more content, thank God.'

'And what of your dark, brooding young lord?'

'Bart?' Karran frowned. 'Badly behaved. Sullen. I really will have to do something about that pony.'

'You won't need to. Look out of the window. A present for your son.'

Karran looked. She'd failed to notice the brown pony that had been on a leading rein behind one of the horses.

'I can't take that!'

'I didn't give it to you.'

'As his mother, I have the right to decide what gifts he can receive.'

'Dear me. How pompous you sound.' O'Ferrall smiled good-humouredly.

'I insist that I pay for it.'

'You owe me nothing. I had some of the furniture I took over valued and discovered that you'd got the worst of the bargain. With the difference, I took the liberty of bringing all three of you a present.' He withdrew two small parcels from his coat-pockets. 'That one's for Johanne.'

'How do I know you're telling the truth?'

'Would a man who tried to undercut your perfectly proper valuation by at least two hundred and fifty guineas be suggesting such a thing if it weren't so?'

'Well—! It does seem unlikely,' she admitted.

'And it's good to have someone to give gifts to at such a time.'

'Have you no family?' Karran asked.

'Neither kith nor kin. Neither wife nor mistress.'

She sat quiet, the warmth of the mulled wine relaxing her body, Johanne's package on her lap. Tom Allen couldn't be a relation then. She'd thought them close as cousins.

'Does the child have to open it herself?' he demanded at last.

Karran unwrapped the present slowly. It was a coral ring with a silver bell attached. 'That's – most thoughtful.' She shook it and the little bell chimed softly.

'What about your own? Would you deny me the pleasure of watching your face as you open that?'

'I don't feel the same about this one. The children perhaps—'

'Stuff and nonsense! I did say I had no longer anyone with whom to share this festive time. Even the Bible says it's more blessed to give than to receive.'

'You surprise me! A bible-thumper who plans to separate fools from their money! You lack credibility, Mr O'Ferrall.'

'Nick. Why don't you call me by my proper name? We've known each other some months now. Must we still stand on ceremony?'

'It's obvious you aren't aware of the small-town mentality, Mr O'Ferrall.'

'Who says so? I came from a small enough place—'

'But you never ran barefoot and uneducated, selling farm produce from a stall. I'll swear you've always slept between silken sheets and used silver spoons and had the likes of me emptying your chamber-pot in the morning.'

He was silent for a time, watching her across the hearth, then he laughed. 'You expect me to believe that? The quality just oozes out of every pore of your very fine body, Mrs Karran Howard.'

'You've obviously had an embarrassingly fruitful encounter with the Blarney stone.'

'It's the effects of the punch. May I have another?'

'Why not? You've come a long way, in uncomfortable conditions, to deliver my belongings.'

Karran put the unopened parcel on the pie-crust table

beside her chair and went to replenish their glasses.

'So. You intend to toss my goodwill offering back in my face?' O'Ferrell asked.

'I've already intimated that my acceptance would put us on a falsely intimate footing. Surely, you can follow my reasoning? You seem an intelligent enough man.'

'I hadn't thought *you* so prudish and small-minded.'

'Someone's been talking to you about me.'

'I've been asking about you,' he admitted, his Irish accent more pronounced than usual.

'Then you know that I did have poor beginnings. That it was only John Howard's interest in me that lifted me from ignorance and poverty?'

'I have only admiration for what you've made of yourself.' This time there was no mistaking his sincerity.

A burning log fell into the ashes, sending up a shower of sparks, then long fingers of flame.

Karran picked up the parcel. She unfastened the ribbon, opened up the glittering paper. Inside was a pair of expensive stockings and a set of shoe-buckles studded with semi-precious stones.

'A very familiar gift.' Karran said drily. 'The sort you might give to either the wife or the mistress you say you have not. You've made your enquiries, Mr O'Ferrall, and discovered that I've made my share of romantic errors of judgement. Well, that's all past and it's my children who concern me now.' She thrust the stockings and buckles inside the costly wrappings and pushed them back at him, the colour staining her face under the wide, high cheek-bones.

'You look very fine in your wrath, Ma'am,' O'Ferrall observed softly, his eyes caught in shafts of red from the fire so that he looked demoniac. 'I'm not used to having my offerings rejected so summarily.'

'You can take yourself off and your gifts with you!'

'What, even the pony? The pony your son does seem to need quite badly? And what would I do with a teething-ring?' There was something irrepressibly comic in his plaintive enquiry and Karran couldn't resist a quick smile she hoped he hadn't seen.

'It's true that Bart does need a new interest. I'll look at the pony and if it's suitable—'

'Suitable! It's of the finest strain, I assure you. An Irishman'd never be fobbed off with anything but the best. And I always get what I want.'

'Really?' Karran crushed down the urge to soften towards him. He *was* attractive, seductive in the way that only the Irish can be with their unpredictable charm. But she'd been a fool in the past and would never be so reckless again.

'I'll pay for the animal if it's as good as you say. Bart's got into bad company of late and I had to teach him a lesson. But I'd want the New Year to start on a better footing. A pony would give him something to think about, to look after.'

'And the infant's teething-ring?'

'Take yourself off and bite on it!'

'Please. It's so small a thing. She's the only girl-child of my acquaintance.'

'Oh, very well! It is Christmas, or will be soon.'

'I'm glad you said that. I had her name engraved on that silver band.'

'Oh, so you did. You were very sure of yourself.'

'And you won't—?' He picked up the spurned parcel.

'No, I won't!'

'One of these days, I'll offer you those things again.'

'Chance will be a fine thing,' Karran responded crisply. 'Now, if we can't agree on a price for the pony, you must take it away.'

They haggled as they'd done over the price for the Ravensdowne estate, and, as before, Karran had her way. She took the requisite sovereigns from a drawer and paid him almost defiantly. 'But don't think I'm not grateful,' she said in reparation. 'I am. Not everyone would have thought of an unhappy boy.'

'Perhaps I had an ulterior motive.'

'Well, it didn't get you very far!' Karran retorted.

'You've heard of that expression, though, haven't you.'

'Which expression?'

'Constant water wears away a stone.'

'That sounds a very lengthy process. Too lengthy for mere mortals.'

'Don't be too sure of that.' O'Ferrall rose, wrapped the scarf around his chin and fastened the warm fur-trimmed coat.

'But I am. I've never been surer of anything.'

'You'll come to my grand opening, though, won't you,' he demanded.

'I don't know—'

'I'll send you the first invitation!' O'Ferrall called over his shoulder as he went out.

Grand opening, she thought, as he shouted for his men in the cold, sharp air. She wouldn't go, not if he sent wild horses to drag her there. She wasn't that stupid!

It was as she turned away from the window after the sledges glided away that she noticed he had left the parcel on the pie-crust table, next to the coral ring. Karran took out the buckles and watched the fiery stones flashing.

Bart was in a ferment of excitement over his new acquisition. He called the pony Tom Beg after a character in one of the fairy tales he'd loved until he felt he'd outgrown them.

It was only when he was with Rosemary Costain that he thought there might still be some foundation in some of the old stories. Man was certainly afflicted with strange mists that came from nowhere to shroud the countryside and the echoing, cobbled streets of Castletown. Yes, he still believed in Mannanen, the mist giant.

Mr O'Ferrall, from whom Mama had purchased the pony, had sent Brand the younger over to give him lessons as soon as the snow and ice had cleared away. Riding by himself was the most wonderful experience of his life. So far he wasn't allowed to go just where he wished, but Mama said he was coming on so well that it wouldn't be long before he could go further afield.

Rosemary, on her next visit, was wild with jealousy.

'Why should you have Tom Beg and no one thinking about me?'

'Perhaps if your mother gets a baby, she'll buy one for you,' Bart suggested.

'How can she since my papa's gone away?'

'Mama had Johanne and Howard died a long time ago.' Bart thinking about John Howard's death, was aware of a horrid tight feeling in his chest. He could almost smell candle-wax, hear the tortured breathing, see the agonized face in the pallid light. It hadn't looked agonized later only white and peaceful—.

'Babies have to grow for a long time. Grandmama told me,' Rosemary said importantly. Bart liked to think he knew more than she did but he didn't know anything about infants and childbirth. Rose had obviously done her fair share of listening at keyholes and behind doors and curtains. She relished the sensation of power such forbidden knowledge gave her.

'Then why are they so small?'

Rosemary bit her lip with vexation. Trust Bart to ask something to which she could give no answer for all her prying.

'My mama screamed and screamed when I was born,' she announced grandly.

'Why do they have us when it hurts so much?' Bart enquired, his attention at last fully diverted from his pony.

Defeated, Rosemary said, '*I* am going to ask for a pony. Why shouldn't I have one?'

'It won't be as lovely as Tom Beg.' Bart looked down fondly.

She stamped her foot crossly. 'It'll be far, far lovelier! Why did you give yours such a silly name?'

'Because Tom Beg met the fairy folk and they took away his hump and made him into a strong, handsome man. I wish—' Bart stopped on the verge of indiscretion.

'What do you wish?' Rose looked very appealing now that she'd stopped being angry. Bart could never hold out against her for long.

'There's someone I know, a boy who's crippled. I wish

he could meet those little beings and be turned back to his real shape.'

'What boy?'

'I'm not supposed to talk about it, Rose.'

'I don't want to know about ugly persons,' she said with distaste.

'He isn't. He's really very handsome. Like a kind of prince.'

'Do tell!'

'I can't.'

'Oh, you are horrible! And so is that fat animal! Just wait till you see mine!'   'I love Tom Beg,' Bart said obstinately. 'You'd have a hard job to match him.'

'Do – do you like him more than you like me?' Rosemary asked, changing her tactics. She was very pretty now that she'd sweetened her expression and softened her voice.

Bart remembered how it felt to have someone else put in your place. 'No,' he answered, unsure if he were really telling the truth, but compelled to reassure her.

'I shall get a pony, then we can ride together.'

'They won't let you. Not till you're older.'

'It's not fair!'

'Lots of things aren't fair.'

'Why do I have to be older?' There were tears in the lovely eyes, but they were tears of anger rather than those of sorrow, and Rosemary's hands were closed into fists.

'You could fall off and break your neck.'

'Would I – be dead?'

'Yes. Even if it wasn't your neck it could be your arm or your leg. Maybe your back.'

'If I broke my back would I die?'

'Perhaps not, but you'd never be able to walk again. You'd just lie in bed for fifty years—'

'Fifty! I'd be terribly bored and I'd never go to balls and meet a prince and wear silk gowns. Just drink medicine all day and get older and older. And sick-rooms smell!'

'You wouldn't like that, Rose, would you? And neither would I.'

'What about arms and legs?'

'They aren't so bad.' Bart stroked Tom Beg's chestnut flank. 'You'd only stay in bed for weeks and weeks but you might limp afterwards if the bones haven't joined together properly. Most people do.'

'You couldn't dance if you limped, could you?'

'No, Rose.'

'How do you know all this?'

'Brand told me. He gave me lessons.'

'Then he could give some to me.'

'I s'pose he could but he doesn't work for Mama any more. He works for Mr O'Ferrall.'

'Who's Mr O'Ferrall?'

'The man who bought Ravensdowne. And he got me this pony.'

Rose was looking calculating and Bart wondered what she was thinking. It could be difficult keeping track of Rose's thoughts.

'D'you s'pose he'd give me one? Your Mr O'Ferrall?'

Bart flushed. 'He isn't my anything!' he responded sharply.

'Don't you like him?'

'Only so long as he doesn't try to marry Mama.'

'D'you think he will?' Rosemary was looking intrigued.

'Gideon's the only person she liked well enough.'

'But he's gone away for good. Grandmama said so. So she'll have to look out for someone else.'

'Your grandmama says a great deal too much if you ask me.' Bart yanked at Tom Beg's bridle in the way Brand said you shouldn't and the startled pony shot away at a dangerous speed.

'I didn't ask you!' Rosemary shouted after him. 'You're going to get everything broken! Neck, back, legs, arms. Everything!'

Pounding along the shore road, the mud spattering his clothes and an icy wind creeping inside his collar, Bart was aware only of the sensation that, deep inside him, something *was* broken. Something intangible that would never knit together even in the unsatisfactory way of bones.

He'd not thought of O'Ferrall in conjunction with his mother until Rose's careless words. Now she'd aroused those memories of Mama he found most disturbing.

Tom Beg raced on, unchecked, along the ragged margin of the sea.

It was Barney who saw the paragraph in the Liverpool paper. He sat staring at the printed words until the letters danced and lost all meaning.

'What is it?' Erin asked, disturbed.

'See for yourself.' Barney pushed the paper at her, his eyes still registering shock.

'God in heaven,' Erin breathed after a long interval. 'How will she take it, d'you think?'

'Badly.'

They sat silently, then Erin said. 'None of the children have had far to look for problems. Why is it, I wonder, that some families seem marked for trouble? The only one who's had any success is Boyce. It's not every mother can say that her son's a member of parliament. If it wasn't for *her*—'

'If it hadn't been for Nina, he'd never have been a member. You've her determination and her papa's money and influence to thank for that. Boyce is never going to stick to anything, left to himself, and well you know it. He needs someone there, prodding at him, all the time.'

'You've always had a down on them, all three.'

'And you've never had a good word to say for Charlotte! Good God, woman, she *is* your child as well!'

Barney stopped, aghast. It was the closest he and Erin had come to a real quarrel for some time. Erin hadn't been herself for a bit. There hadn't been any of her bedroom games lately. He missed those. She'd been pale and curiously distant. Suddenly, he needed some of her Irish warmth and spirit.

'Does anything ail you?' he asked more gently.

Erin shook her head and shrugged. 'Does Charlotte need to know?'

'Of course she does. It'll hurt, but she's not a lass to

shirk reality. Isn't it better she comes to terms with it now? She's young enough to make another life for herself. Anyway, that report's there so that they may hear from his relatives. All they know at present is his name and Liverpool address. The world's a big place. Folk hide in it and leave no trace of their beginnings.'

'None of them good choosers,' Erin murmured, seeming, in a typically Gaelic way, to enjoy brooding over disaster.

'Are you including yourself?' Barney asked directly.

'Why should I?' Her eyes refused to meet his and his heart beat faster.

'You aren't the same towards me,' he accused. 'What's changed?'

She shook her red hair. 'Nothing I know of.'

Barney's mind registered the way she stressed the word know. Consciously or subconsciously? What had he done, or not done? One could be as bad as the other.

'Men get queer notions at a certain age,' she went on. 'Take that old feller Quilliam along the road. His wife dies after devoting the whole of her life to his wants and dislikes and what does he do?'

Barney recognized his cue. 'What has he done?'

'Taken up with the swaggering-arsed little madam who's been looking after the house and she not above twenty-three. And his wife not quite cold in her grave.'

Barney burst out laughing. 'Well, the old dog! I hadn't heard.'

'And that's all you can say, is it!' Erin's large green eyes blazed. 'So that's the sort of behaviour you find amusing. But I didn't think *you'd* find it reprehensible! The dirty old goat that he is!'

'Erin, have you ever tried to picture the man without those straight-up-and-down clothes of his? They look lined with tin. If he took them off in a fit of lust, he'd fall to the floor. They're all that hold him up.'

She didn't laugh. A few weeks ago, Barney reflected, she'd have been unable to contain herself. Erin had always enjoyed a good earthy joke. What was she trying to tell him?

'Has she put your nose out of joint?' he joked. 'Did you fancy him yourself?'

It was the wrong thing to say. Erin turned very pale and her mouth thinned as it always did under the force of her anger.

'Not as much as I think you fancy a certain person whose name will not pass my lips.'

'You're being a fool. I'm not given to dubious attachments, but suspecting me of them could be the quickest way to drive me in that direction. This coldness of yours isn't what I'd imagined or require as my lot for the remainder of my life. D'you understand me?'

'Once, you had *me* living in perpetual winter,' she said in a low voice.

'Ah, but there was very good reason. *I* didn't imagine anything. You have some maggot in your head as usual. Take care it doesn't destroy us,' he warned.

'You swear you don't hanker after someone younger than meself?'

'Would you believe me if I did? It seems, my dear, you've some compelling urge to ruin my peace of mind. But just as an old man like Quilliam can find his blood running unexpectedly hot in his dotage, women can be quite as unpredictable at a certain age. I can only conclude that you've reached it.'

Her swimming eyes reproached him.

Barney's conscience was pricked. 'I'm sorry. That just slipped out.'

Erin turned away to dab at the tears.

'What's the matter?' Charlotte asked from the doorway. 'Something in your eye, Mama?'

Erin nodded and went on with what she was doing.

Belatedly, Barney remembered Abel. 'Charlotte—'

His daughter gave him a clear-eyed look. 'Papa?'

'You meant it, love, when you said you wanted nothing more to do with Abel, didn't you?'

'Yes. You know I did.'

'All, all your feelings for him, were they gone?'

'Whyever are you asking me about him? I'd rather not be reminded.'

'Then, you wouldn't be unduly upset—' Barney floundered.

'You don't mean he's coming back?' Charlotte's throat constricted.

'I mean, he isn't coming back. Ever.'

Charlotte's face registered unexpected horror. 'Ever? What's happened to him?' Her voice was wild. 'I think I misunderstood you. He's not *dead*? He couldn't be.'

'That's what I was trying to say. I hoped you'd not be too unhappy.'

'Unhappy! How? How did he die?' Charlotte, her skin drained of colour, sank on to a chair and made washing movements with her hands. She was obviously in a state of extreme shock.

'They – think he drowned.'

'Think? Don't they know? What do they mean by think? And who are "they"?'

'It's all in the Liverpool paper.' Barney indicated the paragraph.

Charlotte snatched at the stiff sheets. She was trembling violently. The paper crackled as she read, then she allowed it to slide to her lap while her hands lay over it, heavy as stones.

'I know why he did it,' she said tonelessly.

'No one knows!'

'Yes, Papa. He asked me for help and I refused. Somehow I didn't think he could possibly be so destitute, but he must have been, after all. I feel like a murderess.'

'That's foolish talk and you'll be the first to realize it once you're over the shock. If you'd gone on keeping him, he'd never have left you in peace.'

'I – was married to him, Papa. It did mean something. Once—'

'I know, my dear. But he spoiled that himself. I'll write to Liverpool, shall I? Better still, I'll go over there and see whoever is in charge at the docks. Find out as much as I can.'

86

'Will they – find his body?'

'I can't answer that, love. Somewhere, perhaps, one day.'

'They'd know it was Abel. By – his right hand.'

Barney went behind Charlotte's chair and put his hands on her shoulders. 'Try not to think too much. Fill your time with other things. Go to see Karran. She'd be good for you.' His eyes encountered Erin's and he was astonished by the bleakness in hers and the haggardness of her looks. But he wasn't going to retract his suggestion, however much Erin might hate him for it. He'd no time for old scores, and, anyway, no matter how fond he was of Erin, he knew perfectly well that she'd not be as kind to his grieving daughter as Karran Howard. 'Karran will make you laugh, you'll see.'

Erin turned away, standing stiffly by the window.

'I'll go to Liverpool then, Charlotte. I'll not be gone long. A few days at most. And you aren't to blame yourself.' He leaned down to kiss the top of her head, aware of her intense desolation.

Rosemary ran into the room, a picture of prettiness in a green dress trimmed with thick, creamy lace, a matching ribbon in her hair.

'Why are you kissing Mama?'

'Your mama's sad. Something's happened to your papa, child.'

'Something bad?'

'You're a brave lass, Rosie. I can tell you. Your papa's dead.'

The child's face turned curiously blank. 'Did he fall off a horse and break something? His neck? His back?'

'What odd things you do say, my girl. No. He – drowned.'

Rosemary shivered. 'I always knew the sea was wicked. That it would rush over you if you didn't always watch it. I always do. Always.'

'You'll be a good girl for Mama's sake, won't you, while I go to Liverpool? Mama mustn't be bothered with naughtiness. Not just now.' Barney stroked Charlotte's hair, staring at her unresponsive profile with helpless perturbation.

'I feel sad too,' Rosemary said with a catch in her voice. 'Very sad. Can I have a pony? Please, Grandpa?'

'I don't really see why not,' Barney replied a little absently, his thoughts still for his daughter.

Rosemary's expression changed to one of calculation that Barney failed to notice. Only Erin saw, from her place in the shadows.

'Good,' the little girl said. 'Can I have white one?'

'Aren't you glad you're free? I thought that's what you wanted?' Karran asked, pouring tea. She hadn't brought out the bottle of sherry yet because Charlotte looked in a frame of mind to drain one all by herself, and Rosemary would only carry tales to her grandmother. Karran still hadn't forgotten Erin's threatening shadow looming over her weakened body, the fears she'd entertained for her helpless baby in the cot by her side.

'I don't feel free. Abel's fettered me. I wonder if he knew how my conscience would prick me? Don't answer that. Of course he did. But I can't bear to think of him leaving his cape on the dockside and jumping like that. Never coming up. He must have been so unhappy. I didn't visualize that sort of freedom.'

'Was he a good swimmer?'

'He could swim, but certainly not strongly. Those people who witnessed the event didn't see him come up. None of them. Perhaps he had weights in his pockets. Most suicides do.'

'You'll feel better soon. Here, drink that.'

'Nothing stronger?' Charlotte suggested, crouching closer to the fire, eyes haunted.

'Later perhaps, when Rose is in bed.'

Charlotte stared. 'Why? What difference does she make?'

'I hadn't meant to say anything. But—' Karran hesitated.

'But, what? I insist on knowing.'

Bit by bit, Charlotte drew out the story of Erin's

disruptive visit. Her dark skin flushed with anger. 'How *dared* she!'

'I think she was genuinely concerned. Everyone knows how she feels about your father.'

'She had no right,' Charlotte said again, unmollified. 'You must let me know far sooner next time. I wonder what Rosemary said?'

'Enough to raise several hares! I feel sorry for your mother. She's most insecure.'

'I noticed she's been sullen lately. Poor Papa! My sympathies are with him. As if he hadn't enough to worry him. He's found out they're re-opening the Bath shipyard in Douglas. There's more space and deeper water. It's bound to affect Castletown. They're even saying that the House of Keys will eventually be based in Douglas.'

'My mother and her parents came from there. My grandfather was a fisherman. He died in the dreadful storm of, 1789, I think it was. No, it was 1787. There were four hundred herring boats off Clay Head when the gale blew up out of nowhere. One of them ran into the beacon at Douglas Harbour and the rest were left in pitchy darkness. So much for all those lucky pennies under the masts! My mother saw and heard it all. She was only a child.'

'Poor thing. You never told me before.'

'I didn't know myself for a long time. How do you like my new fireplace?'

'That's Poyllvaish marble, isn't it? The black looks very distinguished.' Charlotte, diverted, rose to inspect the polished smoothness. 'You've got a piece with fossils embedded. So decorative and mysterious. Didn't they make the steps of St Paul's Cathedral from it?'

'So I was told. They're no longer there, though. All those hundreds of thousands of worshipping feet wore them away.'

Charlotte returned, sweeping a copy of the *Manx Advertiser* from the arm of a chair. 'Sorry.' She picked it up, then, still restless, paced the floor.

'Your tea's getting cold.'

'So it is. I'm sorry I'm on edge. It must be trying for you.'

'It's not trying. It would be strange if you weren't.'

'How's Bart?' the question coincided with the scream of the wind outside. The casements rattled.

'Better. He loves that pony.'

'I believe Rosemary has wheedled the promise of one out of Papa.'

'I thought she might.'

'She's growing into a minx.' Charlotte smoothed black skirts and recommenced her distrait pacing. 'I see too much of my mother in her.'

'Do you recall laughing at me when I felt that I'd more of my dubious antecedents in me than I cared for?'

'Yes.'

'It's nothing one can help. You said so yourself.'

'I suppose it isn't. But it doesn't make life any easier.'

'Charlotte. Sit down and compose yourself! You'll wear out the carpet.'

'Damn my mother! Please, may I have something other than this tea? I couldn't care less if Rosemary reports we've had a black mass!'

Karran winced. 'Erin would believe that. She knew the Karrans, remember.'

However, she did go to the cupboard where the bottle was kept and poured her friend a generous measure and herself a small amount.

'Thank you,' Charlotte said. 'I understand you are to have a gamblers' paradise at Ravensdowne? Didn't you know?'

'Not at first. O'Ferrall's invited me to his grand opening. But the weather's turned so vicious, that's obviously going to be delayed.'

'Will you go?' Charlotte's face was not so distraught.

They sat for a moment listening to the sough of the wind in the chimneys and the flutter of the flames in the fireplace.

'If I do, it's to return something.'

'What?'

Karran pulled out a small drawer and took out O'Ferrall's parcel. Charlotte pounced on it, diverted.

'An intimate little offering!'

'That's what I told him but it didn't stop him leaving it behind.'

'You know what he's after!'

'No. Tell me.' For all that she tried to infuse amusement into her voice, Karran didn't succeed. 'He thinks I'll be an easy conquest but he doesn't know me.'

'You've not forgotten Gideon, have you.'

'No.' The word seemed drawn from the depths of Karran's being. 'I'm reminded of him almost hourly. Johanne gets more like him every day. Even her eyes have gradually taken on the same colour. Those dark spokes—'

'But you wouldn't have had it otherwise? You don't wish none of it had ever happened?'

Karran shook her head. The shoe-buckles on Charlotte's lap flashed rainbow fire. 'No. I experienced great happiness with Gideon. And little Hanna fills many gaps I'd have found intolerable.'

'Hanna!'

'Yes. I found it evolved quite naturally. It's not quite so hard as Johanne, though she'll be given the choice when she's a little older. She may prefer her full name.'

'Rosemary's all things to all people. Papa calls her Rosie. I give her her proper name. Bart, Mama and Abel tend to call her Rose – Abel used—' suddenly Charlotte broke into violent weeping, her body contorted, her head thrashing from side to side as though in some monstrous fit. The parcel fell from her lap to the hearth-rug.

Karran retrieved the scattered objects quickly, then knelt to put her arms around Charlotte. 'There, my dear. Cry. Get rid of it for once and ever. It's what you needed. Cry it all away. He wasn't really worth that unhappiness. I never yet met the man who was.'

The shadowy corners of the room mocked her words.

The weather had improved but O'Ferrall had not sent the promised invitation. In spite of her previous reservations,

Karran was piqued. At least he might have given her the chance of a dignified refusal.

She re-wrapped his spurned Christmas gift and sent it, with a cool little note, by the carrier who regularly passed Cormorant House. She wished she'd done it sooner, only she'd expected to see the new owner of Ravensdowne before now so that she could have returned it in person. It seemed that O'Ferrall was another man who was easily distracted from his purpose.

The carrier spoke of a lady who was staying at Ravensdowne, but knew nothing about her except that he'd been told she was young and golden-haired. It was an unsatisfactory second-hand account and Karran was left more curious about the enigmatic Irishman than before.

A few more days passed with the weather even better, the air crisp and sharp as wine-apples and the buds beginning to show on the trees. Karran saw the shaggy tribe of the Stark boys riding by, their eyes swivelling towards the windows as though they sought for a glimpse of her beyond the lace curtains. They looked so fierce and barbaric that her stomach muscles contracted. How fortunate that Charlotte and Rosemary were no longer here. The Starks had no cause to feel friendly towards the Costains, though they were beholden to her son.

They said old man Stark had erected a post at his boundary on which rested a gun loaded with rusty nails. Trip wires spread in all directions, the weapon swivelling in the direction of any intruder who touched any wire. Karran didn't care to think about nails fired at speed.

She wondered how many other feuds were being perpetuated all over the island. In such an insular place one had either good friends or bitter enemies. There seemed little neutral ground between.

Disturbed by the noisy passage of the Starks, she went upstairs to tend to Hanna who'd changed subtly from infant to little girl. Her thick, dark hair had grown, not crisply waved like Bart's, but smoother, only the ends curling outwards softly to frame the small, pale face. The eyes were Gideon's, the pupils a violet-grey marked with black lines.

Karran made Hanna comfortable, then held the child to her breast. It was infinitely peaceful with only the soft flicker of the fire and a faint sighing in the chimney, not at all like the savage cacophony of sound that had brutalized the house on the day of Charlotte's breakdown. Her thoughts passed again to her grandfather Kinrade who'd drowned in the year 1787, the same year as the famous, or infamous, Mutiny on the *Bounty*. Three men then living on Man had been involved, Karran remembered, soothed yet stimulated by the tug of the baby's mouth on her nipple. Indeed, Fletcher Christian had been a relative of the Christians who'd taken her mother into their home after she'd been orphaned on that dreadful night of the storm.

There'd been many interesting folk on the island. The famous Stanleys had ruled it for three hundred and fifty years. Oh, why was she sitting here like an old woman reliving the past?

She was missing Ravensdowne, the smell of the smoke-house at Port St Mary, the sight of the red herrings being packed into barrels, ready for shipping to the far-off slave plantations. She wanted to ride to Spanish Head along the cliff-tops, and see the black outline of the Sugarloaf rock rising from a silver sea. The rock did resemble those large sugar cones that were used in the kitchens of grand houses. She found herself remembering O'Ferrall. The first gaming-house, Fort Anne, was at the other end of Douglas Bay. Buck Whaley had been afflicted with a desire to have his home built on Irish soil.

That was it! Karran sat up straighter, laughing. The baby lost its grip on her breast and complained sleepily. Still laughing softly, Karran shifted the infant to her other breast. The fact that she'd forgotten what was so amusing about Whaley had niggled at her thoughts of late. He's married an heiress who could only keep her fortune if she lived on the good earth of Ireland, so he'd had tons of it

93

shipped to Douglas to fill in the foundations of his grandiose mansion! Only true Irish wit could have devised such a scheme. She must remember to tell O'Ferrall when next he came.

If he came.

Karran concentrated upon the less than satisfactory present. She had what she'd wanted, the full amount for Ravensdowne, the cottage enlarged without losing any of its character. The new kitchen would shortly be finished now that the weather showed signs of stability. She couldn't be more pleased with the two completed wings. The small four-poster had been put up in the new guest room and the big rosewood table graced the dining-room, complementing the long sideboard with its battery of old silver. Mrs Quinn had hung the last of the expensive curtains though still she maintained that 'the sea would get at them'.

Something was missing, something vital, the absence of which spoiled the achievement of the rest. Quinn had warned her she'd miss Ravensdowne.

Hanna tugged strongly, her baby lips suddenly whitened with spilled milk. Her face was almost sensual. For the first time, Karran saw herself in the child. She knew what was missing. Fulfilment.

Mrs Quinn was coming upstairs. She came rather more slowly than usual, her feet curiously careful on the treads. Karran wondered what had gone wrong in the kitchen. Perhaps Bart had come back from his ride on Tom Beg earlier than intended and upset the cream. Maybe it was Erin, renewing her old antagonism after another bout of uncertainty— Then, intuition told her that it wasn't the housekeeper. She knew her step too well.

Karran pulled together the front of her bodice and put both arms round the child protectively. She thought of shouting for Mrs Quinn or Molly Quayle who'd be cleaning the old part of the house by this time, and might hear her even through these thick walls.

Remembering the rough, ragged figures of the Starks, her heart beat wildly. There was one of them, Reuben, or was it Will—? who stared—

A tall shadow filled the doorway.

'Oh,' she said, 'it's you. Why on earth did you come creeping upstairs like a felon? If it's your offerings you've come to see me about, I still don't want them. But if you're asking me to visit you at Ravensdowne, then I think that might be arranged, Mr Nick O'Ferrall!' Relief made her light-headed. His grand opening could after all be the diversion she needed to counteract this feeling of loneliness.

'It's neither,' Gideon said and stepped into the light.

Karran could not speak or move. Only the huge black eyes were eloquent, taking in every detail of his appearance, the dark, elegant clothes, the long, well-bred features, the sensual mouth that belied the rest of him.

For a long moment she thought she might faint. Nothing had prepared her for this unexpected confrontation. The vast expanse of sky beyond the window seemed to shift vertiginously. She was aware that something screamed close by and wondered, stupidly, if she herself had cried out. But her throat was clamped tight by the force of shock – and longing, detestation, bitterness—. It seemed an eternity before she realized that the sounds came from the gulls that had just noticed the crusts she'd thrown into the garden an hour ago.

The tick of the clock seemed too loud to bear. She was not sure whether she wanted him to seize and ravish her or if she should grab the water jug and fling the contents in his face. Both would have served the same end. Whatever had died between them would have been stampeded into a conflict larger than life.

Slowly, the impulse to savage him ebbed away. She realized that the strength that had, only moments ago, flared like some consuming forest fire had gone, leaving her sick and shaken, barely able to stand.

Was it anguish she felt, self-pity, or just good old-fashioned anger? The one certainty was that he still maintained that inexplicable power over her, and she despised herself.

'Sorry to disappoint you,' Gideon said in a choked voice.

'How could I have known?' she cried passionately. 'One letter in a year! Should I have put out flags to welcome you? Why did you come?' Her voice dropped almost to a whisper.

'To collect some things held in store. I heard – heard about the child. You never told me.' It was his turn to protest.

She tried to turn a deaf ear to his complaint. That could be a convenient peg on which Gideon could hang her guilt if he wished.

'You never thought to ask! Most men might have wondered. Most adults, that is. I didn't wish to break in upon your idyllic fantasies with cold reality.'

'That's cruel, Karran. You never were before.' His low, hurt tone reproached her.

'I wasn't a widow before. A woman with a young son and – daughter to bring up.'

'You should have known I'd be interested in my own child!'

'*My* child. Her name's Howard, Gideon. You've no claim on her.' She knew the answer to her question now. It *was* red-blooded anger she felt, and directed as much towards herself as him.

'Why didn't you reply to my letter? I was desperate when nothing came. Not one word, affectionate or otherwise. What was I supposed to think? I waited. Waited in vain for some explanation. Pride prevented me from writing again. I thought I'd give myself a month or two. Still silence. Then I knew that it must be over, our dark idyll, that you'd cut free. That was when anger replaced the hurt. I damned you in my mind, thinking that I'd done my part in keeping your name clean—'

'And yours!' she said hotly.

He advanced, his face dark with an emotion she'd never seen. Part anger. Part— Frustration? What else? Oh God, she wanted him, but she didn't trust him an inch.

Hanna had her eyes wide open. Gideon stared down at her, everything about him still as stone. A dribble of milk trickled down the baby's chin. She gave him a brief, toothless smile and held out one chubby hand.

'You should have told me, Karran,' he insisted.

'I might have if you hadn't taken such pains to tell me how happy you were. How Mary depended on you. What pleasure you took in one another's company. How you were busy looking for a new partnership. How you weren't coming back!'

'I never said that!' Again that condemnation that cut her to the quick and left her smarting. But she hadn't written—

'Not in so many words.'

'We had an arrangement, Karran. We were to counteract gossip by remaining apart for long enough for you to get out of mourning blacks for your husband. D'you think a stream of letters from me wouldn't have been noticed? It's *you* who didn't grow up! They'd have been as damning as my appearance. It was just as much your wish that I stayed away. More, if I remember correctly.'

'Perhaps it was,' she admitted. 'But I found it – hard.' Her voice was small and tight with repressed pain.

'Not too hard, though. Where were you to visit Mr O'Ferrall? The gazebo?'

'Now who's cruel! And blind.'

'Not too blind to recognize my own flesh and blood. And a certain note in your voice when you greeted me so erroneously—'

'Go away, Gideon! Go away. I've often thought about the way we'd meet again, if we did, but it was not like this.'

'Did you think I haven't thought? If I'd sent you a letter full of the things we'd already done, and the things I wanted to do in the future, would *that* have been any better than ignoring them? We've both got imaginations. A breathing space was what you demanded and that's what you've had, but I see I stayed away too long. I knew you'd bought the cottage, and some of the furnishings, I had that from Barney Kerruish and Paul Christie. Only I never thought of you taking another lover quite so soon. It took me long enough to get you. O'Ferrall must be an exceptionally persuasive man.'

'I hardly know him.'

Gideon laughed shortly. 'That's not the impression I received.' He looked down again at the child and held out a finger. The small hand clasped it strongly.

'Gideon—'

'She looks like Mary.'

'Oh, damn your clinging vine! Mary sounds like an incubus.'

'You don't know her.'

'And I don't want to! Perhaps we've misinterpreted one another's actions but I want you to leave, Gideon. This is my house now. And it's obvious that too much has changed between us.'

'But this is my daughter. You and I both know it, and, I daresay, the entire population of St Mary's and Castletown.'

'And, if you raise your voice any more, so will my entire staff, not to mention my son. You used to be very concerned about the harm done to developing minds.' Her body was shaking and she saw that his hands too were unsteady, as though he fought for control.

'Karran. What are we doing to one another?' His voice had softened now, either with affection or in calculation, and he'd switched his attention from the child to herself. 'You haven't buttoned yourself up properly.'

'I – I wasn't sure who was coming up the staircase. I'd been feeding my baby. In the dark, at the top, you looked much the height and shape of the man who bought the estate.'

'Who has pestered you to visit him.'

'He's by way of being a card king. He plans to open a casino. Not the kind of man one takes too seriously.' She found herself laughing a little shakily though she couldn't have explained why. The gulls were squawking again, and the fire dropped in on itself as though it were as worn out with turbulence as themselves.

'Surely that's been done before? Buck Whaley and a host of lesser notabilities?'

'Yes. We get a lot of mainland dilettantes with murky

pasts on Man. They enjoy gambling.' Karran saw that he was scarely listening to her reply. It was the child who really concerned him.

'Let me hold her. Whatever her name is,' Gideon demanded softly.

'It's Hanna, though it started as Johanne. After my paternal grandmother.' She was conscious of a danger that threatened, a danger that had not existed before today. Panic made her clutch the child closer.

'Let go of her! Are you afraid I'll run off with her?' he asked, half-irritated, half-amused.

'Yes, I am. Would you?' She wondered if he'd tell her the truth but how would she know?

'How do I answer that? I'm very drawn to her. Already she seems to know me.' He seemed pleased at the thought.

'And I love her very much. You have your sister. Isn't she enough?' It had to be enough. She felt cold after so much passion and the heart-burning that had left only the ashes of emotion.

'We won't talk about either of them for a while. Only ourselves.'

'It's not possible to leave them out. Mary influences you greatly, I fear.'

'But we'll try, shall we? Is there anything to eat? I'm famished. I didn't stop for any food.'

'Oh, Gideon. Of course there is.' The switch to practicalities was a relief after such highly charged emotions.

'Shall we have it up here? Where we won't be disturbed.'

'If that's what you want.'

'Then let me hold – Hanna – while you arrange it? Please?'

Karran said, 'It's not just – an excuse to get me out of the way?' She wavered, touched by his look of genuine pleading. Like a small boy desirous of a sugar plum.

'Of course not. Why should I make such a point of having you to myself? No one will intrude, will they?'

She shook her head. Placing the infant in his arms, she

refastened her bodice.

'I would have done that for you,' Gideon told her with a touch of his old mischief. The light from the window shone on his face and she could see small lines of weariness round his eyes, in spite of the smile.

She would have to trust him. He'd been on the rack just as much as she.

Once downstairs she experienced a little thrust of fear, but so long as she didn't leave the drawing-room, he couldn't go out of the house unnoticed. Calling through the doorway of Gideon's former sitting-room, she gave Mrs Quinn her order for a meal for herself and Mr Collister to be eaten upstairs. A matter of business. There was some cold fowl and beef, wasn't there? But all the time she was wondering what he was doing. Planning—

Mrs Quinn listened, not without an old-fashioned look, 'I'll tell Master Bart you're busy when he comes back? If he does before Mr Collister leaves.'

'No. Don't do that. He'll want to see Gideon. Bart can't be much longer. I knew it was a mistake to give him so much licence. Yet, he so enjoys that added freedom and I want him proficient before he returns to school. He and Tim Clive are to go to the Castle Academy next term. Rose won't like that, but this time she'll not get her own way.' All the time she made herself speak calmly and unhurriedly, Karran wanted to run back. She forced herself to stand there as though time didn't matter, as if nothing was wrong—

'She certainly won't. A foot-stamping little madam who's got her grandfather as soft as putty. Still, that's what we'd all like, isn't it, to be cocks-o-the-walk. But since the Academy don't take children of her age, there's nought she can do.'

Mrs Quinn went off to prepare a tray and Karran returned swiftly to her chamber, where she found Gideon still engrossed with their child.

He looked up at her. 'We'll be left to ourselves?'

'Until Bart comes. He shouldn't be very long.'

'I'd hoped—'

'Oh, I can guess what you hoped!' She laughed abruptly. 'For today you'll get a meal and nothing more. I have to be much surer of my feelings than I am. Things have been said that aren't so easily forgotten. I'll swear you honestly thought me ready to tumble into O'Ferrall's bed – if you hadn't pictured me already having occupied one side of it.'

'I'm sorry.' The old Gideon smile that should put her on her guard!'

'Didn't you expect a certain degree of caution?'

'A year ago, matters would have been vastly different.'

'We all – change.' But the trouble was, she didn't think she had, or that she had the strength to keep up the pretence.

'I haven't changed that much. If I'd written every time I thought of you, would it have made a difference?' He studied her with what looked like real hurt.

'Yes. I'd have known you still loved me. Wanted me—'

'Oh, I certainly want you, Karran. Make no mistake about that.' But he made no move to relinquish the crowing baby.

He's fallen in love with Hanna, Karran thought. He must keep me sweet so that I won't deprive him of her. As if I'd have tried— He's insulting!

Gideon picked up the coral ring with the silver bell and waved it in front of the smiling infant. She chuckled at the pretty, tinkling sound.

He never had a childhood, Karran forced herself to remember. Gideon wants to live it now through Mary and my child. Our child—

She went to the window, restless as Charlotte had been in her agony of guilt over Abel, peering through the curtain for a sight of Bart. Bart who represented safety after the intimacy of the forthcoming meal. She didn't want to be alone with a man as persuasive as Gideon Collister when she was so confused in her emotions. He could pay little attention to her assertion that he must go unsatisfied. Their previous meetings had never ended on so inconclusive a note, however strong her principles initially had been. Yet, misunderstanding had undeniably made a gap that might be hard to bridge.

Mrs Quinn brought the tray herself, invitingly set out with cold meats, soup and wine.

Gideon did at last allow Karran to put a drowsy Hanna into her cradle where she fell instantly asleep. Mrs Quinn's footsteps receded down the echoing stairs. He pulled Karran into his arms and her senses quickened. 'I want you,' he whispered.

'And go off leaving me pregnant? For another year?' Purposely she made her voice sharp, but her senses wanted what he offered her, to be taken again with all of his seductive wiles, to go back to being a woman. Not to be Mrs Howard, the widow, but Karran – Gideon's lover.

'No. I'll make sure I don't leave you with child.' He kissed the side of her neck.

'You'd never have that much self-control. It's all or nothing with you, Gideon.' Desperately, she clung to commonsense.

'Karran, Karran—' Softly he offered her delicious wantonness.

Self-denial made her shrewish.

'You know yourself better than that! And don't tell me you've been celibate since last we met. I'd never believe you.' Ridiculously she was still afraid of allowing him to come too close.

'Nothing that counted.'

Karran was conscious of a stab of anger. Gideon with his fly-by-nights, O'Ferrall with his golden-haired visitor. It was a man's world and suddenly, like Charlotte, she resented it, while realizing her inability to change it.

Decisively she moved out of his embrace. 'I thought you were famished.'

'So I am.' Smiling, as though he'd seen through the pitiful pretence, he sat down and helped himself to food and wine, eating hungrily, watching her across the low fireside table.

Little by little, the magic of her former violent feeling for Gideon returned. She drank some wine, beginning to enjoy the sensation of relaxation. She was with the man she professed to love. It was she who'd sent him away, afterwards regretting the finality of the separation.

'If I hadn't had Hanna,' she asked carefully, 'Would you still have come? Or would you have gathered all those chattels and departed on the next boat?'

'You've grown very suspicious, my dear.'

My love, he'd have called her a year ago. His lovely love. A chill came suddenly over her spirits.

'You haven't answered.'

'Of course I'd have come.'

Was it her imagination or was there an edge to his voice?

'Forgive me if I seem over-cautious. My year hasn't been without its traumas.' The spell was breaking and she wasn't strong enough to face up to the fact. She despised her weakness.

'I can see that.'

'People wanted Ravensdowne but not at my price. I had to fight for that. And Hanna was making her presence felt, increasingly. O'Ferrall, I'm sure, now thinks he had good value.' She strove to return to more level ground. Enchantment had a habit of disappearing as insidiously as it came.

'I'm sure he had.' That edge was more pronounced.

'Gideon, we'll get nowhere if your mind persists in thinking in double-entendres.'

Gideon frowned. 'What's he like?'

'O'Ferrall? Rather like you in many respects,' she was driven to say. 'An opportunist. Kind, when he wants to be. Likes his own way. If he's forced to concede, he usually asks for some small sop to his ego.' She hadn't intended to sound so critical. Gideon had thrown her off balance.

'And what – what was the small sop he demanded for payment in full for Howard's house?' Gideon's voice was dry as dust.

'My attendance at his grand opening. I refused initially, that's why I thought he'd come back to ask a second time. He's a persistent man and makes no bones about it. Quite frankly, he reminded me that constant dripping wears away stones. You made that discovery yourself, Gideon. No one could have battered at my defences more strongly.' She knelt at the hearth and threw a log on to the fire. 'But breached citadels can lose their attraction. I'd not blame you if you've come to that same conclusion. Only, never pretend! I'd find that unacceptable.'

There was a clatter as he pushed aside the laden table. His hand shot out and grasped at her wrist. 'I'm still coming to terms with your description of me. Do you really think me an opportunist?'

Karran nodded, only half amused by his apparent indignation.

'You didn't object too strongly a year ago.'

'Oh, but I did. You didn't listen. Wouldn't—'

'I want to see more of the child. Marry me and come to Glasgow.' His voice vibrated with what sounded like real urgency.

'And live in Mary's house?' Now she must be careful. 'No, thank you. I've no time for a ménage à trois. She wouldn't want me. Can't you realize that? Although we've never met I feel I know your sister. I suspect she'd be eaten up with jealousy!'

'I realize that you are.'

'No, Gideon.' Again she was tormented by her inability to gauge the truth. 'I won't uproot my family. Bart has friends here. He feels as I do about the island. I've made this house as I want it. You must come back if you want us so much. I'd never prevent you from seeing Hanna.'

'I've joined a new company of solicitors. I begin to practise next week. Gilmour and Blackwell.'

'You've severed links completely with Christie's?'

'Yes. I'm surprised you didn't know.'

'I wasn't in a position to ask about you. Remember? Only to think. To listen to snippets of gossip. And wonder—'

'And come to the wrong conclusions! I blame you, Karran.'

They stared at one another, aghast.

Karran was aware of pain in her wrist where his hand

was still clamped fast.

'You're hurting me. I didn't want to shackle you. I'd never bind any man.'

Gideon let her go. The marks of his thumb and fingers showed redly. 'I'm sorry.'

There would be bruises, Karran thought numbly. The sort of bruises Charlotte always had when her husband lived with her.

'I'm sorry,' Gideon repeated, his face pale.

'When must you leave?' she asked.

'On Friday.'

'You'd better go now. We'll only continue hurting one another. Face facts. We've grown too far apart.'

'But I may see Hanna before I go altogether?'

'Of course.'

He looked into the shadowy confines of the crib, his mouth twisted.

Again, Karran was afraid that he might try to remove the child. But he stood back without any attempt to touch her. Turning to Karran, he said. 'I do think you should reconsider my offer of marriage. Bart might not be as averse to changes as you fear. I think he'd accept me.'

'He always gets very upset at the notion of leaving the district.'

'If you went, he'd have to go.' Again that edge of hardness. 'It's your decision.'

'I'd prefer it to be his own choice. He had a bad time before John died. I won't consider unsettling him at present.' Gideon was going to pretend that the chasm between them didn't exist. Gideon could be very good at burying his head in sand. She felt old and responsible, resenting the burden that weighed on her shoulders.

'Does that mean that you might at some future date?'

'I shouldn't build your hopes too high. Why don't you go back and marry someone of your sister's choice? Have a brood of children you *could* call your own?'

Anger transformed his face a second time.

'I said we'd only hurt each other,' Karran whispered. 'We aren't the same people.'

'I'll come on Thursday,' Gideon told her grimly. 'Give some thought to what I've suggested.'

'How could I not?'

He turned at the doorway just before he went from sight. 'Thursday, Karran.'

The words hung on the air like a threat.

She heard him call out to Molly Quayle as he stepped out of the house and his voice was completely different. It was the voice of the old Gideon, carefree and seductive. Karran was lacerated with pain.

Rosemary had her pony. It was white as she'd imperiously requested and she called it Snowball. Shining-eyed, she displayed the pretty animal to Bart.

'However did you manage to get him?' Bart asked.

'Her. My father died and I was sad. So Grandpa thought I should have her.' Rosemary assumed a sorrowing expression she had by this time accepted as genuine. Not that she could remember a good deal about her father. He was a shadowy figure whose breath had usually smelt of spirits and who made Mama cry. *She* wouldn't have cried. She'd have turned on him and bitten his hand! Only, not the damaged one. Misshapen things revolted her. There was no picture of Papa to remind her of his looks. He'd faded to little more than a waiting darkness in the corner of a room.

'Can you ride her?'

'Quite well. Ever since I last came here I've been having lessons with Mrs Lacey, the lady who keeps horses near us. Sometimes for hours! But Mama said I had to persevere or she'd send Snowball back. So I did. It's quite easy.'

'Shall we go for a ride now? Our mamas are very occupied with Hanna and all that eternal talking they seem to like so much. They'll never notice we've gone.'

'Where shall we go?'

'There's a bridle path round the edges of Kentraugh estate. We won't meet anyone up there. And I'm allowed to take it so far, so long as I don't go to Stark's.'

'All right.' Rosemary stood on the mounting-block and

was quickly astride.

Bart tucked her small, booted feet into the stirrups.

It was cold but everything shone brightly after rain. The distant views were very clear. Water drops sparkled on the long grasses. The track was pleasant, following the line of the rise. They could look down on the roof of Bart's home, the plumy smoke banners from the chimneys, the Black Rocks and the sea that shone hurtfully silver. The sound of the carrier's cart as it rumbled along the low road was carried plainly on the breath-catching sharpness of the air.

Rosemary's face stung as though it had been washed in icy water. The motion of the pony was curiously enjoyable. She liked the feel of its broad warm back moving between her legs. Perhaps she'd rather have worn her fur hat, but the hard black one she was forced to adopt was modelled on a grown-up's and not too unflattering.

Birds were making mating noises as though they sensed that spring wasn't far away. A blackbird watched them from a bare branch like a dark sentinel.

Bart didn't have much to say today. Sometimes he was very quiet. Rosemary gave him a sidelong look. How black and white he was, like a pen and ink drawing. She'd never seen another child like him. Most boys were so ordinary, with snivelly noses and mousy hair. But Bart had the look of a dark young prince. He said he *was* the Mist King, Mannanen. Perhaps he told the truth, but maybe he just felt that pretending made him important in her eyes. He was important, of course, more special than anyone else she knew.

The bridle path grew narrower. Bart took the lead. The trees pressed closer and the bird songs had died away as though the little creature never came to this haunted part of the wood. A cold breeze dipped into the back of her collar.

'Shouldn't we go back?' Rosemary said, uneasy at the thought of unseen forces.

Bart shook his head.

She continued to follow, not wanting to lose face. But the light had gone out of the sky and a ghostly greenness lay on their skins and on Snowball's white hide. Her spine prickled. They were in a goblin wood out of which anything might suddenly appear. Was that the sound of sticks breaking? She gasped.

Bart looked back at her, over his shoulder. 'Don't be scared, Rose. I know who it is. A friend of mine.'

Rosemary was not reassured. A friend of an ordinary boy or a friend of Mannanen? For the first time in her life she was conscious of real fear.

'Who? Who is it!' she whispered.

'Ben.'

'Ben who?'

'Just Ben.'

'Is it the boy who's crippled? The one you talked about last time?'

'Yes.'

'I don't want to see him. I didn't even like Papa to touch me, not even with his good hand.'

'There's nothing wrong with Ben's hands.'

'What *is* wrong then?'

'Wait and see.'

The stick noises grew louder. The colour left Rosemary's cheeks and her mouth grew dry. Then the boy appeared further up the track, hanging on a pair of crutches like the terrible old man who lived in one of the mean little houses across the bridge where the brewery stood, and who had a habit of popping out of a dark archway and frightening any children who passed by.

But this boy wasn't terrible. The sun had burst from behind sullen cloud just as she saw him. He was the most beautiful boy she'd ever seen. Bart was handsome and striking, more masculine. Ben was an angel. Rosemary had heard of the Greek gods from Mama, and seen pictures of them. There was one named after a flower. Narcissus. She'd thought it very silly for a man to have such a name, but, looking at Ben, it no longer seemed stupid, only curiously fitting. Greek gods could take the form of anyone, or anything they liked. Animals, people, even children. And they were all gloriously attractive.

'He met a fierce creature in the wood,' Bart said, 'and it took hold of his foot with its terrible teeth and wouldn't let go. He's the bravest person I know.'

Ben approached gaily, and Rosemary saw that one foot indeed was missing. He looked like some beautiful statuette, carelessly dropped. Not all damaged things were ugly. Mama had shown her a picture of Venus with both arms gone. There'd been an odd rightness about it. It was only Papa and persons like the brewery cripple who looked distastefully wrong.

The boys waved. 'My mother says we must never speak to one another again,' Bart told his mysterious friend.

'So does mine.'

'This track is public, though,' Bart said, 'not like that other path. I've promised Mama never to go that way again. This is Tom Beg. Isn't he handsome?'

Rosemary's cheeks coloured again. She'd expected Bart to introduce her first, not his silly old pony which wasn't to be compared with her lovely Snowball.

'Who's she?' Ben asked, propping his crutches against a tree and sitting on a green stump. He seemed totally unaware of his disability and Rosemary thought him braver than even Bart realized.

'Rose Costain.'

'Costain?' Ben frowned. 'Are you from Castletown?'

'Yes. My father's dead. I live with Grandpa and Grandmama.'

'We aren't supposed to have anything to do with all you Starks,' Bart told the boy. 'So you must never mention me or Rose? Promise? Your uncles or our mamas will try to stop us seeing you. I thought we might be secret friends, only ourselves to know.'

'No one at all?' Ben mused. 'Only you, me and Rose? A secret?'

'That's right. We could come on Saturdays. We could come this way on our ponies and meet you here. Would you like to try Tom Beg?'

Ben's face was transformed. 'Oh, yes! Yes!'

'Stand on that tree stump. I'll help you into the saddle.

There. How does it feel?'

Ben made Tom Beg pace slowly up and down.

'Wonderful! I've only been on the shire horse with Uncle Reuben or Uncle Will, but never on a little horse by myself.' He clamped his thighs against the beast's sides and nudged him to a trot, laughing out loud with surprised pleasure.

Bart ran alongside, carrying the crutches, regardless of the prick and scratch of the overhanging branches. Rosemary followed slowly, wishing one of them would notice her. She'd bring something with her next time, cinnamon balls or locust, or home-made toffee. Boys could never resist sweet, sticky things. That was the way to get them to accept her. She'd not envisaged Bart enjoying another boy's company. It was not a realization she cared for, yet, oddly, she couldn't resent Ben's presence.

'Try Snowball!' she called out, not that she'd ever allow anyone else to ride her newest possession. She'd told Virginia she must never touch Snowball. Tim hadn't wanted to.

Ben dismounted and climbed, by way of a large stone covered with patterns of lichen, on to the white pony's back. The thin, greenish light covered animal and boy who were, momentarily, frozen into an unreal tableau.

Rosemary was reminded of the story of Europa and the bull who was really the greatest of the gods disguised. Mam told such lovely stories. She'd advised Rosemary that it wasn't good to hear nothing but Manx tales. She must broaden her mind and her horizons, not that Rosemary was entirely sure what they were.

The branches tossed, breaking the spell.

Ben was thinner and taller than herself and his legs nearly touched the ground.

'A secret! A secret!' he shouted and tossed his fair hair as the pony broke into a restrained gallop, squeezing her fat little body through the encroaching undergrowth. 'We've got a secret!'

'It won't be a secret for long if you make such a din,' Bart said with a grin. 'Come back!'

110

Ben turned the white pony without too much trouble and returned.

'The people up at Kentraugh will hear that,' Bart pointed out. 'People who live in big, grand houses don't want to hear children shouting.'

'Grandpa doesn't either,' Ben said, cheeks flushed, 'and he only lives in a little bit of a farmhouse.'

'There can't be much room when all your uncles are inside.'

'I heard a story,' Rosemary interrupted, 'about a man who was so big that when he went to bed his legs went up the chimney. Sometimes out of the window.'

Ben went off into shrieks of laughter, then, seeing Bart's warning look, covered his mouth with a dirty fist. 'It's so funny,' he spluttered. 'No one tells me things like that. You did mean it?' He was suddenly serious. 'About coming on Saturdays?'

'Whenever possible,' Bart told the boy rather grandly.

'We wouldn't be allowed to if it was wet or snowy or if there was a party,' Rosemary observed.

'Party? What's a party like?'

'People come and wear their best clothes. Extra specially nice food is made—'

'What sort of food?'

'Jelly in moulds. Cakes and biscuits. Chicken—'

'Could I come to one of your parties?' Ben asked wistfully. Rosemary shook her head. 'No.'

'Is it – is it because I'm too dirty? Or you don't like me?'

'No, silly! You've forgotten already. It's our parents. We haven't to be friends. They don't want us to. Bart and I will be smacked if they found out we were with you. So how could we ask you?'

'I never went to a party.'

'Haven't you any cousins, or friends of your own?'

Ben shook his head, all his gaiety quenched.

'We'll have a party here, next Saturday,' Bart said boldy.

'We can't go riding with plates of jelly,' Rosemary told him, practically.

Ben started laughing again at the ridiculous notion.

'We can bring other things, though, in knapsacks.'

'Where are we going to get them, Bart? People in kitchens always notice. If they don't at the time, they do later. And they always know it's us.'

'Yes, Rose. But I'll buy some things. Gideon gave me some money the other day, when he'd called to see my mother.'

'Gideon?'

'Collister. I met him outside just as I came back on Tom Beg.'

'Will you be able to buy lots of food with it?'

'Yes. Quite a lot. And some ginger beer.'

'I like ginger beer,' Ben said. 'I had it when I was ill. After IT seized hold of my foot in the wood.'

'Alligators do that,' Rosemary told him, not without an inward shudder. 'Mamma told me about alligators and crocodiles. They infest rivers. But they go up on to the banks, too.'

'She does seem to know a great deal,' Ben observed. 'Not like my mother. My uncles say she doesn't know anything, except . . . how to . . .'

'Except what?'

'It's something I'm not supposed to talk about. Uncle Will hit me across the ear when I asked what it meant. It hurt.'

'We won't!' Rosemary breathed. 'We wouldn't hit you.'

'It must be something rude and I wouldn't want you to wish we weren't to be friends. Secret friends.'

'You must never mention us, or the rides on our ponies,' Bart said seriously.

'I never will.' Ben hoisted himself on to his crude supports. He looked tired now, Rosemary thought with an unaccustomed pang. It must be dreadful to have a crocodile get hold of you. Did they really inhabit Manx rivers? But if it hadn't been one, whatever else could it have been?

'It wasn't here, was it? Where IT was waiting for you?' she asked.

'Oh, no. That was a long way off, in Grandpa's copse.'

'That's good! If we're to meet you here, I mean,' Rosemary said hastily. 'It wouldn't have been the best place to have our party. We needn't worry now.'

'It's a lovely place,' Ben insisted, his face one shining smile.

Rosemary had never seen such uninhibited happiness. Strangely, it made her sad.

'We'd better go before we're missed,' Bart reminded her.

'We'll see you on Saturday.'

The ponies' heads were turned homewards.

'I can't wait,' Ben said in a thin little voice as they made off.

Rosemary wanted to turn back.

'We can't,' Bart whispered, reading her thoughts. 'The Starks.'

She looked back over her shoulder. Ben hadn't moved. He stood, pressed against a leafless trunk, his pale face intent as though he willed them to return.

Rosemary waved. A turn in the track shut him from sight as if he'd never existed.

'Mr Collister, Ma'am,' Mrs Quinn said and withdrew.

'Gideon. How are you?'

'Well enough.' He stared round the sitting-room that had once been his own. 'You haven't changed it much. I always liked that purple press.'

'I regretted the Chinese elephants.' Karran was wearing a dark crimson gown that accentuated a luminous pallor. She felt nervous and her hands were cold.

'You needn't feel too deprived. I'll give them to you as a wedding gift. If the bridegroom is to be myself, of course.'

Karran laughed. 'How like an advocate to add that necessary caution!'

'Where's my daughter?' he demanded.

'Hanna is upstairs, sleeping.'

'You aren't trying to keep me away from her, are you?'

'Why should I do that? She always sleeps at this time.'

'Now you look unfriendly,' Gideon commented.

'Only because you sound suspicious. I said you could see her and so you shall.'

'You do, however, make it sound like a papal dispensation!'

She said nothing, only returned to the fireplace to hold out her stiff fingers to the heat.

'I'm sorry,' Gideon told her. 'My nerves seem on edge. I haven't slept.'

'Neither have I.'

'Did you do what I asked?' He came to the other side of the hearth and regarded her with shadowed eyes.

Once, Karran thought, numbed, he'd have had me in his arms inside a minute. And I'd have been happy to be there. Now, all I can hope is that he won't touch me.

'Did you?'

'Think, you mean? How could I not. I've done little else.'

'And where did these thoughts take you? I meant what I said. I want to marry you and become Hanna's true father. I want her to have my name.'

But he doesn't say he wants me to be his true wife. It's only the baby he desires now. Well, I want none of that sort of arrangement.

'I'm afraid that won't be possible. You've given me no indication that you have the feeling for me that a wife should expect. According to law, Hanna is John's posthumous daughter and no one can prove otherwise. I think you are being selfish, Gideon. You haven't even troubled to pretend that you've any other motive for proposing to me.'

'How remiss of me! I thought you knew that I find you no less attractive. I'm sure we'd be as accomplished lovers as in the past.' His tone was faintly mocking.

'You've said nothing about love.'

'My dear. D'you expect to be wooed? I hadn't envisaged having to do that a second time. You're right, I am selfish. But I thought we'd passed those enticing portals quite decidedly already.'

114

'If it's your intention to make me appear cheap and foolish, you're succeeding. I *didn't* expect a spate of facile endearments. Only to feel that you want me for myself and that you still would, Hanna or no Hanna.'

'My dear, I'm trained to see matters as they are. Hanna exists. How can I know if I'd love you any differently if she didn't?'

'If I agreed – and I'm only saying if – would we have a house of our own? I wouldn't be expected to share a house with your sister?'

'Now, what could be so dreadful about such an arrangement? Naturally Mary would have to share our lives. Mary will always lean on others, through no fault of her own. That's what my father and aunt have done to her. I'm her guardian. How can I cast her off? Did it ever occur to you that you might come to care for her?'

'No. I've given it no serious consideration.'

'Remember your loyalty to John Howard?'

'Yes.'

'I regretted it but I didn't take you to task for it. It strikes me, my dear, that you make your own rules.' His face had darkened.

'The situation was different. Our relationships were not the same.'

'You would not leave him when he was ill.'

'John was old and I knew he was dying.'

'And Mary is young and might live for another fifty years?'

'Already, I have a jealous child to contend with. At times, I almost fear for Hanna's safety . . .' Karran stopped, wishing she hadn't said that.

'You mean that Bart might . . . attack her?' Gideon's face registered alarmed anger.

'I have to keep a watch, always. Other mothers must do the same. Who's to say that your Mary mightn't find your baby an even greater rival? You admit she's far from stable.'

'And who's to say she might not prefer to mother Hanna?'

115

'That's what I am! Hanna's mother. I have thought, Gideon. I don't want to take that risk. Everyone at each other's throats! You standing up for Mary. Me taking Bart's side. Hanna caught at the very heart of dissension. She'd grow up as miserable as we were in our childhoods, however much you and I might care for her. If she *is* allowed to grow up.'

'And what about Bart?'

'I can cope with him. Already there are distractions. Rosemary Costain. The ponies. A new, interesting school. There won't be too much time to brood in future. He'll outgrow the resentment. Unless I put other strains on him and I've no intention of doing that.'

'So you'll cut me off from Hanna?'

'No. You're welcome to see her from time to time. I've already made that plain.'

'And I suppose I am to become an uncle! Perhaps, one of a long stream of supposed uncles? Knowing your passionate nature . . .'

'How dare you, Gideon!' Karran struck him across the cheek. The strength in the blow knocked his head against the mantelshelf.

'I warn you, Karran!' He made a move towards her, then held himself in check.

'Come and say your farewells to Hanna,' she said coldly. 'I'm sure you'll congratulate yourself, in time, for having escaped my undesirable clutches.'

He followed her up the narrow stair that led to her bedchamber. She watched him as he looked into the oak cradle.

Gideon remained there for a long time, just staring at Hanna's sleeping face. Once, he touched the lace edge of the little cap she wore over her dark curls, and smoothed the corner of sheet and pillowcase. Then he turned, his face impassive, and went down the staircase and out of the house without a word.

Out of her life? Karran ran to the window and watched him ride off, his body straight, no backward look. The hoofbeats grew softer, then were replaced by the rhythmic thudding of rain on the roof, a gigantic heartbeat.

She threw herself on to the bed in a torment of weeping, stifling the ugly sounds into the rumpled linen, knowing she'd acted cruelly but having been unable to prevent herself.

The baby stirred and began to cry as though something had been taken away from her.

PART FOUR

The Grand Opening

Erin wished that the evening were over. She wasn't in the mood for company but Barney had insisted on asking George Seyler and the Bascombes to dine with them. He'd thought Charlotte still needed cheering up after the trauma of Abel's death.

It was odd they hadn't yet fished his body out of the harbour, but it had turned stormy after the suicide and he could have been swept heaven knew where by this time. Erin asked Barney why Seyler had been invited and he'd told her that Seyler was interested in boat design. They had mutual interests.

Seyler was connected with a Scottish firm with a thrice-weekly steamship service running between Greenock and Liverpool, via Douglas. Seyler was their Man representative, a kind of liaison officer, Barney explained. But Erin suspected that he was there for Charlotte's benefit.

Erin's lip had curled at the news that he patronized the poetry group to which Charlotte belonged. Hadn't her daughter had enough problems with an unbalanced artist without seeking the acquaintance of some effeminate word-lover?

Any doubts as to Mr George Seyler's virility abated when he was shown into the parlour, his strong, compact figure clothed in dark blue material, plainly cut, his skin darkened as though he spent much time out of doors. His gaze was uncompromisingly direct and his eyes were the kind that seemed to see beyond the obvious.

Erin had the strangest sensation, on first encountering that all-seeing gaze, that something inside her scuttled for cover. Previously Barney had been the only person capable of arousing such a defensive reaction. Studying Seyler unobtrusively as he was given pre-prandial sherry and introduced to the Bascombes, Erin decided that there was indeed some strong hint of Barney about him, though he was more conventionally good-looking in a rugged way. Imagine such a person finding pleasure in tinkling imagery!

Listening with only half an ear to her long-time acquaintance, Muriel Bascombe, Erin was not unaware of Charlotte's change of colour when she entered the room and saw that Seyler had already arrived. She noted, also, that Charlotte had taken unusual pains with her appearance. Her hair was particularly well-groomed and the girl's eyes looked more attractive. If it wasn't so far-fetched an idea, Erin might have suspected the discreet use of cosmetics. But Charlotte had always resisted the aid of such false blandishments. 'I want to be seen as I really am,' she'd say annoyingly, ad nauseam.

Grudgingly, Erin approved the improvement in her ugly duckling, while resenting the subtle change. She herself was looking haggard through loss of sleep and worry over Barney's seeming indifference since their inconclusive quarrel. Why hadn't she let well alone? She should have accepted Karran's version of events more whole-heartedly, but every now and again that sensation of having been cleverly duped rose up in her, threatening to boil over.

'What was that?' Erin enquired, realizing that Muriel had been speaking and that she hadn't heard a word.

'I said you were looking tired. Not at all yourself.'

'I've been suffering from sleeplessness.'

'That's not like you,' Muriel said, then added in a hoarse whisper, 'is it Barney who's keeping you awake? Having a final fling, is he? The gay dog. They all do!'

Not long ago, Erin would have enjoyed the fun. Tonight

119

she was furious with Muriel for her tactlessness. She could have spat in the foolish, pink face so frivolously framed in suspiciously blonde curls.

Some of that repressed anger communicated itself to her guest.

'Don't mind me,' Muriel went on uncertainly. 'My George always says I let my silly tongue run away with me.' She sipped at her sherry to recover her confidence.

Your George is right, Erin thought. Aloud, she said, 'He says that, does he?'

Muriel nodded. 'But your Charlotte's looking well! I always thought her the plainest girl but you've got to admit she looks distinctive tonight. Don't you agree?'

'I thought she appeared much as usual.' Erin's headache grew more pronounced. Even Muriel, harmless as she was, took on the aspect of an enemy who sought to demoralize her by insinuations that she'd finally lost those attibutes by which she'd set such store. Her only assets, Erin realized painfully. People overlooked much for beauty. She had no reserves of goodness or gentleness which might have alleviated the insidious changes and ravages of time.

'Oh, no!' Muriel prattled on. 'Charlotte's really taken on some looks at last. Even my George has noticed and he's blind as a bat about other women. I wonder what could be the cause of such belated blooming? One would have expected the opposite with the grim news of Abel. Oh, I forgot, we were not to refer to that! You see, Erin, I can't be sensible. You must forgive me. I do mean well.'

'Excuse me,' Erin murmured. 'I must see to the supper.'

She moved away, aware of Muriel's surprised regard. Outside the door she leaned against the panels, trying to control her breathing, pushing down the anguished panic that almost overwhelmed her. Her mind seethed with conflicting emotions. Despair in case she'd alienated Barney predominated, closely followed by jealousy of Charlotte who, indeed, seemed to have come into her own. Unreasoning dislike of Murial Bascombe who still maintained a blowsy attraction and vitality.

Inside the parlour, the men burst into guffaws of laughter. Erin felt that she hated them all. Even Bascombe had forgotten to show his usual gallantry or to praise her hair or her large green eyes. Tonight he'd seemed not to notice her.

Erin dredged up the remainder of her courage. Somehow she must survive this supper party. She must remain polite and sociable, avoiding another breach between herself and her husband. He'd not forgive her if she antagonized two of their closest friends or the steam-packet man with the look of a sailor. Someone had once told her that sailors took up knitting and tapestry-work to dispel the boredom of an overlong voyage. She tried to picture Seyler with a needle and thread and experienced a ridiculous compulsion to laugh. To go on laughing . . .

She went to ascertain the progress of the meal then returned, holding herself severely in check, to say that they could now adjourn to the dining-room.

Bascombe, seated next to Charlotte, began to carry on a clumsy flirtation with her. Erin intercepted a glance of cool amusement between Seyler and her daughter. Was he, then, the reason for Charlotte's transformation? She'd been going to the Roses' meetings for a long time now but she'd never mentioned George Seyler at home, at least, not in Erin's hearing. She'd be far more prone to unburden herself to Barney. The deceitful miss! All that supposed grief for her lost husband. So much eyewash!

Erin came to the conclusion, during the course of the excellent meal, that Seyler was indeed sniffing after Charlotte. Those amused glances had continued, betraying an unmistakable familiarity. Was Charlotte, Erin wondered, always at Cormorant House when she said she was? Not that Mr Seyler looked raffish. On the contrary, he seemed the opposite. He spoke with authority tinged with humour. He was intelligent without being arrogant. Barney, undoubtedly, was taken with him.

'I'd like to see those plans of yours,' Barney said to Seyler when they'd reached the stage where no one could eat or drink any more and returned, pleasantly relaxed, to sink into the comfortable sofas and armchairs in the parlour that Erin wanted so badly to turn into a proper drawing-room, only Barney preferred it as it was.

'They are for a luxury vessel,' Seyler warned. 'A small schooner for private cruising, perhaps.'

'Where will you find anyone rich enough to buy anything like that?'

'It's not improbable, Mr Bascombe.'

'George. Call me George. Everyone else does.'

'You've the same name as myself,' Seyler pointed out. 'I've always found that constraining.'

There was some badinage about both Georges and it being a king's name, then Seyler said, 'It's becoming popular, among the upper classes, to have one's own ship. The more expensive and outlandish the fittings, the better. They like to outdo their friends, and, better still, their enemies.' He smiled and Charlotte responded.

'I've only dealt in working boats up to now,' Barney said. 'There's always a call for those.'

'Ah, but there's a deal of money to be had from the bored rich. There's always a call for penny buns, but it's surprising how many people can afford a lavish cake if that's what takes their fancy.'

'Imagine being so rich that you're bored!' Charlotte expostulated. 'It only goes to show that the wrong people have money in that quantity. There's no need for anyone to find life tedious and without meaning!'

'And what would you do, Mrs Costain, if you had unlimited funds?' Seyler asked.

'Travel. Travel and travel. Buy books and travel some more. Build orphanages, or endow hospitals. Have soup kitchens anywhere they're necessary—'

'Well, love, you'd very soon become a pauper,' Barney teased. 'I'm glad you decided to travel first. And haven't you done enough reading yet?'

'No, Papa. I'll never read sufficient.' Charlotte laughed and looked quite pretty.

The talk returned to boats and shipyards, the advantages of Douglas as opposed to Castletown. Muriel was disapproving, Barney thoughtful, Bascombe downright angry. 'It's all wrong the way folk seek to denigrate Castletown these days! It's too backward. There's little room for expansion. Before we know where we are, they'll be transferring all our privileges to Douglas. The Keys, the main shipping traffic. I don't like to contemplate our good little town becoming a secondary backwater!'

'Calm down,' Barney said pleasantly. 'It's not going to happen tomorrow.'

'Sooner perhaps than you think, then Castletown will become a place in which nets are made and herrings smoked and old women sit in doorways. And we can get out our clay pipes and prepare to meet our Maker.'

'Or move to the seat of activity.'

'Barney! What if our roots are here? Homes? Friends? The neighbourhood one grows up in?' Muriel sounded upset. 'I like living here.'

'Douglas isn't the end of the world. Transport's improved a lot since my young days. It's like the great continents gradually growing closer.'

'Move!' Erin couldn't help the cry of distress. Leave her fine house to be lost in a trough of mediocrity! Here she was well-known, a personality. Over in Douglas she'd be just one more aging nonentity. 'I wouldn't go.'

'You should read your Bible, Erin,' Barney said with deceptive gentleness. 'Whither thou goest, I will go? That's what's required of a wife, my dear.'

'Of course,' Muriel put in uneasily, aware of Erin's taut pallor, 'as Barney says, it's not going to happen in our lifetime. That's a problem for the likes of Charlotte and Mr Seyler, or your grandchildren. How are the little dears?'

'The twins are good, industrious children,' Barney told her, pouring brandy for himself, Bascombe and Seyler. 'As for my flighty little Rosie, she's more trouble than the rest of the household put together and cast out to sea in a sack, but she gives me the most pleasure. She makes me feel seventeen again. That's how Rosie affects old men.'

'Papa! You're not old!'

'Aren't I, Charlotte? Well, I can tell you this, just lately I've begun to feel it. What I need is a bit of excitement, someone to make me feel more than merely a – provider.'

Bascombe gave a bellow of laughter. 'You must be referring to old Quilliam. What if he does drop dead in his tracks one sultry evening, eh? His shade would be the first to agree it had been worthwhile. She's a seductive young piece.'

'Really,' Erin said stiffly. 'We aren't by ourselves this evening. We do have Mr Seyler here.'

'George!' Bascombe said loudly and laughed again. 'You don't mind us being ourselves, do you?'

Seyler shook his head, smiling as though he enjoyed some secret thought. 'She's a lovely child, Charlotte's daughter.'

'If she's grown into a handful,' Erin said, 'it could be that she's been in the wrong sort of company.'

There was a silence while everyone digested the import of what Erin said.

'Rosie's never been anywhere she was liable to pick up wrong habits,' Barney insisted quietly. 'I'm perfectly happy with her choice of friends.'

Erin could not help herself. 'You would be.'

'And so am I,' Charlotte said a little sharply. 'And that's what really matters.'

'Do you really think that glowering chip off Luke Karran's block is the best Rosie could do for herself?'

'We won't discuss that here, Mama, if you don't mind. As you pointed out, we aren't by ourselves. They've been very happy, the pair of them, since they both acquired their first horseflesh. It's perfectly safe for them up the Kentraugh bridle path. They've taken to having Saturday picnics. Bart's mother discovered him stuffing his saddle bag with enough food for a regiment—'

'There!' Erin exclaimed. 'The boy's a thief!'

124

'Not at all, Mama. He'd been given a sovereign and wanted to treat Rosemary—'

'Why can't you call her Rosie like the rest of the household?' Barney asked.

'Because that isn't her name.'

'You're fighting a losing battle,' Barney warned. 'It's too much of a mouthful. All children should have pet names. Makes them feel special.'

'Muriel had one when she was a child. Moo,' Bascombe said wickedly.

Even Charlotte had to laugh.

There wasn't much one could do with George, Seyler told her, except to lengthen it to Georgie, as so often happened. Erin's intransigence was forgotten in the light-hearted dissertation on the unchanging ridiculousness of the human race. Everyone relaxed.

Erin couldn't help wondering who'd given Bart that large sum of money. Karran was such a dark horse and so conveniently tucked away at Black Rocks. Erin had ceased to repudiate the picture of Barney's arm round Karran's shoulders. Daily, the image became more real. Karran had lied.

She got up and passed round a box of sugared figs and another of preserved ginger. Muriel made her usual protest about being stout enough, thank you, this being disclaimed with normal alacrity by Bascombe who gave her backside a surreptitious pinch while his other hand removed a fig from the fancy box.

Would the evening never end? Erin nibbled a piece of the preserved ginger she didn't especially want as the conversation returned to luxury craft.

'It's no new vogue,' George Seyler propounded. 'Charles II enjoyed cruising.'

'A king may have what the rest of us might never achieve.'

'Not only kings. But they were expensive in their day. Charles was reputed to own one that cost two and a half thousand guineas.'

'Really!' Charlotte remarked. 'When I think of all the poor who could have lived off that amount!'

'Don't be such a wet-blanket,' Barney ordered good-naturedly and turned again to their guest. 'Go on, Geroge. There must have been others.'

'It was Nelson who brought the vogue to the ordinary seamen who so admired him.'

'Ordinary seamen with heavy purses?'

'Perhaps I expressed myself badly. One no longer needed to be royal or titled. Only rich.'

'Interesting.'

'Most. I was at Deptford when the *Royal Sovereign* was launched in 1804. A comely vessel. Copper-bottomed and coloured blue and yellow. There were paintings of women in frames of gilt, and gilded greenery carved to best advantage, and I seem to recall a dolphin gambolling round a replica of Neptune—'

'My dear Seyler! Surely we are going quite out of our depth?'

'Oh, quite! I was merely carried away by the memory. A young boy thinks nothing of the material side of so magnificent a venture. But I do remember the splendour and the sense of adventure as they set sail.'

'I see. *Did* they have this splendid adventure?'

Seyler shook his head. 'They made an expedition to the site of the battle of Waterloo where they found nothing but vandalism. Broken walls and bullet-holes. Spoiled trees and soil made rich by dead men's blood. Desolation—'

Erin shivered at the grim description. That sounded like her own soul. Jesse—

Barney broke the dark spell. 'Well! I'll admit I'd have gone somewhere a bit livelier. White beaches and palms, and bright birds—'

'I'd have chosen Europe, but Italy or Greece,' Charlotte said eagerly. 'Spain—'

'And I'd have tried the Isle of Wight,' Muriel Bascombe offered triumphantly.

'I have a job to shift her from the back door,' her

husband revealed, grinning. 'You'd only need to sit her by a bathtub filled with water and stick an aspidistra or two beside it. She'd be perfectly content. That's what I like about my wife.'

'What about you, Mrs Kerruish?' George Seyler said softly. 'Where would you have gone?'

Erin stared at them, disorientated. She'd just been somewhere. Hell, that was where she'd found herself. Purgatory—

'Oh, twenty-five years backwards, I think,' she whispered at last.

They laughed dutifully, thinking she joked. But she hadn't. She longed to be there where she'd been desired, where life had had meaning. Where she was young.

A tear trickled down her cheek and she wiped it away before anyone saw.

Crying was only for fools.

A large number of people received invitations to the belated opening of O'Ferrall's by now well-discussed rooms; the Kerruishes and Charlotte, the Bascombes and other influential business folk, Mr George Seyler, who, O'Ferrall had decided, could be a useful contact with his privileged position in that shipping company. Not all of his prospective 'guests' would have their own vessels and there might be useful rebates if he attracted sufficient trade to the line.

The grand opening had been delayed of necessity when the steamship carrying his essential tables had foundered, taking the much-needed gaming equipment to the bottom of the sea. There'd been the usual insurance delays and it was summer before Ravensdowne was properly equipped for card-play and occupation.

Port St Mary had benefited by O'Ferrall's presence in their neighbourhood. There'd been a constant stream of would-be staff and tradesmen, much bulk buying of linens, dry goods, liquor and wines; planting of roses and exotic shrubs, repainting, re-slating, tidying of the grounds until the place lost much of its former not unattractive wildness.

There was great excitement in the village when, on the night before the occasion, visiting yachts could be seen at anchor, while dinghies plied industriously between the exotic craft and the shore, each with its complement of well-dressed passengers.

A good deal of repainting of traps and carriages took place, gowns and coats cleaned and furbished, jewellery taken out of places of safety.

'You *must* go, Ma'am!' Mrs Quinn said when she saw Karran's handsome invitation. 'You have most right to be there. Not that I'm saying I approve of all that gambling and taking liberties with Mr Howard's house.'

'Mr *O'Ferrall's* house. And he *has* tidied up those gardens and shrubberies. It should have been done long ago.' But Karran's tone was wistful.

'T'was a good, natural-looking place wi' little wrong wi' it. But there's one place he couldn't touch! No one could spoil them windows out to sea.'

'No,' Karran said slowly, and a great wave of home-sickness struck her as she remembered the panorama of rock and water, the swooping gulls, moonlight on the water of the bay, the dark preening of cormorants.

'Don't look so sad, Ma'am. You've a nice, tidy place here. More homely, and better for your children. And your money troubles have sorted themselves out. That was what you wanted, wasn't it?'

'Yes,' Karran agreed in a stifled voice. 'I did want all that. But memories are hard to kill.'

'I'll see to the baking, then, and you go and choose a gown to be pressed. And none of that miserable black, mind! You aren't in mourning now.'

But I am, Karran thought dully, for the Gideon of last year. No one would ever know what it had cost her to send him away a second time, but she'd never have been happy with a man who'd appeared to have fallen out of love with herself. Her children needed stability and security, not conflict. Gideon's recent hurt and angry letter had not helped to restore her peace of mind.

She went to attend to her child. Hanna had begun to respond very satisfactorily to her mother's affection, but Karran felt that even that pleasure had been spoiled by the knowledge that Gideon set such unexpected store by the child. Her refusal to wed him and leave the island so that he might share in the upbringing of his daughter had caused such bad feeling as might never be dispelled. He'd called her jealous and unnatural.

Hanna began to cry for no apparent reason. Was she aware of her mother's deep disturbance? Karran decided that it was more likely to be the result of teething and gave the baby a teaspoonful of the colourless soothing fluid that seemed to settle her.

Bart rushed in to ask for some of Mrs Quinn's baking as Rose would be coming next day and they were to have one of their pony-picnics. There was some colour in his normally pale face and he seemed not to notice the child now quiet in her arms.

'Of course,' she told him. 'And there's ginger beer in the pantry. Oranges too.'

'Good.' Bart's dark eyes glanced at the baby who stared back at him with an intentness that was curiously adult. Obviously Hanna knew her half-brother, young as she was.

'Would you like to hold her while I get a clean napkin?' Karran suggested.

Bart grimaced. 'No! I'm going to tell Mrs Quinn it's all right about the picnic.'

'She says that you and Rose manage to eat great quantities of food.'

'Does she?' Bart said carelessly. 'It must be all the fresh air. You don't mind, do you? About the things to eat?'

'Good gracious, no! I'm only glad you're enjoying yourself. Rose, too. Is she very angry about the Castle school? About not being eligible?'

'I'm afraid so. You know Rose.'

'Indeed, I do!'

It was peaceful after Bart had gone and Hanna restored to her cot under the open window where she'd get the benefit of the air. The house was quiet now that the last of the workmen had departed. They'd taken longer than Karran had imagined, but at last everything was decorated, the new kitchen in use and the roof weather-tight and ready to withstand the gales that so often beset the Manx coasts.

The wind rose during the night and flapped sheets of rain against the panes. It abated after breakfast and a watery sun appeared. Distances turned blue and purple, their outlines sharp and clear.

'Lucky it's better, Ma'am. All them folks going to Ravensdowne. Don't want to arrive all mussed up,' Mrs Quinn said in the late afternoon.

'They certainly won't. Are you sure it's all right to leave Hanna?'

'She's used to me and it's no trouble, Ma'am. Truly. And it's not far away, is it.'

'She may be teething. That's the stuff over there.'

'Very well. Don't you concern yourself. And I'll make sure she's not left alone with Master Bart.'

'Is it – very unnatural? To dislike one's sister so?'

Mrs Quinn laughed. 'Bless you, no! Never cared for my own brother. Couldn't wait to see the last of him, I can tell you! Happens in most families, that does, unless they're very unusual.'

Except in Gideon's, Karran thought. She'd been right not to go to Glasgow. She'd had enough trouble with Martha Kenyon, Howard's sister. She *had* been right, hadn't she?

Rose hadn't come today and Karran realized that it must be because both Charlotte and the Kerruish family had been invited to O'Ferrall's. No one would be free to bring and collect the child. Oddly, Bart hadn't made a fuss, only went off to picnic on his own, returning flushed and windswept, with the powdery green off ancient trees all over his clothes and a far-away look in his eyes. Karran suddenly wanted to hug him.

With a sense of shcok, Karran realized that she knew nothing about her son. He'd never divulge where he'd been or what he'd done when he was out of her sight or not at school. Occasionally she'd find him in the orchard, lying on his stomach under the old apple and plum trees, lost in a world of books. She understood that, as she did the times he came down from the cobwebbed attics, his face streaked with dust, hands grimy. But the essential Bart was lost to her and she couldn't escape a weight of grief.

Molly Quayle was to see to the boy's supper while Mrs Quinn took charge of little Hanna. The baby liked the short, dolly-peg figure as much as her mother did. The tiny hands would clutch at the polished red cheeks as though they plucked apples.

Karran, aware that the eyes of O'Farrell's guests would be on her, looking for signs of wantonness, chose a dark purple gown, long-sleeved, simply cut. Its colour emphasized the whiteness of her skin and the blackness of eyes and hair. She wore pearls to offsett the sombre effect, and coloured her pale mouth. One could go to the opposite extreme. She took a fan of white feathers and mother-of-pearl out of a drawer. It would be stuffy at Ravensdowne with so many guests and on such a muggy evening.

As she climbed into the trap, the damp west wind slapped her face boisterously. The trees were tossing and the sea was whipped into white horses. Mrs Quinn waved from upstairs, Molly Quayle from the front door. The white house did look homely and welcoming, Karran thought. It was a fine place, perfect for children, and Bart liked being closer to Castletown. Still, Ravensdowne called her.

The trap bounced and swayed. Karran pulled the hood of her cloak over her hair. If much more of it escaped she'd arrive looking like a trollop, and for the children's sake she wished to make a favourable impression.

At Port St Mary she was sandwiched between other

vehicles obviously bound for the same destination. The cobbled streets of the village resounded with the rumble of wheels and folk looked out of their windows at the unusual activity. Small boys darted in and out of the press of traffic, performing feats of daring that made Karran gasp. Suppose one of them was too slow and was run over? Would O'Ferrall be blamed?

The boys had charmed lives but she breathed more easily once she was up the slope and on the flatter approach to Ravensdown. The wind was much stronger up here, buffeting the plumy tops of the trees, making the trap creak alarmingly. Horses' manes streamed like banners. Out in the deep water, the anaemic lights on the yachts dipped and swung. The warm breath of the southerly gale, maliciously human, puffed at the extravagant hair-styles of those just arriving.

The guests from the pleasure-boats had been ferried to Port St Mary last night, according to the carrier, and would have the advantage of having had all day to rest and primp themselves at the gaming-house.

It wasn't until Karran had brought the vehicle to a stop outside Ravensdowne that she fully realized that she was no longer the mistress of the house returning from a journey, but a guest of short duration and unaccompanied at that. She hesitated.

'Karran? Karran!'

Charlotte was coming down the steps. Against the candle-glow in the hall, the folds of her skirts appeared almost diaphanous. Karran stared. Surely that wasn't Charlotte's usual taste? But she was overwhelmingly glad to see her friend and to be spared the ordeal of entering alone.

A groom appeared to lead away the trap. Karran hurried across the windy gap, clutching reticule and fan.

'That was good of you. I'm beginning to feel like a Hottentot!'

'How do you know so much about Hottentots?' Charlotte asked, lifting delicate black lace flounces away from the

132

large, invading feet of a bucolic gentleman in a brocade coat. They passed banked flowers and plants in ornate pots. It was all quite grand.

'They do have wild hair. That's a new gown, surely?'

Charlotte nodded. 'Papa insisted.'

'And a lovely brooch.' Karran handed her cloak to a waiting footman and patted her hair into place.

'He insisted about that too.'

'I wish someone would be as insistent where I'm concerned,' Karran teased.

'What about a certain pair of shoe-buckles and silk stockings?' Charlotte whispered.

'Where is O'Ferrall anyway?' Annoyingly, Karran found herself blushing.

She glimpsed him over the heads of recent arrivals awaiting announcement.

The names of two advocates from Douglas and their wives were called out.

'He obviously intends to keep on the right side of the law,' Charlotte murmured. 'One can hardly eat a man's bread and salt, then hand him over to the Keys.'

'Can't they? You don't know advocates!' Karran assured her with feeling.

'You never did say much about Gideon's visit.'

'Oh, that, it was ages ago. I've almost forgotten it.'

'D'you think he'll come back.'

Karran shrugged. 'I wish I knew for certain.'

'But you've heard from him, haven't you?'

Karran nodded. 'Yes.'

'You don't sound happy about it.'

'He's become possessive about Hanna. Much too possessive.'

'I see. Oh, dear!'

Brand the younger, unnaturally neat in a sober black coat and smart breeches, shouted, 'Mrs Charlotte Costain! Mrs Karran Howard.'

The effect of his words was astonishing. All the myriad low-voiced conversations stopped in mid-flow. Dozens of pairs of eyes swivelled in the direction of the two young women, some curious, some condemnatory, others assessing. One broad, fleshy-faced man with a shark-like mouth stared openly, his eyes travelling over Karran from head to toe with slow deliberation.

'He's detestable,' Karran whispered angrily. 'Who is he, Charlotte?'

'I don't know. One of the yacht people, I expect.'

'I hope he doesn't try to speak to me. Oh, God! I wish I hadn't come.'

O'Ferrall came forward, shutting out her view of the shark-mouthed man and most of the other arrivals. Conversations were resumed but the atmosphere was still full of conjecture and murmured disapproval, a few muted sniggers.

Why hadn't she thought more carefully about this possible reception? A discreet gown couldn't alter anyone's opinion, Karran admitted belatedly. She remained Karran the witch, Karran the whore.

Loyally Charlotte stayed close to her side, ignoring the cold glance of her mother who stood at the other end of the room. Karran opened the white fan and tried to dispel some of the effect of the multitude of candles that turned the place into a hot-house.

'Well,' O'Ferrall said softly, candle-flame reflected in his eyes. 'So you did come.'

'And wish I hadn't,' Karran told him more sharply than she meant.

'Why?' He raised his brows. 'What have I done?'

'Nothing. I was stupid to feel that matters between the locals and myself could be forgotten or forgiven. You might as well have invited an adder into your presence.'

'I've never considered such a course of action.' He smiled with outward charm but who knew what went on behind his contemplative gaze?

'It could also present enormous difficulties,' Charlotte observed wickedly. 'Since I doubt there are snakes on Man. I'll take myself off, Karran dear. George Seyler is over there and I have to give him a message from Peregrine Rose.'

She hurried away before Karran could stop her.

'You look very beautiful,' O'Ferrall said, 'and so self-possessed.'

'I don't feel it. Everyone looking this way—'

'They are all jealous, my dear. All wishing that they looked like you. That they had the same power to change the universe.'

'That's ridiculous! More of your blarney.'

O'Ferrall shook his head. 'Oh, no, it isn't. You'll still be turning heads when you're eighty.'

'No—'

'But, yes! The most refreshing thing about you is that total unawareness of your own attraction. You seem, actually, to shy away from the notion as though it were something of which to be ashamed. Well, you'd better get used to the idea that men are going to pursue you for another sixty years.'

'Sixty! That's indecent!'

'Some persons are born to be desirable at any age. The moment I saw you—'

'You decided that I was a vulnerable widow whose property could fall into your predatory lap, well below the approved valuation.'

O'Ferral smiled brilliantly. 'There, you've spoiled it all! That lovely mouth should never bring out words like valuation.'

'I have dependants—'

'Oh, forget about your children for tonight! Just for this evening you're free to do as you like. To be admired as any such magnetic woman should be.'

'Mr James Quilliam and Mrs Quilliam!' Brand bawled.

O'Ferrall shook hands with the Quilliams, murmured something agreeable and turned back to Karran who'd taken temporary refuge behind the fan of feather and mother-of-pearl.

'You should attend to your other guests,' she said,

swishing the fan vigorously.

He shrugged carelessly. 'Most were asked out of expedience. The only one I invited out of genuine feeling was yourself, though I have to admit that Mrs Costain has gained my admiration by her championship. A splendid young woman.' O'Ferrall snapped his fingers at a passing flunkey. 'Two glasses of champagne, if you please. And quickly.'

'Why quickly?'

'In case, like a woman in a fairy tale, you choose to disappear when I turn my back.'

'You sound like my son.'

'I can assure you that the feelings you rouse in me are most certainly not filial.'

'And I am assuring you that they aren't reciprocated.' Karran, breathing more quickly, held his ironic gaze with her own.

'You sound – over-emphatic?' he suggested smoothly.

She shook her head. 'I've had enough of uncomfortable relationships.'

'Is that how I make you feel? Then there's hope for me. I can wait.'

He'd be good at waiting, Karran thought, and shivered.

'You're not cold?' Instantly he was considerate.

'A goose walked over my grave.'

'That sounds – uncomfortable. I'm sorry I'll have to leave you to entertain yourself for the next hour. Contacts to follow up while I have the chance. But later, we'll talk properly.' O'Ferrall smiled. It was a tight reflex, all brilliance and charm departed. The champagne arrived. They sipped for a moment in broody silence.

'Oh, come!' A new voice broke into that hint of unwelcome seriousness of purpose. 'Must you keep all the most interesting guests to yourself, O'Ferrall?' The shark-mouthed man grinned over O'Ferrall's shoulder. Karran's stomach muscles tightened.

'It's you,' O'Ferrall said without noticeable enthusiasm. 'My dear, this is Sir Miles Standish. Standish, this is

136

Karran Howard. Mrs Howard. She used to own this place.'

'Enchanted, Ma'am.' The fleshy face was beaded with perspiration. When Standish moved closer, Karran could smell sweat on his clothing which was inclined to garishness. He took her hand and kissed the back of it.

Suddenly O'Ferrall's face was bleak and unfriendly. 'I must go,' he said. 'I've things to attend to, people to see.' He drained his glass and replaced it on a nearby tray. 'I'll see you later, Karran. It's plain you won't be left unattended.' Then he bowed and went swiftly between the gossiping groups.

Any relief Karran might have felt at his departure was dispelled by Sir Miles Standish's presence, the knowing familiarity of a man, who, when he wanted something, was unable to conceal the fact with any show of finesse.

She schooled her features to hide her troubled thoughts.

'So you are from the same part of Ireland as myself,' Erin said. 'I don't recall any mention of your name. Of course, I was very young when I left Wicklow.'

O'Ferrall said, 'Before I moved to Dublin we were at the other side of the county, Kilmichael way.'

'Oh, yes, I'd an uncle over there.' She was not yet altogether at ease with this host who seemed to be indulging in secret amusement over his ill-assorted guests. They were a mixed bag, Erin admitted, then wondered if her gown really was in good taste. It was that purplish thing of Karran's that made most of the women here look like overstuffed sofas. It was not pleasant to feel like an overstuffed sofa. And her dress had cost enough to make Barney blench when the bill arrived. Had green satin been a mistake? She longed for another glass of wine.

'Did anyone tell you that you've eyes the colour of a four-leaved clover, Mrs Kerruish?'

'Not for a long time.' Erin was still woman enough to pat her carefully coiffed hair, a shade redder than usual but reasonably natural-looking in the smoky candle-glow that

137

concealed those increasing lines on her skin.

'They are remarkable. Mr Kerruish is a lucky man.'

'You're too kind.' Had O'Ferrall just concealed a yawn? Erin was devastated. Had she indeed come to that time in her life when she'd become merely another boring old woman to be tolerated? Or pitied?

'You'd know the O'Neills!' she insisted desperately. 'Dermot O'Neill?'

O'Ferrall's eyes widened, then narrowed. 'Why, yes. Dermot O'Neill. I do know him!' And he laughed. The quality of that laughter left Erin confused.

'I knew Dermot,' she said rapidly. 'Very well. That was a long time ago, of course.'

'Oh, come! It couldn't have been *that* long, surely?' Was there the slightest tinge of mockery in the implied compliment? Was she never to trust anyone again? Erin grew steadily more unhappy and confused.

'I assure you that it was.'

O'Ferrall seized two tall glasses from a tray carried by a young flunkey in a too tight costume that showed straining calves and biceps. Following the direction of Erin's gaze as he walked away, O'Ferrall said, 'You can never conceal a lad's true origins, not even dressed in silks and satins. And that doesn't just apply to lads.' He pressed a glass into her hand, then lifted his own. 'Present company is always excepted, naturally.' And he smiled that vaguely derisive smile, drank the champagne and glanced around for another bumpkin with a silver tray. He had not far to look.

Erin, who'd already had more champagne than was discreet, drank both glasses greedily. It was Barney's fault if she over-indulged. He'd gone to every Tom, Dick and Harry at this incredible affair, pleading urgent business with each. And Charlotte had been just as inconsiderate. Both of them must realize that none of her own cronies was present. O'Ferrall had been discerning about silk purses and sows' ears. She leaned towards her host confidingly. 'There was good blood in the O'Neills.' She seemed unable to stop chattering.

Disconcertingly, O'Ferrall's face appeared to have retreated a little. All but those bright grey eyes now seemed slightly out of focus. Only the eyes seemed to bore right inside her, searching out all those mean little secrets. Erin tried to pull together the dingy remnants of her past self-esteem. 'We were the best of friends, Dermot and myself. My father never considered him good enough for me, but that didn't put Dermot off. Very per – per – persuasive, Dermot could be. Too – too persuasive if you must know. And I – I was innocent till then.'

'My dear Mrs Kerruish! Should you be telling me—?' O'Ferrall looked startled.

'No. No. Don't try to stop me. Dermot thought me good enough and I was beautiful enough in those – those days for any man. It was his miserable old pig of a father squashed the thought of any wedding, and a wedding there surely should have been. Mr O'Ferrall, are you listening?'

Erin's head had grown curiously light and her body no longer seemed to belong to her. O'Ferrall was smiling like a satyr. She heard him snap his fingers and one of the ploughboy flunkeys arrived almost instantly like a genie out of a bottle. O'Ferrall whispered something and the youth vanished.

Erin laughed. 'You're a – mag – magician, Mr O'Ferrall. You snap your fing – fingers and men disappear. I was telling you about Dermot. I, I had his son. Did you know that? Boyce is grandson to that old pig who wouldn't let us wed. That would be a slap in the eye, if only he knew!' She giggled.

'It would be, if he wasn't in his grave,' O'Ferrall observed, his voice seeming to come from the bottom of an echoing well. 'This ten years or so.'

'I'm del – delighted to hear it. He'll be stoking the fires in hell, so he will! And he'll never know the boy's in Parliament. None – none of Dermot's other children can have done so well for them – themselves.'

'None of them have, Mrs Kerruish,' O'Ferrall assured her from an immense distance to which even that all-seeing gaze had retreated. Sinisterly, his face looked covered with muslin.

'I'm – glad of that.'

'I think your wife is a – little unwell,' O'Ferrall murmured politely and then Barney was beside her, his arm supporting her. Erin felt herself swaying.

'She's been under a strain,' Barney said without expression. He was still angry with her!

'There's a small room just there,' O'Ferrall told him. 'Go in there until she feels better. It'll be the heat of these damned candles. It's like a forcing-house.'

'You've been very kind.'

'Yes, he has,' Erin supplemented hazily. 'Mr – O'Ferrall's the kind – of man a lady can – converse – with. Mr O'F – O'Ferrall listens.'

'I'm sorry,' Barney went on, dragging her remorselessly towards a door that looked no larger than that of a doll's house and wavered mysteriously as though it were under water.

'There's – no – need to be – sorry,' Erin mumbled, only just aware that her green satin skirts were making noises like waves. She was beginning to feel submerged in unreality. Part of her wanted to cry.

'Oh, but there is,' Barney insisted softly, and gave her a push.

She was lying on the sea-bed, drowning. It was not an unpleasant sensation. Erin giggled. She wanted to tell Barney that he must come with her but her tongue seemed tied. She just had time to reflect that it was the first time it ever had been, when someone put out the light and all the sounds floated away like bits of bladderwrack.

Something touched her gently and was gone.

Barney came upon Charlotte and George Seyler returning from the card rooms.

The French windows stood slightly open because of the heat but the wind was too boisterous and flickered the candles, putting half of them out. Female guests screamed happily and crowded closer together. A flunkey closed the windows hastily and opened inner doors instead. A slate crashed on to the patio outside.

'What a night! Look, I'll have to take your mother home. I think she was overtired and the champagne's gone to her head. This wind could well rise. Reminds me of that night at Clay Head when the fishing fleet went to the bottom of the sea. That *was* before your time! I feel that if I've to go it should be now, but I don't want to spoil your fun, Charlotte. Enjoying it, are you?'

'Surprisingly, yes.' Charlotte laughed as the flunkeys went round with tapers, re-lighting the candles. 'I had reservations about coming but I'm glad I did. At least it's an experience. I want to look for Karran. When I saw her last she was in the centre of a rather raffish crowd. They've all been round her like bees round honey, which should raise her morale, but I'd like to find out if she's really happy, and if not, do something about it. I thought, perhaps, that I'd go back with her to Cormorant House? She could have difficulty in leaving alone. There's at least one guest with unmistakably ulterior motives! Perhaps my presence will put him off.'

'Don't wait until the wind gets much stronger. Karran's trap is rather small. I don't want you being overturned on that hill down to the village.' Barney warned. 'Where's Karran at the moment?'

'Somewhere upstairs, at the tables. The predatory gentleman maintains that she's bringing him luck. And luck is everything to a confirmed gambler.

'The things they do to ensure it! Scruffy talismans, obviously used a thousand times, or not wearing a certain colour. They'd have run shrieking from Mama's gown! Where is she, by the way?'

Barney jerked his head in the direction of the ante-room. 'Lying on a sofa. I blame myself. Kept getting involved and forgetting to make sure she was with someone else.'

'I should have done that,' Charlotte said. 'But I do seem to constrain Mama. We find communication difficult, and anyway, one doesn't come to an occasion like this to stand in corners. O'Ferrall meant us to circulate.'

'And to get a taste for his tables,' Seyler pointed out, smiling.

'And that,' Charlotte agreed. 'What a strange way of life! Based on weakness and superstition. You'd never believe the money that can change hands.'

'Oh, but I would,' Barney said. 'That's why I've stayed away from those enticements, and if you've any sense, so will you. But George won't let you make a fool of yourself. I'll go back to Erin now. A pity the Bascombes couldn't come after all. Erin'd have been all right if Muriel had been here. Bad luck she was ill at the last minute. I think it's a good idea of yours to go to Black Rocks afterwards. I shouldn't leave it much longer. O'Ferrall's treated us all very handsomely and must want to be left to get on with the real purpose of the affair by this time. There's a hard core of gamblers who'll refuse to leave the seductive delights of Lady Chance. You'll see that the two girls do leave safely, won't you, George?'

'Certainly. My pleasure. O'Ferrall's invited me to stay the night.'

'Good. Take care, my dear.'

'Do you want any assistance?' Seyler asked, 'with Mrs Kerruish?'

Barney shook his head. 'O'Ferrall's had our carriage brought round to the side door and one of his flunkeys is poised to help. I'm too old to carry my wife over any more thresholds.'

'You'll never be old,' Charlotte insisted quickly.

'Wishful thinking, my love.' Barney patted her arm. 'You must accept the fact that I'm too old and wise a dog now to court trouble.' He kissed Charlotte's cheek and hurried off.

'Have you really enjoyed the evening?' Seyler asked.

Charlotte looked up at him, eyes glowing, cheeks flushed. 'Yes. I thought I'd hate it but I haven't. This incredible display! Excitement. The house is filled with it!

It's not like the old Ravensdowne. And yet, there *is* something missing.'

'Tranquillity?'

'No. Certainly not that. There are still faint echoes of long-gone hostility. There's always been more than a hint of discord about this place. I can't recall that anyone's ever lived at peace inside these walls. Always undercurrents.'

'What a sensitive little person you must be.' Seyler's voice was very gentle.

Charlotte hadn't known that his tones could ever become so muted. So intimate. She shook her head positively. 'That's a fallacy. I'm tough as boots.'

'No, you aren't. You like people to think you self-sufficient, but there's more under the surface. Much more.'

Her cheeks burned. 'Are you such an infallible judge of character?'

'In this case, yes.'

She laughed uncertainly. 'Haven't you a good opinion of yourself!'

'No. Only the certainty that beneath what the rest of the world sees there's something I want to discover, bit by bit—'

'Please, George—'

'I'm not asking you to commit yourself here and now, but since you are free and no longer out of reach as once you were, I want you to know that I've admired you for a very long time. My feelings amount to more than admiration. I wondered whether yours might ever come to match them? There, I've said nothing that could offend a single soul of your acquaintance! What do you say, my dear Charlotte? Knowing you not to be a silly, prevaricating sort of woman, in fact, a painfully honest one, don't hesitate to speak the truth.'

Charlotte stared. In spite of the fact that the French windows were tightly closed, the candle-flames still danced like will-o-the-wisps, sending the little trails of grey smoke to diffuse in the air. Another slate crashed on to the stone outside and the sound was like a great

143

knocking on the door of her heart, a door she'd imagined to be barred and bolted for ever. She'd liked George Seyler well enough but there had never before been this powerful sense of almost terrible closeness, as though, by sending him away, her spirit might be transformed into a dusty prison with no exit, where no one would come again.

She drew a deep, uneven breath. At one and the same time she felt safe, yet most thrillingly in danger.

'Don't tell me I've had that much effect on you!' he said at last. 'To take away the power of speech. I'd not thought myself capable.'

'I think,' Charlotte brought out in a small jerky voice that didn't seem to be her own, 'that there's every possibility that we are intended to know one another better. A great deal better. And I do wish it with all my heart.'

'Charlotte—'

'And now, shall we go in search of Karran? Because if we don't, I fear I may be tempted to behave very foolishly.'

George Seyler took her arm with a highly satisfactory possessiveness. They walked together towards the staircase, seeing no one, not even noticing the sullen rage of the wind in the chimneys, sending the soot pattering into the big fireplaces like a foretaste of evil.

Karran had had enough of present company. Standish and his party had clung close as leeches, blocking every attempt at escape. She thought she hated O'Ferrall for inviting her, then abandoning her to the mercies of his dubious acquaintances. But she couldn't reasonably have expected anything more. He owed it to the success of his grand opening to go to everyone in turn. Each time he'd looked around for her she'd been with someone else, George and Charlotte, or this motley group who'd adopted her as some sort of mascot. One or two were tolerably amusing.

She wondered what they'd say if she told them she was

reputed to be a witch and granddaughter to another, that everyone with whom she'd come into contact suffered from bad luck and not the good fortune they so obviously sought.

There was an Irishman with a flower in his hat. He hadn't liked it when she'd laughed at that. It was his symbol to stave off the fickleness of chance.

Every now and again she had painful thoughts of Gideon, a Gideon she scarcely recognized. What had happened to the exciting person who'd swept her off her feet? And on to the first available bed.

She encountered Standish's gaze and detested him afresh. He deposited a handful of sovereigns on to the green baize and said a little thickly, 'There you are, my dear. Try your luck.'

'Not at anyone else's expense,' she replied clearly. 'If I gamble, I use my own stakes.'

For a moment, she seemed circled by hostility. Standish's friends pressed closer to stare at her with varying emotions, some owlishly, some suspiciously, resentfully, lasciviously. Karran realized that she'd become very angry.

'That's not very friendly.'

'Whatever did you take me for? Some hanger-on trying to milk you out of your gold? You're mistaken, if that's what you thought.'

She was aware of other faces in the background, familiar faces that watched discreetly, betraying another range of conflicting feelings.

'I meant no harm,' Standish offered, his voice slurred.

One of the women gave vent to a high-pitched bray of laughter. 'You've never tried to buy me, Miles! But I swear I'd not be so arrogant!'

'Don't be a fool,' he dismissed her contemptuously.

'If you'll excuse me,' Karran said coldly, 'I'm tired and I intend to go home.'

'Not so fast,' Standish murmured and grabbed at her wrist.

'How dare you?' she whispered, not wanting to attract

any more adverse attention. His shark mouth curved upwards, cruelly.

'You must have known that I expected to accompany you. You aren't a child.'

'I made no such promise.'

'Nevertheless, you did know.' There was an ugliness in his tone that frightened her. 'Why else should I have attended you hand and foot?'

'If I were truthful, I'd admit I've wanted to be free of you this last hour.'

The trees in the shrubbery swept the window-panes with scratching talons. Something large and heavy crashed to the gravel. One of the chimney-pots? One less chimney on which to pay the smoke-tax!

Standish pulled Karran close to him. 'You did know what was required of you,' he insisted, his heavy face only an inch away. 'I made sure first you were no innocent to be led astray.'

'Let go of me,' she expostulated, swept by impotent distaste. 'I've a child at home and must return to her.'

'I'll take you there.'

'I think not.'

'The whisper is that you only came to find—'

'How dare you repeat slander!' She tried to ignore the insinuation in his tone and his eyes, to free her hand from his hurtful grasp, but could not.

'Oh, there you are, Mrs Howard. Charlotte and I are ready to take you home.' George Seyler's voice broke coldly into her feelings of desperation. Karran had never been so thankful to see anyone. Damn O'Ferrall and his house of chance! She'd not set foot in it again, not if she lived to be a hundred.

'Thank you,' she murmured. 'I'll fetch my cloak and see you downstairs.'

The hot, heavy hand was removed reluctantly. Standish remained silent, though the slitted gaze spoke volumes. The look he gave George Seyler was murderous. No one spoke.

Seyler smiled thinly and drew Karran away, gently but firmly.

'I'm glad you came,' she told him as they crossed the room.

'Charlotte thought you might be in difficulty. It seems she was right. By the way, she intends to spend the night with you. Her parents have already left, taking the carriage.'

'I would like that!' They were out into the long hall. One door stood ajar.

'That's where the cloaks are. Tell Charlotte I won't be long.'

'Very well.' Seyler moved away, humming the refrain of 'Greensleeves', the bulk of his dark figure comforting. He seemed in good humour. She wondered why.

Inside the cloakroom which had once been a guest room, she stared at her pale face in the glass and automatically tidied her hair, then slid her arms into the warm outer garment. She'd need it now that the weather had turned so wild. The wind howled like a banshee. Erin would know all about banshees. Karran wondered why she'd gone before the evening had properly ended. It wasn't like Erin to miss anything.

Slipping the pearl-handed fan over her arm, Karran went out.

'You're going nowhere,' Standish said, stepping out from an adjacent doorway. 'Not without me.'

'Get out of my way, you drunken pest.'

'That's not what you usually say, is it,' Standish sneered, planting himself in her way, 'not according to some of my evening's informants.'

Karran thought of screaming but that would attract too many bystanders. In any case, O'Ferrall had been generous with his refreshments. Hardly anyone would be sober enough to care that she'd been accosted. All they would remember was that Mrs Howard had a reputation for being free with her favours and had met her match.

Any idea of taking flight in the other direction was

dashed when she was seized by Standish who wrapped powerful arms around hers and forced his wet lips over her mouth.

She struggled furiously but he was imbued with a bull-like strength that brought back unwelcome sensations of fear. Even if she wanted to scream she couldn't, not with that shark mouth clamped on hers. Karran felt physically sick.

There was a snapping sound and she realized that the sticks of the treasured fan had broken in the undignified struggle.

Someone was coming swiftly. Karran had time only to see a shadow fall over herself and Standish, then she was hurled against the wall as her attacker was yanked away to stand for a moment, swaying uncertainly, his face distorted with a kind of anger she wished never to see again.

A fist crashed into the shark face, breaking up the furious stare. His eyes closed as he rocked, then pitched full-length on to the carpeted floor of the passage.

O'Ferrall gestured peremptorily at the flunkey who'd appeared at the end of the hall. 'Take him to his room. Get someone to help you. If I know Sir Miles, he's going to be in an unpleasant mood when he wakes up. But that won't be for some time.' The reflection seemed to please him.

'Aye, sir.'

O'Ferrall stared contemptuously at the fallen man. 'I'm sorry you should have suffered such a distasteful experience under my roof.'

Under mine, she thought swiftly, knowing too late that she regretted having left this house. Not even the recent struggle with this drunken brute had spoiled what she still felt for Ravensdowne. She should have tried harder to keep it.

Karran lifted her hand and detached the broken fan from her wrist. 'The main damage seems to have been to my pride, and to this.'

O'Ferrall surveyed the recumbent figure coldly. Karran

148

had the certainty that he wanted very much to kick Standish.

'I apologize,' he said, 'that this has had to happen. If I'd had my way, you'd never have been introduced. But if I were too particular about my clients I'd go out of business. And the object of the opening was to foster goodwill and interest and to do as much business as was possible. In that respect, the evening has been more than satisfactory.'

'I realize that.'

'The yellow room,' O'Ferrall said, as two brawny flunkeys appeared.

'Aye, sir.'

'And you needn't bother to use kid gloves.'

'No, sir.'

'But isn't that going to be bad for business?' Karran enquired as the lolling body was carted away, none too gently.

O'Ferrall shrugged. 'It's of no consequence. I've no time for anyone who'd treat you with disrespect.'

'Don't you mean anyone? Anyone at all?'

'No, I mean you in particular. I don't waste words. Life's too short.'

Life would be too short for a man like O'Ferrall. Too restricted. But what about that golden-haired woman someone mentioned some time ago? Wasn't she equally important?

'Thank you,' Karran said, rubbing a bruised shoulder.

'What for?'

'Rescuing me.' She shivered. 'I'd never have got away. He'd some – mistaken idea I was there for the taking. In reality, I'm fastidious.' It seemed important that O'Ferrall believed that.

'Come into the study for a moment. You look cold and shaken.'

He closed the door behind them. 'The sot's damaged that fan worse than I thought. You must allow me to replace it.'

'No.'

'Yes. I left you in his accursed company!' O'Ferrall raised an elegant foot and kicked at the fire.

'Why did you?'

'I told you. I had half a hundred people to talk to.'

'I thought you were – angry with me.'

'Not with you. I know Standish's type and I was annoyed because I could do no other than to make introductions. Not that I haven't been watching the progress of your evening so far. So long as you were adequately surrounded I decided to leave well alone. Then I noticed that both you and he had gone. Did he hurt your shoulder? You keep rubbing it.'

Karran shook her head. 'It happened when you wrenched Standish away from me. I lost my balance.'

'That's a pity.'

'Shouldn't you go back to your guests?'

'They've had all they're getting of me. I want to talk to you now. Unless you're dead set on going this instant?'

Karran didn't want to get up. The fire was flickering strongly with the aid of that rumbustious wind in the chimney. The night was as unquiet as her thoughts. But she had a curious compulsion to remain.

'Oh! I've just remembered that I was to meet Mr Seyler and Mrs Costain in the hall. Charlotte's going to Black Rocks with me for the night.'

'They can't object to remaining a little longer.' O'Ferrall tugged the brocaded bell pull at the side of the fireplace and asked the flunkey who answered the summons to tell Mr Seyler that Mrs Howard was taking a little refreshment with him, and would leave in another half an hour.

'I'd like to have said in an hour but I felt you'd disagree.' O'Ferrall poured brandy into two glasses and gave one to Karran.

'I most certainly would! And you knew, I think, that I wouldn't argue in front of your manservant to undermine your authority.'

He smiled and raised his glass. 'Always fight from a

position of vantage.'

'That sounds like the sort of remark Napoleon or Wellington might have made.

'Are you an admirer of the martial arts?' He cut the end off a cigar and lit it.

Karran shook her head. 'I've a cousin of sorts who was. It upset Boyce greatly that the Napoleonic wars hadn't gone on indefinitely.'

'Boyce? Would that be Mrs Kerruish's son by any chance?'

'How did you know that?' The brandy trickled down Karran's throat in a thread of fire.

O'Ferrall tilted his chair back and scrutinized her through a thin haze of cigar smoke, legs outstretched. He appeared immensely tall, full of self-confidence. There was a strength in him that seemed lacking in Gideon. Gideon—

'Your – aunt? – and I talked at great length. Rather, she did.' O'Ferrall smiled secretly. 'Some of her revelations were embarrassing to say the least. But you must know all about those.'

'I've never been so favoured. But Charlotte says that Erin has taken to referring to Boyce as though the King himself was his father. It seems he's from privileged stock. Blood blue as a violet. Fitting for a future member of the House of Lords.'

O'Ferrall laughed lazily and blew a perfect smoke ring. 'Blue blood my Aunt Sarah's garter! He, it seems, is son to a piddling little squireen without one brass farthing to rub against another. The passage of time has cast some charmed mantle over the lady's recollections. I know Dermot O'Neill. There's not one generous bone in his miserable carcase.'

Karran gasped pleasurably. 'Should you be telling me all this?'

'Well, it's all in the family, surely?'

She shook her head. 'Erin does have delusions of grandeur. I've never come up to her expectations. Not that

151

it bothers me unduly.'

'She's not fit to kiss the hem of your skirt.'

'Well, that's blunt enough!'

'As I've already told you, I never mince words. But Kerruish is a different kettle of fish. He's the sort of man I'd enjoy doing business with.'

'Barney's a good man.'

'I think you meant that.'

'Like you, I don't care for pretence.'

'Then I can ask you what you think of an Irish adventurer in expectation of a truthful reply?'

'How can my opinion matter?' she prevaricated.

'It could matter to me.' He rose and dropped the ash from his cigar into the fire.

'I prefer to reserve judgement, Mr O'Ferrall.'

'More brandy?'

'I'd better not.'

'Then please me by calling me Nick. Surely we've known one another long enough by now?'

'I suppose we have.'

'Then say it.'

'Nick.'

'There, was that so difficult?'

Karran smiled. 'Not really. But shouldn't you be asking that opinion from someone else?'

'And who might that be?'

'I heard mention of a lady. A lady with yellow hair.'

'My God! I should have known Philly wouldn't pass unnoticed. Is that why I've had so much trouble getting you here?'

'No.'

'I believe it was.'

'Believe what you like! It's of no consequence. I can't imagine why I mentioned her in the first place.'

'Oh, yes, you can! Well, I won't disappoint you. I could have passed her off as a cousin, but Philly occasionally visits me from Douglas. Life can be difficult for a man when he's spurned by the object of his affections. There

152

must be some substitute. Philly doesn't object to the arrangement. She knows my real interests lie elsewhere. In inaccessible places. Has anyone told you how desirable you look when you widen your eyes to their fullest extent? Like two dark jewels in a mask of ivory.'

'Very poetic,' Karran managed to say and set down the brandy glass. 'I really have to go—'

'While we are on the subject of other attachments, I understand that Hanna's father has visited you.'

'Why shouldn't he?'

'Why didn't he, a long time ago? It says little for the advocate—'

'You presume,' Karran said icily. 'He never knew about the child. I didn't tell him.'

'And no one else did?'

'No, not that it's any business of yours!'

'Any more than my poor brassy-haired Philly is of yours.'

'I suppose I asked for that.'

'It's a question I'd have wanted to ask, anyway. About your erstwhile friend, Collister.'

'You needn't sound so condemnatory. He asked me to marry him once he knew about my baby.'

'Is it in order to ask what you said?'

'No. Certainly not!'

'When I think how close you two must have been, I'll never understand why he went, or why it took him a year to come back.' He'd re-lit the cigar and his face was, annoyingly, half-hazed with the fragrant fug. But seeing her furious look, he said, mock-contritely, 'Oh, did I omit to ask you if I might smoke? Does the fact offend you?'

'You know perfectly well that the wretched cigar doesn't worry me in the least! It's your colossal impudence!'

O'Ferrall laughed.

Karran got up stormily. 'I'll be glad if you don't send me any more of your gilt-edged invitations. If only your guests came up to their quality.'

'Touché! But I wasn't entirely responsible for Standish's

behaviour. And when a man comes all the way from London, complete with entourage and obviously inclined to spend money, I could hardly turn him away in case he should by chance insult a lady.'

'You should have kept your invitations for the Phillys of this world!'

'You mustn't malign my friends. Particularly those you've never met,' he said quietly.

'No. I apologize. That was unfair. Many people would bracket us together and they mightn't be so wrong. Once again, I'm obliged to you for settling the score with Standish. I know where to find Charlotte and George. Please don't trouble to come with me.'

Karran wrenched at the door-knob and hurried along the passageway as if the devil himself were in pursuit. She'd had enough of whispers and false expectations, the hidden whirlpools of emotion. She longed for the now familiar comforts of Cormorant House, the genuine companionship of Mrs Quinn, Hanna's soft little arms about her neck, Bart's shadow as he bent over some book or other. Ravensdowne had gone for good. No one there would look out over the bay in moonlight or watch the shags preening on the dark rocks. Those green-covered tables glowing in pools of lamplight were all that interested these new, alien inhabitants.

'Oh, there you are,' Charlotte was saying, and Seyler took her arm as though he cared what became of her.

'Let's go. Please, Charlotte.'

'Of course, my dear. I'm ready.'

Seyler opened the door and a great gust of wind met them, scratching and screaming like one of the Furies. Karran clutched at her cloak and fastened it with trembling fingers. She fancied she heard O'Ferrall's mocking voice and let the door bang behind her with tremendous force.

They ran towards the waiting trap.

'What's that?' Charlotte pulled at Karran's sleeve.

Seyler had already stopped, his hand cupped over one

ear. 'Trouble!' he shouted above the wind's gusting. 'Where's the quickest route to the cliff-top?'

'This way.' Karran, her cloak whipping around her, led the way round the side of the house. There were other people there before them, pointing and gesticulating in the direction of the water.

Moonlight showed the the white crests of giant waves and the blurred, anaemic bobbing of the lanterns on the distant yachts. But there was one light that was closer. Thin masts rose from the flurries of angry spume. The uncertain light picked out the shape of a vessel that plunged and rose, that disappeared behind veils of spray only to reappear, endlessly tossing, helpless without the sails that the crew had had no time to raise before the cable had broken, sending them on a journey that could have no end but death.

A terrible whiteness roared about the Shag Rocks. Karran was reminded of lions waiting with mouths agape, those dark maws filled with teeth.

Someone pushed her aside regardlessly and cried out, 'Tom? Tom, keep her away from the Shag!' But O'Ferrall's words were useless. Faint cries reached the watchers on the cliff, then the graceful hull and the slender, dancing masts cracked sharply against the black, waiting fangs. The distant screams, the bobbing timbers were drawn into a maelstrom of agony, then oblivion.

PART FIVE

Family Reunion

The fierce gales left a trail of destruction that had far-reaching repercussions. Nick O'Ferrall's pleasure-boat was not the only one that had broken adrift and been driven on to rocks and smashed with great force. Crews drowned within sound of the people of Port St Mary who watched, as impotent to go to their aid as O'Ferrall and his guests had been.

The locals began to speak of O'Ferrall's luck. Hadn't his gaming tables ended up in the sea some months earlier? The expression slid easily into Manx conversation. O'Ferrall's luck was a kiss of death.

He'd been grim and quiet for a time, grieving for his drowned friend, Tom Allen, shunning public places, running his strange, unreal business from the sanctum of Ravensdowne, sending others to Douglas when there was need for contact.

Karran became used to the sight of Brand riding past the house on O'Ferrall's errands. He didn't always ride past. Occasionally he came in to see how she was and how Hanna was progressing. It was Brand who brought back the fan that Standish had so brutally broken, very neatly and unobtrusively repaired and as beautiful as ever. As always in her feelings towards Nick O'Ferrall, Karran was both irritated yet inexplicably pleased. She'd never expected to see the fan again after having left Ravensdowne without it.

She'd also grown accustomed to the sight of the carriage

that took the woman she knew only as Philly towards Nick's house. There was little to be seen but pink cheeks and bits of yellow hair under a bonnet, but the distant impression always reminded Karran of the woman Laurence had known before they came to mean so much to one another. The sharpness of her youthful jealousy returned to lacerate her thoughts. Philly was a ghost returned and Karran could not understand the strength of her dislike. Why should it matter that Nick had mistresses?

She sent a brief note of thanks via Brand for the return of the fan and commiserations on the loss of Tom and the vessel, and made herself push thoughts of Nick and the fair-haired woman from her mind. There were more immediate problems of daily living with which to contend. There was Bart's increasing urge for more freedom than she felt was right for a boy of his age. But he'd always been older than his years and was perfectly well able to take care of himself. Hanna experienced the normal troubles of teething and childish ailments, yet continued to thrive. Life was busy.

Karran had a sense of time slipping by and taking her youth with it.

Charlotte, too, unsettled her by speaking of George Seyler. 'He wants to marry me.'

'And what's so unexpected about that?' Karran teased. 'I could have told you that more than a year ago. When we both went to the Roses'.'

'They ask when you are coming again.'

'How could I? The Standish affair must be all round the district. I'm fated to remain a femme fatale, my dear. I'm sorry I went.'

'I wish I could say the same, but it was that evening that I knew I loved George.'

'Is it – anything like your feelings for Abel? Your initial feeling?'

'Oh, no! Nothing so wild and unhappy. It's the most wonderful thing that ever happened to me. I pray that it will to you.'

Karran shrugged. 'I think I've had enough of men.'

'That's nonsense, of course. You're disenchanted with that brute, Standish, and even more with Gideon. And it doesn't help that I have a wonderful man.'

'Have?'

'Oh, not in that sense, not yet. George is almost annoyingly correct on that score. I'm the one who wouldn't scruple to bed with him. I'm afraid I'm as weak as ever. I miss being a wife. Not Abel's wife, just a woman. I've never subscribed to the school of thought that says it's immodest for a good woman to feel passion. Why should such pleasures be reserved for harlots?'

Karran, beset by images of Philly and O'Ferrall, still could not help laughing.

'Something tells me that George is due to become far less proper.'

'I sincerely hope so.'

'Is it true that your beloved is to design a new yacht for Nick?'

'Oh, so it's Nick nowadays, is it? You always held out so strenuously on that point. Can it be—?'

'No, it can't! About the yacht—'

'Yes.'

'How can he spare so much time? He has that responsible post with the Scots line.'

'That's what I really came to tell you. Papa is very taken with my husband-to-be. They get on almost like father and son. Of course, they've both similar natures. George has some money – inherited, need I say – and a good deal of the sort of acumen Papa most admires and needs. Karran, they are to throw in their lot together! Papa would like to spend less time in his various offices, says he's getting old and the pace is too hot, not that I believe that.

'George will leave the shipping line and become a junior partner. He'll draw up plans for a new kind of vessel to be built alongside the bread and butter variety. Nick's is the first order. Oh, and George has arranged passenger service for some of Nick's prospective customers from Scotland.

There are any number of tobacco lords, mine and mill owners, East Indiamen and plantation owners all wanting diversion.

'George will take over the routines Papa finds most wearing, like going to Foxdale to deal with the affairs of the mines. I will ride with him once we're wed. Oh, why are there these difficulties about the remarriage of widows? Why should it be so indecent to become someone else's wife before twelve months have passed? I want him now!'

'I can't answer that. I don't make the laws.' Karran noting Charlotte's happy absorption, thought, 'She's going away from me. She'll become enmeshed in her fine new family life and she won't need me. And I'll miss her.'

'Oh, my dear!' Charlotte's voice broke into Karran's sense of desolation. 'It won't make any different to us. You transformed my life that day we encountered at Poyllvaish. We'll go on being friends, always.'

'It can't be the same, though. You won't have the freedom that exists now. You won't have to escape any more. You won't want to leave a home that shows promise of being – how was it that you, yourself put it? The most wonderful thing that ever happened to you.'

'So it is! But you'd never be excluded. George, as I said, does resemble Papa, who couldn't live without his fingers in a thousand pies. I think that's why Mama has to fill in her time with those gossipy women she always seems to favour. But she'll be indiscreet one day and then her erstwhile friends will tear her to pieces as they've done everyone else.'

That day, Karran reflected, could be closer than Charlotte imagined. Erin had been positively foolish the night of the ill-fated grand opening. She'd stripped her soul bare to Nick O'Ferrall's clear gaze. He might repeat her disclosure in the wrong quarter. How would Erin stand up to the results of *her* past becoming common knowledge? Nick might tell Philly in some vulnerable, intimate moment. Women like Philly weren't always discreet.

'Have you heard from Boyce recently?' Karran asked abruptly.

'Boyce?' Charlotte wrinkled her brows. 'What made you think of him? As a matter of fact, he's asked Mama and Papa to visit himself and Nina. He thought she'd enjoy sitting in the gallery at the Commons and listening to the debates. She'll probably swell with pride. Not that she wouldn't turn a few heads, even at her age. Mama can still look beautiful when she puts her mind to it.'

'Will your father go?'

'If you'd asked me that a few months ago I'd have said no. But they've grown closer again recently. To my surprise, I'm relieved. She can never be good enough for him but he's never really happy unless they're on good terms, and I want him always to be happy. In any case, he's been tired of late and could well do with the change. The moment George takes over his share of the responsibility they'll be off to London. Rosemary's wildly jealous. She wants to see all the royal princes. In order to make her eventual choice, I suspect! She thinks they'll be riding about in carriages, looking solely for glimpses of herself. As I've always said, there's a deal too much of Mama in my only child. I've not been able to think of a way to break the news that the King has no sons.'

'She's not going to remain an only child for ever, though, is she?' Karran teased, diverted at last from her attack of depression.

'I hope not. I intend to give George what he wants. He likes the thought of children. Then I'll have your problems! Rosemary's sure to resent them, little minx that she is. Thank heaven she's got that pony and is still thick as thieves with your Bart. What do you suppose they do on all those picnics they have?'

'I've always wondered. They manage to look so secretive. But being at different schools could push them apart to a certain extent. Seeing different people.'

Charlotte got up. 'I'm sick of the sound of my own

160

voice! I seem to have monopolized the conversation. Forgive me?'

'Forgive? What odd things you say. I hope you're going to have a truly splendid future. and you must warn me about those occasions when George is likely to become "less proper" so that I won't call at inconvenient moments.'

Charlotte laughed. 'Don't worry, I will. There's so much to look forward to, when only a short time ago life had too many arid periods.' She bent to kiss Hanna gently on the forehead before picking up her gloves. 'One can't blame Gideon for being so besotted by the child. Do you still hear from him?'

'Oh, yes. He wants me to go over there, with Hanna. He says I may feel differently about Mary if we met.'

'Why don't you? You needn't commit yourself to anything. I do think this has to be resolved, don't you. You've had a face as long as a fiddle for quite some time. I knew you were troubled.'

'Have I? Was it so obvious?' Karran was chagrined.

'It was. Do it, Karran. You can't know that you won't get on with a person you've never met. It's unlike you to be so indecisive and so short-sighted. It smacks of prejudice. Something I find hard to connect with you.'

'I was going to write to Gideon this evening—'

'Well, tell him you intend to go. So long as you remain free to return at any time should you find your position untenable. You're afraid it will be, aren't you. It's a sort of cowardice alien to the Karran I know.'

'I thought you were going!'

'I'd better, before I disrupt your day any further. I – haven't spoken out of turn, have I?'

'No. I needed someone to put the case so plainly. But I don't have to like the fact that you're right.'

'You could find Gideon totally different on his own ground.'

'What is his own ground?'

'That's what you're going to find out.'

'In my own good time. Hanna's too small yet for such a journey. After her birthday, perhaps.'

'That might be sensible. Goodbye, my dear.'

Karran, as she watched the obviously radiant Charlotte depart, experienced some of the feelings of a woman standing before a guillotine. But she did go to her desk to get out a sheet of writing-paper. Dipping the quill into the blue glass inkwell, she began to write with a resolution that surprised her.

Sanding the finished epistle, she sealed it quickly and took it to Molly Quayle who was bound for Castletown to replenish the stores, to post before she could change her mind.

Watching the trap bowling along the shore road, she thought she stood on dangerous quicksand. She called out for Molly to return but the wind cast her words in the opposite direction. The small vehicle vanished into distance.

She needn't go. But over this matter, Karran felt that Gideon, for once, might be stronger than she wished.

Time was flying faster than ever. Bart was absorbed by his new, exciting school. Hanna was on the verge of walking. It had become appropriate for George Seyler and Charlotte Costain to make their wedding plans known. Not that the announcement caused too many raised brows. The partnership between Kerruish and Seyler was, by this time, firmly established.

Barney had accompanied Erin to London to stay in the grand house occupied by Boyce Kerruish, MP, and his forceful little wife, Nina. Not that Nina was quite as small as usual. She was some months pregnant and pregnancy can be unkind to short, slender women. Nina disliked her state.

Erin, who'd lost weight over the past year, took delight in parading her new and shapely figure on every occasion. She'd never liked Nina, who made her feel like a peasant, and her daughter-in-law's present embarrassment put her in good spirits.

Nina yawned as Erin told Boyce the island news, that a musical society was to be founded. 'That'll put paid to those nonsensical poetry meetings,' Erin said, not without satisfaction. 'Oh, and did I mention that we are to be counted?'

'Counted, Mama?' Boyce raised his brows.

'What is it that they call it, Barney? The method of ascertaining the number of island residents?'

'A census, my dear.'

Boyce said, 'Then it looks as if they are to decide on a change of capitals. If most people reside at Douglas, it would make sense to give Douglas the proper status. In view of the harbour facilities alone, especially with the new Red Pier. I'm surprised it hasn't happened before.'

Erin looked agitated and Barney swiftly changed the subject. 'Mark Cosnahan is to part with the *Victory* at last. He couldn't get shot of her to a Manx buyer. But now she's to take Sir John Ross to the Arctic. Fame indeed.'

Inevitably, Barney's remark led to a discussion of Captain Ross's Arctic expedition ten years ago, and the meeting with the bemused Eskimos of Prince Regent's Bay in their primitive furs.

The talk slid more comfortably to the frozen wastes and the certain discomforts of such another epic journey, then proceeded to the more mundane suggestion that a group of businessmen and ship-builders discuss the possibility of subscribing to build a steamship owned by Manxmen and captained and crewed by islanders. There was even a tentative name put forward for the venture that met almost universal favour, the Mona's Isle Company, Mona being the ancient name for the Isle of Man.

'Who are these men?' Boyce asked, leaning back in his chair and lighting a long black cheroot, having disdained Barney's offer of one of his own thick aromatic cigars.

'Moore of Cronkbourne, Wood the shipbuilder, Sam Harris, Harry Noble, Dr Garrett, the Gell brothers,

Gawne of Kentraugh, Forbes the banker and Quirk.'

'Which Quirk?' The island was full of them.

'The High Bailiff. Oh, and Captain Banks.' Barney ticked them off on his fingers.

'An impressive list. Will it come to anything?'

'It could. They mentioned it to me.'

'Would you be interested?'

'I might if it had been mooted before George and I went into partnership. I don't, however, want to stretch our mutual liabilities too greatly. But we thought we'd take out some shares if it should ever come to anything. Such matters have been brought up in the past and come to nought.'

'Not the sort of vessel that could be built locally, though.'

'It would have to go to the Clyde. There'd be a deal of money involved.'

Erin, bored by the business discussion, went to the window to look out at the view of the river. Cheyne Walk was so pleasantly situated and she could never tire of watching the promenaders, all so fashionably dressed, and the variety of vessels that slid down the great, glittering waterway.

Elizabeth and Nat Gelling had been persuaded to pay a brief visit to London while the Kerruishes were ensconced with Boyce and a not too enthusiastic Nina. Thank God, Erin thought, that there need be no awkwardness about Sebastian. There was no question of him being able to appear on the doorstep. That black sheep was safely tucked away at the back of beyond. Yet the spectre of his eventual return could never quite be dismissed. The smell of the river jarred suddenly, spoiling her pleasure.

Erin concentrated on the parade and forced herself to contemplate the advent of her daughter. Elizabeth had always been a beauty, but Gelling might not be able to provide the fine feathers that had hitherto enhanced his wife's good looks, so she herself needn't worry about being totally outshone.

Erin looked down with satisfaction at the expensive folds of her own new gown. The eau-de-nil had been an admirable choice. Barney had helped her to choose it. Thank God they were on easier terms. Only last night— She smiled secretly as the thought of their mutual sleeplessness in the strange house and the good use to which they'd put the annoyance. The hooting of tugs had accompanied the bounce of bedsprings she'd half-hoped might keep Nina awake, supercilious cat!

Nina's portliness had kept her at home the day before yesterday when her parents-in-law had attended the House of Commons. Boyce, of course, was still a back-bencher, but Erin's fertile imagination was sufficiently active to enable her to see him seated before long beside Viscount Goderich and the imposing Wellington who'd so recently superseded him as Prime Minister. She secretly thought the House an untidy, disorderly place where men behaved more like schoolboys and badly behaved ones at that, all shouting and waving their order papers. Some women among them might improve the atmosphere and provide commonsense.

Better by far was their exploration of the city yesterday, Nina having pleaded fatigue – a lie if ever there was one! The woman had the constitution of an ox! – and Boyce being required at the House. Barney had hired a cab for the entire day. Erin's eyes still glistened at the memory. The Burlington Arcade was best. She'd never seen such elegance, not that they'd been able to do much but feast their eyes. Barney was comfortably off but the prices of some of the goods they'd seen would make your hair stand on end. All they'd bought were some gloves at Lord's and a pair of shoes at Dawson's.

Someone had pointed out Cranbourn Alley, choc-a-bloc with cheap bonnet shops, and she'd found one to match the eau-de-nil gown. They'd purchased figs from Smyrna at Fortnum and Masons, and some Jamaican ginger for the Bascombes, snuff and cigars from Fribourg and Treyer's in the Haymarket, Barney loved a good cigar.

Then they'd stopped at Hatchard's for books for Tim and Virginia, and skirted the premises of the Grafton Fur Company, for the temptation was too great to allow oneself the mistake of entering and being seduced by some garment quite out of one's reach.

Erin had never seen so many people outside of Liverpool. The pavements were thronged. She liked the small shops, the bakers, butchers and greengrocers as much as Barney liked the secondhand-book stalls and the fishmongers. She came to recognize the pawnbrokers' signs and the barbers' poles.

'But what are those odd dishes beside the poles?' she'd asked, mystified.

'Gallipots,' Barney told her, puffing at one of his new cigars. 'Bleeding-dishes. Barbers are also surgeons. Didn't you know?'

'I'd forgotten. I don't care to see them on display.'

'If you were suddenly taken with a stroke, you'd forget those qualms.'

'Barney!'

'Don't take that too seriously. You look blooming. The change has done you good already. Both of us.' He reached out and covered the hand that was presently neatly covered in one of the recently purchased and wildy extravagant gloves. 'You won't get any more daft bees in your bonnet about me, will you?'

'No.' She had never felt so sure of him.

'Well, in that case, there's a place I heard Nina mention, a Mrs Bell's. Her husband sells French books . . .'

'But a French book's little use to me,' Erin expostulated. 'Our tastes are plain different. The way Nina goes on about that German Ackerman and his wretched periodical on the arts! And the fact that the King's bed-hangings are made from Ackerman's chintzes! If she can make me feel a bumpkin, she's happy!'

'Erin, you've got hold of the wrong end of the stick. It's not Bell and his French books we're going to see about. There's a Mrs Bell and by all accounts she makes corsets for royalty. She even made one for Princess Victoria's mother, the Duchess of Kent. *Now* do you see what I'm getting at? You'll have a better figure than most of the grand ladies who are her customers. I want you to have one. A gift from myself.'

Erin couldn't help giggling. 'You've got corsets on the brain.'

They were both laughing and Barney choking over the rich cigar smoke.

'I can think of worse afflictions. Quilliam's tin trousers.'

They rattled up to Mrs Bell's establishment in high good humour, and Erin had her measurements taken and the promise of an early delivery of her new foundation which was to be made in daring black. She hadn't mentioned this to Barney. Let him find out for himself.

The Gellings arrived that evening just in time for dinner, Elizabeth looking paler and thinner than of old, but even more beautiful with those hollows under her cheekbones, and her narrow waist. Nat Gelling was broader and sleeker, still quiet, yet outspoken when he had something to say.

It must be Nat's fault that they had no children, Erin decided, yet he presented an aura of virility. Elizabeth said nothing nowadays about their private lives. She came to life however when told of Charlotte's wedding plans.

'Imagine Charlotte! *Two* husbands!'

'And why not?' Barney asked sharply. 'Hadn't your mother?'

'She was always so . . . so quiet.'

Thank God Elizabeth hadn't said plain, which was the word most probably in her mind, Erin thought. Barney had always been angry at her own children's patronizing attitude towards his less well-favoured daughter.

'You're all to come to her wedding,' Erin put in quickly. 'She and George sent their invitations via ourselves.'

'I won't be able to travel so far,' Nina said, with a downward scowl at the unbecoming lump, 'but Boyce must, since it's family.'

'You can, of course,' Erin told her daughter, with inward relief at the thought of Nina's absence. 'You aren't expecting, Elizabeth.'

'I had enough with the twins,' Elizabeth replied avoiding Barney's eye. 'How are they? Still their father's children?'

'Yours too, surely!' Barney couldn't help saying forcefully.

'They're happy enough, aren't they?' Elizabeth asked. 'It wasn't possible to take them at the time. I doubt if they'd want to come to me now. Even if there was room, which there isn't.' Then she changed the subject by asking Nina what she wanted herself, a boy or a girl.

'Oh, a boy, of course! Papa won't forgive me if I don't give him a soldier or two. No sailors, priests or girls for him!'

Barney looked as if he meant to speak further about the twins, but each time Erin headed him off by talking of something else. This wasn't the time or the place to take Elizabeth to task. It was all old water under the bridge, and Barney would be the first to miss Timothy if his mother ever expressed a wish to remove him from his grandfather's custody. It seemed that Barney eventually realized this himself, for he left off his attempts to engage Elizabeth in recriminations and confined himself almost solely to conversation with a by now monosyllabic Nat.

Barney had a lasting dislike of Boyce, who had always been a thorn in his flesh. He'd only accompanied Erin on the understanding that they spent most of their time out of the house, seeing as much of London as was possible.

'We had a letter from Bastian recently,' Boyce remarked as the beef was served, enjoying the flicker of distaste that showed in Barney's eyes.

'I expect ours came after we left home,' Erin said swiftly. 'What does he say?'

'That the uncle is in poor health and that he has passed all his architect's examinations, and is beginning to receive modest commissions for work.'

'Timothy is not the only boy in the family to be brought up by someone not his parent.' Elizabeth could not resist saying.

There was a silence that was broken unexpectedly by Barney. 'I must take care, in future, to remember that old saying.'

'What saying?' Nina asked, diverted, her small head lifted sharply as a dog's on the scent.

'People in glass houses. Sorry, Elizabeth.' Barney's mouth twisted.

Erin's tightened stomach muscles relaxed. She accepted more wine, admitting to herself that it might be a mistake, remembering the night at O'Ferrall's.

Elizabeth smiled stiffly and Nat, who had obviously been out of humour with Barney for his implied disapproval of his wife, looked more friendly.

I might as well be the mother of a litter of hedgehogs, Erin thought a little desperately. She'd had her reservations about the possible direction of the evening's events, but it would have looked odd if no attempt had been made to have some sort of family reunion. All families must come together sometime.

'I wonder what Bastian will do if anything happens to the uncle?' Boyce mused lazily, not missing the conflicting emotions so patently visible on each and every face. Nina knew about Sebastian, of course. It had been little shock to a soldier's daughter, especially one with an outspoken father.

'He's not that ill?' Erin asked anxiously, her world about to crash about her.

'Bad enough,' Boyce told her. 'Come to my study after we finish, Mama, and I'll let you see what he had to say.'

The rest of the meal passed in uneasy spasms of conversation, interspersed by silences into which Nina, as hostess, was obliged to throw items of news that were of little interest to her husband's relatives but which helped to span the awkwardnesses. Everyone drank more than usual. Gradually the atmosphere grew superficially friendlier.

Erin was forced into the realization that her children had grown so far away from her as to be strangers. She mustn't lose them all. Boyce. She must keep him at least.

It was a relief to be ushered into his leather-scented, book-lined sanctum with its sporting prints and equine portraits, the large painting of the battle of Waterloo that covered the upper part of the dark-papered chimney-breast. Firelight flickered on the buttoned chairs and gleaming bureau, the gilt frames and fire-irons.

'It's a nice room,' Erin said, her head reeling, not unexpectedly, from over indulgence.

'Sit down, Mama. Not the most comfortable of evenings, was it! Here, have a brandy. Go on, a night-cap never hurt anyone. It'll help you sleep.'

'I confess I am aware of the Thames traffic.'

'We're used to it now.'

'I expect you are. You're quite grand these days. But it's what I always expected for you in particular.'

'Good heavens, why? A gaolbird's son? Stepson to a boat-builder?' Boyce's lip curled unpleasantly. 'Not that I ever told Nina about my real father, so be discreet, won't you. It's nothing I'm proud of.'

'Jesse Kinrade wasn't your father,' Erin said flatly.

Boyce stared, his brandy-glass halfway to his lips.

'Your father's an Irish gentleman. Sir Dermot O'Neill.'

Boyce began to laugh. 'Mama! You're being ridiculous. You've had too much wine. You don't have to tell me stories now. I'm a big boy.'

'It's true. I was pregnant when I left home for the Liverpool boat. Dermot's father refused to acknowledge your existence and whisked him away to his uncle's place for an extended visit. My own father'd have killed me. So I had to go. Jesse was never sure about you. I made out you were premature. There's good blood in you. I'm told Dermot's still in Wicklow, though his wicked old father's gone to his grave and good riddance!'

170

'Married, I suppose?' Boyce had begun to take Erin seriously.

'Oh, yes. His father saw to that. You've brothers and sisters though I don't know how many.'

'My God! You're not just making it up?'

'Would I do that to you, Boyce? You know you've always been my favourite. Aye, you should have been a legitimate O'Neill. Your father's heir.'

'Instead of which—'

'But you've done well for yourself.' Erin drained the glass, a warmth filling her belly and her thoughts. She'd always wanted to tell Boyce the truth and now she had. He seemed, suddenly, twice the size as he stood against the glow of the fire, his hair a red nimbus. Any mother would be more than proud of such a personable son. And any father, even a squireen.

'Well, Mama,' he said after a long pause. 'I'm glad you told me. Bar sinister or no, I no longer feel the shame of thinking myself son to a hanged murderer.'

'It was Barney who made us respectable, though. Never forget that!'

'No, Mama. I'll never bring myself to like him but I recognize the debt that's owed.'

'I wonder if I've done right? Telling you now. Unsettling you—'

'Oh, you have, Mama. You have. I've gone up in my own esteem. There's the letter from Bastian.' He threw it across to land, crackling, in the lap of her gown. 'You read it while I think of my new status.' And he poured himself another brandy, turning his back to her to stare into the heart of the fire. She wondered what Boyce was thinking. Planning—'

But though she read Sebastian's letter, the words danced in Erin's brain, making no real sense after the report of his uncle's illness. The old man would die, she could feel it in her bones. And then her younger son would return. There'd be little to keep him in Australia. If he had a gift for designing buildings it would be of greater use to

171

him here in England or elsewhere in Europe.

Or Man! She could not bear to contemplate the thought of him near her. Not Sebastian. Not that unnatural young man.

She shivered in spite of the warmth, and thrust the letter away from her to fall unnoticed on to the carpet. Think of something else. Anything but her son. Rosie. They'd not bought her a present yet. Erin had dissuaded Barney from getting the child a book when they were in Hatchard's. Rosie liked pretty things. A fan, perhaps? There were such attractive ones of ivory and mother-of-pearl. Hand-painted. Be-feathered. But all the fans Erin imagined were not decorated with elegant French figures but were stamped with one face. Sebastian's.

Hanna's brithday was imminent and Cormorant House was in a state of enjoyable ferment. Mrs Quinn, red-faced and perspiring, was a tower of strength. Molly Quayle had worked slavishly to finish the polishing and cleaning, and displayed a hitherto unrecognized skill at arranging plants and flowers to best advantage.

'Always liked growing things, Ma'am,' she'd told Karran quietly when she was complimented on this unexpected creativity. 'And your little treasure deserves to remember her own special day.'

'She won't remember!' Bart put in scornfully on his way to saddle his pony. 'She's got no brains to speak of.'

'She has as many as you, young man,' Molly asserted a little sharply. She'd always had a weakness for little Hanna who so resembled Gideon Collister. Folks hadn't, after all, been wrong about the advocate and Mrs Howard. It must be uncomfortable to present such unmistakable proof of infidelity to the world. She'd been jealous for a whole weekend when she'd first noticed the resemblance, for all that she'd known Mr Gideon was inclined to flightiness. Commonsense had prevailed. She had a good place and the Mistress would turn anyone's head with her looks. Besides which, Mrs Howard was kind and understanding. A pity she hadn't married Mr Collister when she was able.

Molly went outside to put the remainder of the stalks and leaves on to the compost heap. Coming back, she saw the carrier's cart slowing to a crawl and a tall man springing down, then reaching up for a carpet bag and an assortment of parcels. Her heart seemed to stop, as it always did at the sight of Gideon. She had the absurd notion she could smell gorse, that her hair hung down dark and shining as a raven's wing, under a hot, languorous sun.

Gideon Collister smiled. Today he looked happy, not hagridden and scowling as on his last visit, when he appeared beset with a futile anger.

'It's good to see you, Molly.'

He looked as though he meant it, she thought with painful pleasure. He didn't of course. That was Mr Gideon's way. She still could dream.

'Come in,' Molly said. 'Mrs Howard is expecting you?' She tucked away a lock of the greying hair that had, momentarily, been so black and youthful, bound with rowan berries as in long past days.

'Well, as a matter of fact, she isn't.' Gideon said carefully. 'Can I ask you to pave the way, my dear?'

'Yes, sir.' Molly took him into what had been his own parlour and saw his eyes turn towards the purplish press that once was his. His expression was faintly acquisitive, as though there was something here that he meant to repossess.

She went in search of Mrs Howard.

It wasn't fair, Molly reflected, that when her outside was sixty and looked it, the secret compartment inside held the distilled youth and magic of sixteen. Molly was almost ashamed of the knowledge. 'Really,' she told herself angrily, 'you're a daft old fool. Haven't you grown out of those feelings yet?'

Molly was still frowning when she found Karran in the quietest corner of the back garden, watching a well-wrapped Hanna lurching round a patch of Michaelmas daisies with a delirious joy.

Hanna held out her arms to Molly when she saw her coming. She was like a child who enjoyed being liked and was actively miserable when rejected. Bart took pleasure in playing upon this exposed nerve. Molly had grown to dislike Bart.

'Little darling,' Molly said and took the small hand in hers. 'You've a visitor, Ma'am.'

'Good heavens! When we're so busy. Couldn't you make some excuse?'

'That I couldn't, Ma'am. It's Mr Collister.'

Karran's features smoothed themselves to blankness. 'Oh, well. We can hardly be inhospitable when he's come so far. Thank you, Molly. Will you go and tell Mrs Quinn to send refreshments to the parlour? There's a good fire in there.'

'That's where I left Mr Collister.'

'Very well, Molly. You know what to do.'

'Yes, Ma'am.'

Karran swept Hanna into her arms and made her way slowly towards the parlour. Gideon stood by the fireplace, smiling. He kissed Karran then took the child from her firmly yet with great tenderness, cuddling the little girl close, whispering endearments that only Hanna heard. She did not try to wriggle away from this tall stranger, only listened gravely, seduced by the soft magic of his murmured words. Though she couldn't know what they meant, the way in which they were spoken must tell her that she was beloved.

Over the small dark head Gideon said, 'I hope you didn't mind me coming today. I had a desire to participate in her brithday. That's not too difficult to understand, is it?'

Karran, anxiety held in check, said, 'Not at all.'

'And you did say you'd come to us after her first year, when she was better equipped to travel. That's really why I came. To take you back. You and my daughter.'

'What about my son?'

'You said he was at the Castle school. That you felt he should stay there in order to preserve the continuity of his education. Remember?'

'You told me once how being separated from your home and family affected you. That description was graphic, to say the least.'

'Then he'd have to leave the Castle school. There are others.'

'I should have to give the matter a good deal of thought. He's settled at last.'

Gideon rubbed his cheek against Hanna's. 'But please decide before we leave.'

'It's not like choosing a new gown! Bart's important to me.'

'Then you'll understand how I feel about Hanna. It seems years since I saw her. Held her close. I want more of her than I have at present. And – talking of presents – I have some with me. To be opened tomorrow, of course.'

'I'd better arrange for a room to be got ready for you.'

Gideon stared at Karran and she was unable to look away. 'Why bother?' he enquired softly. 'There's enough room in that four-poster of yours for us both.'

Colour flowed in and out of her face. 'I haven't gone far enough along your road to have decided if that's feasible at this stage.'

'Sensible!' he mocked, exuding that lazy attraction that had had such an effect on Karran in their stormy past. 'Why must we always be so sensible? I recall several occasions when we were not. They – were memorable.'

'Gideon—'

He put the child down on the floor and came towards her. Her reaction to his grasping arms was violent. 'You still want me,' he whispered. 'I know.'

'More than you want me.'

'That's only what you've made yourself believe and you're wrong.' He kissed her again, then slid his mouth down the sides of her neck, still kissing as he went.

'Even if – someone still would have to prepare the room.

175

For appearances' sake.'

'Oh, appearances!' he mocked again, and his gaze followed small Hanna's progress across the carpet with fond amusement.

'Which were vastly more important to you when you lived on the island.'

'I no longer do.' He pressed his mouth to the hollow at the base of her throat.

'But I do and I'm no longer free to follow my own whims! There are the children to consider. I want them to be respected, not reviled or pitied.'

'They will be. You'll be far away where no one knows you. You'll be my wife, won't you, Karran?' His voice had dropped to the almost mesmeric murmuring that had so entranced Hanna.

'You know I can't decide that until I see Mary and know her better than by hearsay.'

'And you know that if I picked you up in my arms and took you upstairs, you wouldn't protest. That's important about marriage. If there's no pleasure between the sheets there's none elsewhere. If there is, then that satisfaction permeates the rest and makes everything more bearable.'

'You sound as analytical as ever.'

'It's my training, my dear. But I'm feeling far from such hide-bound restrictions. A year ago I'd have taken you on the floor or the hearth-rug, but with Quinns and Mollys about the place we'll have to be more circumspect. Tonight, however, I'll listen to no protestations. I know they sleep in the old part of the house.'

'Our affair was shabby. Just as this one would be. For once in my life I'd like a relationship that would be honest and open. One like Charlotte's.'

'What's this about Charlotte?'

'She's been widowed for a long while—'

'Widowed? I thought Costain left her?'

'He committed suicide. Jumped into the harbour in front of witnesses, according to the Liverpool paper, and never came up. Barney went over to find out for himself.

The report was true.'

'A man would need to be desperate to do that.'

'He never recovered from the loss of that hand. Painting was his life. I remember once Bart spoiled a picture of Abel's – it was when Bart was only Hanna's age – and I've never seen so devilish an expression of rage and hatred. Abel never forgave us.'

'And who's Charlotte's so exemplary replacement?' Gideon released Karran almost absent-mindedly and went to kneel beside the baby who was studying a group of flowers on the carpet and trying to pick them off with scrabbling fingers. 'I'll give you real flowers,' he told Hanna. 'Hundreds of them, my own darling. Thousands.'

'Oh, no you won't!' her mother said forcibly. 'She'd only eat them. And Charlotte plans to marry Seyler.'

'Seyler, eh? She could do a great deal worse. Charlotte will be safe with him.'

'It's more than that. She appreciates his dependability – who wouldn't! But he respects her enough to wait for what, obviously, they both want very much.'

Gideon looked up at her from his lounging position beside the absorbed child. 'Is this intended to ram home a point, my dear? Must I now become conveniently celibate in a relationship during which we've enjoyed one another more than most and after which you bore my child? I've made it plain that I intend to marry you. I respected your wishes during my last visit. No one need know we've been together and there is no way in which I can obtain the necessary legal documents allowing us to be wed, the day I arrive.

'But it's been a long time since I had you and it seems unnecessary to deny ourselves when it can hurt no one. Tell me the truth. There's still enough left of your affection for me to make the proceeding extremely pleasant, isn't there? Isn't there, Karran?'

A discreet knock saved her from replying. Gideon went to the door, opening it on to the sight of Mrs Quinn with a laden tray.

'Allow me, Mrs Quinn.' He deposited the tray on to a pie-crust table.

Hanna scuttled crab-wise towards it.

'No, darling.' Karran picked her up before she could upset the tea. 'Would you air a bed for Mr Collister, Mrs Quinn?'

'How long will you be wanting it, sir?' Mrs Quinn asked practically.

'A few days. Perhaps a week. I've arranged for my clients to be attended, if necessary, by my partners during my absence. You've no objection, Karran, my love, have you?'

'I hadn't thought—' she began evasively.

'But we have important matters to resolve. And I still have loose ends to tie up with Paul Christie. Going from one business to another is never clear-cut.'

'George Seyler said the same,' Karran agreed with a sensation of seeing prison bars closing around her. Gideon seemed implacable where this business of marriage and gaining legal possession of Hanna was concerned. Remembering how once she'd longed to go away with Laurence Richards in the face of fierce opposition, she couldn't really understand her present qualms. Most people would consider her lucky to have achieved so satisfactory a solution to her problems. Many would envy her. But it wasn't in her nature to be pressurized into doing anything so important out of expedience. Gideon must allow her time to think. It must seem right.

'Will there be enough there to put you off till supper, Ma'am?'

'It's all quite splendid,' Gideon said easily. 'Isn't it, Karran?'

She realized that she didn't like having him answer for her, but she smiled at Mrs Quinn and nodded her assent. Hanna was squirming energetically in her embrace and by the time Karran had put her down, the door was shut and Mrs Quinn gone.

'I suppose these are for her.' Gideon held out a plate of small buttered rusks.

'Yes. They're Hanna's,' she replied stiffly.

'Karran,' he said carefully, 'you did write in the sort of terms that gave me an entirely different impression from the one I now have. Why are matters suddenly so difficult?'

'You're moving too fast. I say that Hanna must be older before she can face the long journey and you decide that the day after tomorrow is quite in order. I've a household to run. Problems you know nothing about, engagements that would have to be broken. Luggage to see to. And you think that forgetting all that and anticipating the wedding you say we are to have will smooth out everything.'

'It could be very relaxing,' he commented wryly.

'Please, don't joke. If you'd written—'

'You'd have put me off with a hundred arguments. Just as you are doing now that we're face to face.'

'You take everything for granted. I only agreed to think about the proposal.'

'And I have to make sure that you'll agree, otherwise our lives will be spent in continual misery. You have a conscience, Karran, and for once I'm glad of it. It would torment you once we were apart. And what if anything were to happen to you, not that I wish it! Hanna has only us two. I must know that I've the legal right to have my daughter in the event of her becoming motherless.'

'What a careful, sly, lawyer's mind!'

'Legal matters always sound cold and calculated. But I swear my feelings are not. I love the child and I want you, if anything, more than before.'

'And Bart?'

'Must come with us. I'll try to treat him as my own son.'

'It may not be easy.'

'It could be easier for Bart to accept me than another man. There – there is no other man, is there?'

Hanna clamoured for a rusk. 'Mama. Mama!' she said quite clearly.

179

'Perhaps we should follow her example and eat,' Karran told Gideon.

'You haven't answered my question.'

'I don't know that I want to answer anything for a few days. You said you intend to stay for a week. Give me breathing space. I want to do the right thing. Believe me.'

'It's halcyon weather. Couldn't we take Hanna and the trap and spend time out of doors? I've a yen to see some favourite haunts.' Gideon smiled engagingly as he changed the subject.

'Why not? Bart has his pony. He could come with us. There's no school for the present. Some epidemic he seems to have escaped,' Karran explained, relieved by the switch of conversation.

'Where is he just now?'

'He went out immediately prior to your arrival. Have some of that pie. It's Mrs Quinn's tour de force. And you pour the tea for me. Hanna wants to hang on to my hair with buttery fingers.'

'That epidemic—'

'Bart hasn't succumbed. I told you.'

'Incubation—'

'My dear Gideon, you only have to look at Hanna to see that she's in perfect health. I'm a very careful mother.'

'I'm sure you are. You had advice from Doctor Gresham naturally?'

'Gideon, I'm trying to tell you that there's been no reason to do so! Hanna is her usual self. If I notice the slightest change I'd send for him immediately.'

'Well, I suppose you know best.' Gideon frowned.

'Is this how you intend to behave if or when we are married?' she demanded.

Gideon, seeing the danger signals in time, said, 'I'm sorry if I appear to fuss. But you have Hanna every instant of her life. It's not the same where I'm concerned. This is only the third time I've seen her and I've the same feelings as any fond father returned from one war in far-off places and due to go back into battle again. I never dreamed one could love one's own flesh and blood so desperately. I'd never given much thought to parenthood, not with a father like mine. My boyhood was the kind of experience that turns one against trying out the same hell oneself. Perhaps I imagined that the outcome of all such relationships was fated to be the same as mine. Such ideas can become deeply ingrained. Yet the moment I saw our child I experienced such joy! You couldn't deprive me of the chance to prove that life *can* give back what it once took away? Could you, my far from heartless Karran?'

How could she! How?

'There's someone knocking. Come in!' Karran called, reprieved a second time.

Mrs Quinn poked a flushed face round the door. 'It's the day for visitors, Ma'am. It's Mr O'Ferrall this time. He remembered Hanna's birthday.'

'Then he must come in and have some tea. There's more than we can do justice to, isn't there, Gideon?'

'You haven't eaten enough to feed a fly,' he observed coolly.

'Just send up an extra cup and plate,' Karran ordered.

Nick O'Ferrall appeared almost immediately, his faintly amused gaze taking in the intimacy of the tableau, only Hanna seeming pleased by such a surfeit of attention.

Nick laughed. 'It's like the court of some infant queen.'

'You haven't met Gideon before, have you? This is Gideon Collister. Gideon, this is Nick O'Ferrall. You've heard me speak of him.'

Gideon inclined his head.

'Interesting to meet you at last,' Nick drawled with slight emphasis on the 'last', turning to Hanna as though she were of superior interest.

'I shouldn't come too close to her,' Karran warned, aware of the slow tide of antagonism that eddied between the two men who might have passed for brothers. 'Those chewed rusks can be lethal weapons. My hair and my gown are quite disreputable.'

'I see nothing wrong,' Nick said gallantly. 'I don't

intrude, I hope?'

'Of course not. We don't see enough of you these days. Are you kept very busy?'

'Busy enough. Enough to recoup my initial losses.'

'That must be encouraging.'

'My dear Karran, you don't fool me for a moment! There's nothing you'd like better than to see my venture crumble and for that jinx of a house of yours to return to its uneasy slumber. There's a guest chamber that's positively haunted. Women run screaming from it. The large room near the head of the staircase.'

Karran knew which he meant. The bedchamber where John had lain ill and in which he'd died. Her skin crept.

'Why do they do that?'

'Some atmosphere they dislike. And they say they smell candle-wax when none has been lit. One even saw a little eddy of grey smoke—'

'An unlikely tale,' Gideon interposed coldly. 'An over-indulgence in claret, we presume. It's a familiar hazard in a place like yours.'

'Not only in places like mine! The fact remains that there have been several such reactions, none in the least way connected. But it's an old house. It would be strange if there'd been no such manifestation. Conflict and past events seem to cling to the fabric of a place.'

'Irish taradiddle!' Gideon said with barely concealed contempt.

'Gideon!'

'I'm sorry, Karran. I find it hard to accept ghosts, seen or unseen.'

'Then we must agree to differ,' Nick murmured with ostentatious indifference. 'As I feel we would over most things.' He accepted a cup of tea and sat back in his chair with every expression of enjoyment.

'How did you know it was Hanna's birthday tomorrow? You've been such a recluse.'

'Brand told me. He could hardly miss the excitement being engendered.'

'Oh, I thought you might have remembered how she arrived so precipitately the moment the bed was set up.'

'There could be some connection between the two events,' Nick agreed, grinning. 'I seem to recall you were extremely active for someone in your state. An unfortunate time to uproot yourself. But the result was an enormous success. Little Miss Howard is going to be an attractive young lady. Your husband would have been proud of her.'

'Yes, he would,' Karran agreed mechanically.

Gideon got up, frowning. 'Let me take Hanna outside for a few minutes. I'm sure you and O'Ferrall must have much to say to one another.' He removed the child firmly and walked to the door. 'We'll be in the garden should you want us.'

'Put something round her. It's colder than it was earlier. Mrs Quinn will give you a shawl.'

Once she and Nick were alone, Karran busied herself with the contents of the tray.

'You didn't come by chance,' she said. 'Someone told you, didn't they, that Gideon was on his way here.'

'No,' Nick assured her. 'But I'm glad I saw him. I've wondered a good deal about your precious Collister.'

'He's not—'

'Oh, it's fairly obvious that you're at loggerheads even if it is only temporary. I suppose it's none of my business but I had a sudden urge to take him by the scruff of the neck and boot him on his way.'

'You haven't the right—'

'Haven't I? If I'd been in his place, I'd never have gone off, not if every tongue on the island had wagged itself to a standstill. There's something lacking in a man who professes to love a woman yet can go away for as long as a year, then expect to find everything as it was. Your advocate's a sulky overgrown schoolboy, my dear. Don't do anything so decisive as marrying him unless you're certain you won't regret it.'

'And what gives you the right to dispense advice?'

'The fact that I care very much what happens to you. A

fact I suspect you already know. I'd go further—'

'No. You mustn't say it.' Karran had grown very pale.

'I don't need to, do I?'

She wanted to ask him how Philly from Douglas was but that would have been cheap and unnecessary. Suddenly Karran was emotionally exhausted.

Nick, as pale as herself, got up and put a small parcel on the table. 'I had her initials put on it. J.H. Better not let Collister see it, eh? He looks possessive. If you get into deep waters, come to Ravensdown, whatever time of night or day. Promise? If I'm not there, the Brands will take care of you until I am.'

She nodded speechlessly.

'Best get it all out of your system. There'd be no peace for either of us until you do. And, if by chance you choose the other way, make sure you don't stay where I can see you, for I'd try to take you away. That I swear.'

'You – make it sound as though I'm committed to one or other of you.'

'Aren't you?'

She shook her head. 'For the first time in my life I'm my own mistress.'

'But it's a lonely sort of state. Don't waste yourself on an empty freedom.'

'I'd no idea you were a philosopher.' She managed a smile.

'There are a great number of things you have to find out.'

'If that's what I choose.'

'Let me help you to make up your mind.' He put his hands on her shoulders and kissed her. It was a strange kiss, filled with restrained urgency. When he released her, Karran had an impulse to draw him back so that he might finish whatever it was that had been begun.

But he had gone from the room quickly, leaving her restless and unsatisfied.

It was quarter of an hour later than Gideon returned. 'He didn't stay long,' he observed, setting Hanna on the floor. He'd tucked a flower in Hanna's hair and her cheeks were flushed with fresh air. She turned towards him, tugging at his legs. He responded immediately with an almost pathetic pleasure. 'You see, she likes me!'

'I didn't, while Nick was here. You were extremely rude to a guest of mine. Am I only to have friends of whom *you* approve? There's a good deal about you that *is* likeable, but I'm discovering that there's another side to you.'

'My dear Karran! There are other sides to anyone you care to mention! People are like icebergs.'

'You're jealous, aren't you.'

'What else do you expect? I haven't forgotten the first thing you said when I arrived unexpectedly and you thought I was O'Ferrall. You made it sound as though he were in the habit of coming straight upstairs, unannounced. Yes, I was jealous. I am jealous. I suppose I'll go on being jealous until you decide to show me that my suspicions have no foundation.'

Karran remained silent. She could no longer assure Gideon that there was no bond between herself and an Irish gambler. Was she about to make yet another mess of her life?

'In the face of your seeming inability to refute the idea, let me say that I'd never countenance a child of mine being brought up in an establishment like that man's! Do you understand? You'll never take Hanna to Ravensdowne as long as I have breath in my body to prevent it!'

Gideon was shouting now and the child took fright, crawling towards her mother, whimpering for reassurance.

Karran knelt to comfort the tiny girl, 'You see what you're doing, don't you,' she said in a repressed voice that struggled for composure. 'This is the sort of situation I feared from the beginning. Do you think this will be the last time you'll scare Hanna out of her wits? It won't and I beg you to think about that very seriously. Your childhood was spoiled by silences. I won't have my daughter's ruined by storms of anger and bitterness.

'Is this what you really want? To have a hitherto happy

185

child reduced to such a state? Perhaps daily? Each upset eroding a little more of her confidence until she becomes another pitiable Mary? But perhaps that's what you *do* want. Another creature afraid to face life, dependent only on you. Does that give you a kind of gratification? A strength you can't obtain any other way? Perhaps you are more like your aunt than you think! I won't let you disrupt our existence.'

Gideon's face reflected horror. He was obviously shaken, and Karran was aware of a spark of pity that threatened to grow.

'None of this would have happened if you'd told me you were expecting a child.'

'When you left, I didn't know myself. After I had your letter I didn't want you to feel any sense of obligation towards our relationship. After a time it began to seem like an infatuation you'd decided should be allowed to die a natural death. That, I swear, is the truth. In any case, the child *might* have been John's. Until he took to his bed—'

'I don't want to hear confidences of that nature!'

'I should have thought an advocate would have to listen to a great many confidences before presuming to make judgements on a case.'

'Anyone with ordinary eyesight could see that Hanna—'

'Resembles you? Yes, now it's not difficult. Until she was born, and for some time afterwards, it wasn't so easy to decide. It was only when her eyes changed that I knew for certain. But she's registered as my husband's child and you know you can't do much against that. I've looked after her properly and shunned a way of life that could encourage gossip—'

'Until you involved yourself with O'Ferrall.'

'He bought my property. I can't pretend not to know him.'

'I warn you, Karran, that if you plan to set up house with him, I'll try to remove Hanna on the grounds that you're an unfit mother for introducing your children to such an environment. I may not have as much difficulty in proving that she's my daughter as you seem to think.'

'Would you really drag our names through courts, making Hanna a bastard, ruining all our good characters?'

'Why did you let me think you were willing to come to Glasgow?'

'Charlotte caught me in a moment of weakness. She persuaded me. Instead of waiting until I'd thought it over, I acted on impulse. It was a mistake. I see it now and I apologize for misleading you. You'll have to be patient a while longer. So long as you don't bully and shout your disapproval, you may still visit us. But I don't plan to make another mistaken marriage. And I'd certainly want to be much more confident that your feelings for me would last. I can't get rid of the notion that the minute the ring was slipped over my finger I wouldn't mean a jot outside of running your household and warming your bed. And you could come to dispensing with even that after a time.'

They stared at one another incredulously, both breathing hard, both appalled by the near destruction of what had once been a seemingly permanent relationship.

'We should never have separated,' Gideon said.

'At the time it seemed the only course. I was thinking only of you.'

'And now you have O'Ferrall—'

'And you have Mary! Not to mention those solaces. The ones you say don't matter.'

'Neither they do.' The anger had died from his face and his voice. Gideon went to Karran and seized her. The quarrel had wearied her and she was past struggling.

'I must put Hanna into her cot. It's time for her rest.'

'Very well.'

They went towards the stair that led to the bedchamber.

Upstairs, Karran laid the child between the sheets, rocking the cot gently for a minute, watching Hanna's eyes close. Behind her, Gideon slid the bolt on the door then came to her, sliding his arms around her from the back, clasping his hands over her midriff. He kissed the nape of her neck, the side of her throat, her shoulder.

Karran could not have pushed him away however much she might have wished. 'Gideon—'

But he would not let her speak. Turning her round to face him, he kissed her. Went on kissing and letting his hands rove where they would. It seemed easier to let it happen, to have Gideon solve the tangle once and for all. Yet, lying on the bed, her mind purposely empty to everything but the violent present, still she had a glimpse of Nick O'Ferrall riding away into barren distances. Poor O'Ferrall's luck!

The image held a brief lacerating pain.

PART SIX

Caldwell

They travelled on the *Robert Bruce*, returning from its weekly visit to Liverpool and stopping only at Portpatrick, on the Mull of Galloway, before proceeding back to Greenock, its starting point.

Karran had never been on any kind of vessel larger than a rowing-boat and a steamship journey was the kind of adventure she'd scarcely envisaged, being so attached to her own little corner of Man.

Bart, by his own choice, was left behind in the care of Mrs Quinn and Molly and with promises of visits to and from George Seyler, Charlotte and Rose. He'd told his mother he didn't wish to be taken from the Castle school and Tom Beg, who'd fret for him, and Karran, half-relieved and half-vexed, had warned him about the foolhardiness of trespassing over at the Starks. She'd been perplexed by the strange little smile he'd been unable to repress at the stricture.

'You do know they say he's set a trap? A particularly unpleasant one?'

Bart nodded. 'But I'll never be in any danger from that.'

'How can you be so sure?'

'I just am. Don't worry about me. I'm happy at school and I have my friends.'

Karran noticed his use of the plural. So there was someone else apart from Rose Costain. She was pleased about that at least. Her son was growing up and should have friends of his own sex.

'And I can still have picnics?' he asked, almost as an afterthought.

'If you promise to return at the times you are told.'

'I promise.'

'Very well. Be good until I come back. You will go to Scotland another time.'

Bart had not looked particularly interested and Karran was driven to say, 'You aren't excited about the prospect of travelling in a steamship?'

'Someday.' He'd looked evasive and again Karran realized the lack of communication between them since Gideon's child had been born. Bart thought she was going away for a holiday. She'd found it impossible to speak to him of the likelihood of a marriage taking place, knowing his deep-rooted dislike of the idea after that bad period that had ended in John Howard's death.

Charlotte had been pleased that Karran had, after all, decided to take one step in the direction of commonsense. Not that she knew the whole story. Karran had kept to herself the fact that she'd taken Gideon back into her bed.

'You must come to my wedding, though,' Charlotte had insisted, her hair dressed very fetchingly under a new bonnet, and looking young and eager.

'I'll be at the church,' Karran had said, wondering if indeed she would.

'And afterwards! At the wedding breakfast! You must. Both of us insist.'

'We'll see. You don't want skeletons at the feast, do you?'

'Who says so? I'll have who I choose and George will back me up. Oh, I do love him. I couldn't bear it should anything come between us now!'

'What could?' Karran had asked reassuringly. 'All will come right. It's what you deserve.'

'I had a nightmare, though—'

'Nightmare?'

'I thought – that Abel was there on our bridal night. Watching. Smiling—'

'You great goose! There'll be nobody but your two selves. Be happy, always.'

And they'd parted, hugging one another as though for the last time, and Karran had brushed away the tears that pricked at her eyes like scalding water.

At Douglas she'd seen a wedding party strolling round the beacon on the Red Pier, everyone gaily dressed, smiling and beflowered for all that it was autumn, dance-music wafting from half-open windows.

Karran wondered if it was an omen for herself and Gideon. Since he had reclaimed her in that storm of passion he'd succeeded almost too well in making her doubt all her former objections. But Gideon had always been a persuasive lover. It wouldn't be the last time she'd flounder on the rock of his sexual dominance.

They'd stood together at the ship's rail, staring at the huddle of picturesque buildings, lanes and shops receding, the Tower of Refuge that was a sentinel that greeted every seaman and traveller to the island, or bade them farewell.

Karran could not describe her feelings as the island began to slip away from her. Straining her eyes to retain the picture of the old quayside houses she saw a familiar figure ride along to the pier's end. Nick O'Ferrall had heard of her departure and had come to watch her go.

She raised her arm and waved to him, then saw his own salutation. It wasn't until both he and his horse had merged into a blur along with the rest of the waterfront that she noticed Gideon's frown. She said nothing and he allowed the incident to pass unremarked, but she knew that he resented the Irishman's appearance at the last moment and wouldn't forget what he'd term O'Ferrall's impertinence.

It was one of those burnished autumn days when the world was bronze and purple, subtle browns and blues. There was a high arc of sky with thick white cloud castles and a tangy freshness in the atmosphere that was clean and sharp but not cold.

The gulls came so far with the ship, swooping and

sailing on the air currents, diving for the bits of bread thrown by the experienced passengers who knew they'd follow the steamship. There was noise and clanking and smells of hot oil that kept Karran and her lover in the open for as long as possible.

Hanna, cuddled close in Gideon's arms, was entranced by the creamy passage of the sea and the glistening waves, the sharp cries of the birds that grew fainter then died out altogether. Man became a long grape-blue shadow.

The hair on Karran's neck prickled almost painfully. What was she doing here in this confusion of sound and water, sailing away from the only land she had ever known? She moved closer to Gideon, needing the reassurance of his warmth.

Gideon pointed out landmarks familiar to him. She'd never seen the Point of Ayre. Here in this immensity of sea, the thought was ridiculous. Karran stared at the long climb to Snaefell's summit, her gaze sliding to the island's end which was flat and monotonous compared with the mountains to the south. The breeze caught in her throat so that she felt choked with conflicting emotions. The distances were very clear. She could make out the coasts of Lancashire and Cumberland, dim traces of Ireland that were the faint faery blue of harebells.

They went inside eventually to tend to Hanna's needs and to refresh themselves from Mrs Quinn's picnichamper. Hanna asleep again in Gideon's arms, Karran couldn't wait to explore the ship by herself, to gape at the juddering engines, then to escape from the hot queasiness of their proximity, to mount the metal stairs and find new perches and higher viewpoints. The wind tore at her hair and she wanted to laugh.

Galloway began to show itself beyond the folds of Cumberland. There were humped hills of indigo patched with rust and vivid greens. Who would have thought the world so large?

Not until she was weary did she return to Gideon, who smiled at her enthusiasms and wonderment and who made her sit beside him on the hard bench to slide his free arm round her waist. A long time later, it seemed, she jerked to wakefulness, her head on his shoulder and her neck full of aches. She was chilled and stiff and Hanna had started to cry.

'Here,' Gideon said, 'have some of that.' He held out a chased silver flask and Karran took a swallow of what turned out to be a fiery brandy that made her choke and cough.

Gideon grinned. 'Not so fast.'

But the brandy did its work and soon Karran felt quite cheerful again, enjoying the resumed adventure, soothing Hanna and making her comfortable, feeding her from the stock of food so lovingly packed by Mrs Quinn. Homesickness touched Karran briefly, to be dispelled by the advent of Portpatrick and the new sensation of being surrounded by landscapes. Ireland, Galloway and Scotland pressed around them like far-off, sleeping lions. It was odd to feel so enclosed, to realize that the sea was not so limitless as it had hitherto seemed.

They sailed on, the horizon ever-changing. A great rock grew out of the water, a harsh, craggy protuberance towards which they travelled for what seemed an age, eventually so close that she saw every groove and scratch upon its inhospitable sides. They passed it, but she couldn't help but look back until it had receded to the size and shape of a cottage loaf.

Beyond Ailsa Craig another island beckoned, a sprawl of dim blue beauty that caught at her senses and ensnared them. There was a hinterland of wild, sharp peaks. She could have cried at their loveliness. 'Are we going there?' she asked.

'Arran? No. Well, not this time. When you decide to marry me and come to live in these parts there's no reason why we shouldn't. A perfect place for a honeymoon.'

She didn't answer, just feasted her eyes on the mountainous panorama that arranged itself in the semblance of a huge sleeping man. An islet lay at his amethyst feet like a crouched beast.

Suddenly, she didn't want to reach their destination because Mary awaited them, and the remembrance of Gideon's unknown sister touched her, as always, with a frisson of danger.

Karran took Hanna and cradled her closely, aware that Gideon had noted the defensive action and the fact that she'd said nothing about his suggestion that they honeymoon on that bewitching stretch of purple that blotted out most of Kintyre. He told her, rather coolly, that they were approaching the Kyles of Bute.

They watched the advent of the Ayrshire coast in silence.

They spent the night in a Greenock inn with a too soft bed and where the cook had a heavy hand with supper. Hanna grizzled and Karran slept fitfully, her stomach rebelling against greasy chops and leaden pastry. She'd been so weary that she'd not expected to lie so unpeacefully at Gideon's side.

Lighting the candle to attend to the child in the small hours, she'd stared down at Gideon's unconscious face almost with dislike. But, Hanna quieted, and night's dark silence wrapping her in a mind of peace, the sleepy fumbling of his arm across her body weakened the beginnings of an anger she found hard to explain. The tentative exploration grew more purposeful. Gideon raised himself on one elbow to lean over her.

'Wide awake?' he whispered.

'Yes. Hanna was restless. I fear we are both bitten.'

'A few flea-bites won't matter too much.'

'I suppose not.'

His hand slid under the shift she was using as a bedgown and the light touch of his fingers on her skin dispelled lingering remnants of her inexplicable resentment.

'That woman who acts as housekeeper to your sister,' Karran murmured. 'What will she think of Hanna and me?'

194

'It's not her business to approve or disapprove.'

'She's bound to think the whole business rather odd.'

'You are the widow of a friend of mine, to whom I owe much, and who is in need of a complete change, having been left alone to bring up her two children.'

'Did you warn them that you might bring us back with you?'

The busy hand grew still, then resumed its soft stroking. He laughed softly. 'No. I believe in the element of surprise. There was no point in unsettling either Mary or Mrs Grace if you'd refused point-blank.'

Had he ever meant to resume their relationship? Had it been only his discovery of Hanna's existence that had brought him to Black Rocks that day? How could she ever be sure?

Lying beside him in such pleasurable closeness dispelled her anguished questioning for a time, but afterwards, with dawn's redness creeping between the gaps in the curtain, and a space between herself and Gideon's bare back, the doubts returned, one by one, to torment her. Yet hadn't she burnt her boats already by her present indiscretion?

In cold daylight, hurrying to board the coach for Glasgow and soothing a Hanna frightened by her strange surroundings and missing the familiar faces of Mrs Quinn and Molly, there was no time to dwell on her secret fears.

Gideon, refreshed and smiling gaily, saw to the luggage, then took the little girl in a close embrace, whispering those foolish endearments that Hanna loved. Everyone liked Gideon, Karran thought, and felt herself ensnared.

Leaving the busyness of the port that was so different from Douglas, both the inside and the top of the coach filled to bulging capacity, the journey continued. There was little to see, wedged as she was between two stout persons, and the leather window-flaps admitting only tantalizing glimpses of greenness and shining water, the smoke from a thatched roof or a copse of thin birches struggling for survival. Opposite her, Gideon clasped their daughter, his eyes and Hanna's comfortably shut as though they disregarded everyone but themselves. Something in their oblivious closeness frightened Karran. She could not help but feel left out.

Karran forced herself to believe that Gideon meant only to help her through the difficulties of the long journey. How could she blame him for loving Hanna? Disgusted by her own selfishness she concentrated on the brief, bright snatches of a Scotland that promised beauty as well as the industry and soot she knew she must expect.

The sea turned to a broad river after Dumbarton Rock. Karran, wearied of the pressure of the stout sweating bodies that flanked her own, wished that she had eaten and drunk more at breakfast and that she did not itch so annoyingly. And that Gideon had not to go as far as Glasgow where he had business to attend to.

Clydebank oppressed her. The flat-fronted houses were tall and grimed and the cobblestones crude, jolting the coach as the metal wheels encroached on their humped surfaces. Leaning forward, she noted grander houses after a time, pink and dove-grey, with greenery and gardens, then more squalor and noise, yelling urchins and a darkness over the interior of the conveyance as it passed, jolting and clattering between high, overhanging walls.

Gideon came back to life, his white smile wooing her. 'All right?'

She nodded. 'Is this – the end?'

'Not yet, my sweet. But we'll have a meal here. I know a good place where the food will be to your liking, I promise you.'

'Hanna?'

'Is fast asleep and likely to remain so.'

Karran climbed down stiffly. She was aware of bridges, a tall church spire, the thin etching of boats' masts. A round building was surrounded by horses and carts, beyond which trees lined the riverbank on either side. Houses stretched into the distances, hazed by the drifting smoke from high chimneys.

'I'm here,' Gideon said, obviously recognizing her sense

of strangeness and abandonment. 'I'll look after you. Both of you. Don't worry.'

'I won't. There's – so much of it.' Her voice was awed.

'You're broadening your horizons. Don't you think it's time you did?'

Karran, with a swift, sickening longing for the moonlit bay beneath Ravensdowne, made herself nod agreement. 'Is this where you work?'

'Until now. But I am being transferred to the Paisley office. It's nearer the house, you see. More convenient.'

'So there's still some way to go.'

'A few more miles. Here, boy! Sixpence to keep an eye on these boxes for half an hour.'

'Is that wise?' Karran whispered. 'Couldn't he just – disappear?'

'I know him. He always meets the coach. In any case, he gets the sixpence when we return, don't you, young Jock.'

'Aye, sir.' Young Jock squared his broad shoulders, shook back violently red hair and stood guard.

'In here,' Gideon said a few minutes later. The eating-house was dark but warm and welcoming, with a fire whose light flickered across an array of pewter pots on an oak dresser. Hanna was deposited on to a leather sofa where she lay unmoving.

The food was as appetising as Gideon had promised. The bright images of the journey passed in procession through Karran's mind, tiring, yet, now that she was refreshed and fortified, exhilarating.

He left her by the fire while he went in search of his business contact. She was nodding in the smoky warmth when he returned.

It was a different coach that took them on the last stage of their travels. They had window seats this time and Karran was able to see much more. There were so many people and some of the ladies were most fashionably dressed. Of course, there were many more poorly dressed folk, most with rather brutish faces, but perhaps that was more a result of having led hard lives than of bad dispositions.

There were green places between the dingy patches and fine houses near a great area of parkland with a distant view of an elegant grey building of some size. Scattered cottages with thatched roofs increased in numbers against a backcloth of low, rolling hills.

Paisley was badly paved with crooked streets in which lingered bad smells. People on the narrow pavements had to shrink aside from the advent of the wide vehicle that bounced and juddered, its leather straps creaking and complaining.

Karran began to feel that her bones would never recover from the treatment they had received in the last hours. A picture of a hip bath formed in her mind, and copper cans filled with steaming water. Scented soap and thick, soft towels. Lavender water to cool her dry, tired skin.

She had glimpses of looms through open doorways, then realized that the unpleasant stench came from the open middens and privies behind each house. There seemed an astonishing number of public-houses to the one coffee-shop in the wynd that twisted uphill. She noted a sweet shop and many signs belonging in turn to a tin-smith, a printer, a house-painter, a sweep and a dyer. Paisley shawls were arranged in a cramped shop window. They were the only beautiful things she had so far seen in this alien town.

Every now and again there was a well or a small stream that ran eventually, Gideon told her, into the River Cart.

'Will you prefer working here?' she asked, wishing that Hanna was not being subjected to the bad air that was wafted into the coach's interior.

'The office is not in this part of the town. This is the weavers' area.'

'But you must pass through it each day?'

'If it's fine, I'll ride over the fell. Coachman, will you set us down at that lane end? We are to be met by trap.'

'Met?' Karran was startled.

'I knew when I must return. I told you so. The house is over that hill. We couldn't walk that far and there is the accumulation of luggage.'

'Yes, I see. I'm glad the place is so far off.'

'The folk hereabouts are not so bad. Hard-working. Inclined to be radical.'

'I can see why they might be!'

'I forgot that you and Charlotte were the defenders of the downtrodden.' Gideon sounded amused.

'You needn't laugh. But I notice that though you were mightily concerned for Hanna's state of health when Bart was quarantined, you seem not to mind that she breathes in this – miasma!'

He looked vexed. 'Go as far as you can up the lane,' he ordered. 'I'll give the coachman something for his trouble in helping me to carry the baggage. The trap will come at any time. The coach is not late today.'

She was glad to escape, clutching Hanna tightly as though to shield her from pestilence. There was fresh air in the lane, and a cool wind from the high fell. In the distance she saw, with thankfulness, the light glancing off the polished sides of the trap and hurried to meet it.

She'd half-expected Mary to be in the small conveyance but it was driven by a heavily-built, middle-aged man who turned out to be Mr Grace. He seemed dour and uncommunicative, staring at her with what could well have been disapproval. His conversation with Gideon consisted mainly of grunts and monosyllables.

'You explained to Mary that I asked you to come alone?'

'Aye, Mr Collister.'

'I was not sure that Mrs Howard would come.'

'No.' The man bent down to pick up a heavy box and deposit it on the ledge behind the seat, lifting it as though it were a feather.

'Is all well?'

'Aye. As usual.'

Gideon seemed satisfied by his responses and, the boxes now secured by strong leather thongs, they crowded into the trap. Grace flicked his whip and the sturdy brown cob began to climb the long, gradual ascent towards the summit.

Staring back, Karran saw the valley hazed with the smoke from a multitude of chimneys and the broad glimmer of the canal. There were hills beyond the weavers' town, fold upon fold of dim blue. She could regret the intrusion of civilization into that splendid isolation.

Once on the level ground the trap bowled along at a spanking pace. They passed moor and hedge, small, unexpected sheets of water where trees cast indigo reflections, a cottage or two, low and burdened with thatch held in place by stones. It grew colder.

Hanna clung to Karran, eyes round with wonder after her long sleep, diverted by the squawking of startled hens surprised near a farm gate. They reached a crude crossroad and followed the fork that led downhill towards a small stream under a frowning fell, and glimpses of a tiny loch.

A house stood inside the fringes of a birch wood that flanked the steep banks of a stream.

'That's it,' Gideon told Karran, and smiled with unmistakable satisfaction.

'Your Aunt Madeline made sure you wouldn't find her too easily.'

Gideon's voice hardened. 'That's all past. I confess, though, that it gives me great satisfaction to live under the roof from which I was, for so long, proscribed like some Highland criminal.'

How bitter he was! His expression was as grim as that unaccustomed tone. It was borne upon Karran that there was much to find out about this man who wished her, for whatever motive, to become his wife.

'She must have been wealthy to have been able to buy such a retreat and to keep it in such excellent repair.'

'She was. Our rich aunt and uncle doted on her and left her the bulk of what they had. She in turn was obsessed by my sister. I can see by that all too expressive face that you find us an odd family.'

'Gideon—'

'And you are worried about what you'll find. Little that's exceptional. My two admirable Graces. Nettie the maid. Mrs Orr, the cook, Macdonald, the gardener, two women who come daily from the village to clean and – Mary.'

Karran's heart jumped like a trout at a May fly. Everything came back to the enigmatic figure of Mary who must not be transplanted, abandoned or upset. Yet, if she were only a year younger than Gideon, she must be a grown woman. Since Gideon's lengthy letter, describing Mary, Karran had, for some reason, retained an image of a young girl.

The trap rattled up a pebbled drive and came to a halt at a porch overhung with virginia creeper. The splash of bright colour was welcoming.

Grace lowered himself to the ground and Karran found her gaze drawn irresistibly towards a window just above the porch and framed in red and yellow leaves. There was a blurred impression of something having been withdrawn, leaving a shadowy darkness.

Simultaneously, a woman, the housekeeper judging by the dark wool dress and the bunch of keys at her waist, came out on to the step nodded briefly at Grace and then favoured first Karran, then Hanna, with a searching look. 'Mr Collister, sir. Coach on time, I see.'

'You'll notice also that I've brought visitors, Mrs Grace.'

Mrs Grace folded her hands, listening gravely to the story Gideon had concocted last night in bed, but Karran didn't miss the faint, satirical spark at the back of the woman's pale eyes. Those folded hands looked large enough and strong enough to be a man's.

'You'll be wanting to freshen up, Ma'am,' she said, 'you and the little one.'

'Oh, I would like that! I'm afraid I have some soiled things of the baby's too—'

'No need to worry about those. I'll get Nettie to see to all that.'

201

'The flowered room,' Gideon said smoothly. 'And you'd doubtless like a bath?'

'I would.' Karran had been waiting for Mary's appearance but the house was wrapped in a curious silence.

'You and Hanna go with Mrs Grace, my dear. We'll all meet for refreshment later.'

Karran followed the housekeeper up carpeted stairs to a pleasant room. She experienced an odd sensation as they passed a door that was slightly ajar. That room was probably the one in which Karran had seen movement near the window. Did she merely imagine that feeling of hostility lying in wait?

Mrs Grace took Hanna from her with hands that could have broken the child's bones with utmost ease.

'You take your things off, ma'am. There, little one. It's a fine, pretty thing you are, and what big eyes you have. There's not many such eyes.'

Ruefully, Karran realized that if Gideon had hoped to pull wool over Mrs Grace's, he had little chance of success. She seemed to know perfectly well whose daughter Hanna was.

Mrs Grace bustled away once Karran had deposited her outdoor clothes on the bed. By the time Hanna was unwrapped, a thin mousy-haired maid had brought hot water and towels and just the sort of expensive soap that Karran had dreamt of on the way through Paisley's crooked wynds.

Her luggage arrived just as Hanna was washed and dried and ready for a clean gown. Nettie brought the hip bath, an extravagant affair painted with large chrysanthemums and exotic birds, then a succession of jugs of scalding water tempered with cold.

Karran, sure she heard Gideon's foot on the stair, waited for him to come into the room, but the footsteps stopped. She heard a soft whisper and the creak of a hinge, a stifled cry, then the murmur of voices cut off almost immediately by the closing of a door.

She looked out when Nettie had gone and saw that the

door that had been ajar was now shut. She'd have given much to be the sort of woman who'd have eavesdropped on the reunion between Gideon and his sister, but she couldn't bring herself to do it.

Making Hanna safe on the top of the wide bed with its flowered hangings, she stepped into the bath and seized the soap and sponge. She had known nothing so blissful. The room, with its elegant silky paper and fine plaster cornices, was soothing enough almost to send her to sleep. It was only when an energetic Hanna seemed likely to roll off the counterpane that Karran stretched her wet body reluctantly and wrapped herself in the large towel.

'Naughty Hanna,' she chided gently. 'You'll hurt yourself. Then, what will your father say!'

Hanna grinned, displaying her few teeth. She looked delighted at the prospect of Gideon's disapproval, but none of that was likely to touch her, in her child's world. Any reproof would be for her mother. Not for the first time Karran regretted the loss of the old John. He would never have reproached her. Karran became intensely aware of her lack of security and her need for love.

She dried herself slowly and let down her disordered hair, then was seized by the conviction that she was being watched. Turning quickly, she saw that the door had swung open noiselessly. Something moved quietly just out of sight. Perhaps Nettie had been sent upstairs and had seen that Karran was far from ready to present herself, withdrawing tactfully to save embarrassment on either side.

Karran began to dress herself swiftly in fresh linen and a more suitable dress taken from her luggage, then attended to her hair. Her skin glowed. But she wasn't entirely at peace. The thought of Mary nagged at her, an unwanted ache. It might have been Mary who'd stared at her, naked and disadvantaged. The supposition was disagreeable.

Once ready, with Hanna squirming in her arms, the child absorbed in taking in all that she could of her strange but not unpleasing surroundings, Karran went out into the passage. As if by magic, Gideon appeared, darkly handsome in a fresh shirt and fine coat. He tickled Hanna under the chin and her laughter echoed in the recesses of the staircase. He could not hide his pride and pleasure in the little girl.

Turning his attention to Karran, he said, 'You look quite rested. Have you forgiven me for inflicting the rigours of the journey upon you?'

'Yes. It's a fine house. I am only – surprised that I haven't yet met its mistress.'

'Mary was lying down when we arrived. Now she is ready to see you.'

As though she is an empress, Karran thought, and I am some envoy from a far-off country. An inconvenient visitor who cannot yet be turned away. And then what?

All of her reservations came crowding back, spoiling the sense of relaxation induced by the bath.

'She won't eat you,' Gideon murmured.

'I don't suppose she will. She'd find me very indigestible, I assure you!'

'You look very beautiful.'

'And you are quite impressive.'

'Come, then. I'm famished.'

Gideon was always hungry for something, Karran reflected, but then, he'd been denied so much. Her children should never suffer as he had.

Delicious smells of cooking drove everything else from Karran's mind. She was ushered into a dii .g-room in which the fire leapt blazing. She didn't, at first, see Mary, then there was a movement inside the window embrasure and Gideon's sister stepped into view.

Karran had a curious sense of familiarity. It was almost as though she'd seen Mary before. Of course, she did have Gideon's eyes. She was dressed in a white garment that might have been made for a sixteen-year-old girl and which looked out of place, in spite of her extreme slenderness and still youthful features.

Karran became aware of a pity that was unexpected,

since for so long she'd harboured for this woman much stronger, far less kind feelings.

'Mary, my dear. This is Mrs Howard.'

Mary held out her hand. 'How do you do?' Her voice was thin and childish, lacking expression. Then her gaze passed on to Hanna and her face came to vivid life, holding an almost frightening beauty. 'What's her name?'

'I told you,' Gideon said patiently. 'Hanna.'

'Oh, yes. Hanna.'

'I hope our visit is not an intrusion,' Karran said quickly. 'Gideon said not, but this is your house and I feel that you should have decided.'

'It's Gideon's as much as mine,' the young voice declaimed, parrot-like. Mary could have been a child repeating a lesson in school.

'You see?' Gideon stared challengingly at Karran. 'I told you it would be all right.'

'I am sorry you have lost your husband. It must have been terrible for you. I saw – Aunt Madeline in her coffin. She looked so strange and – empty. Mrs Grace said it was only her body. Not really Aunt Madeline. I shouldn't like to go away and leave only part of myself.' All of the brief brilliance had left Mary's features and she hunched her back like an old woman.

'Nothing is going to happen to you,' Gideon said firmly, going to her and patting her shoulder comfortingly.

Mary swung round swiftly and grasped at his hand. 'Why did you stay away so long! I hate it when you aren't here.'

'You must get used to my absences, my dear. We have spoken about the necessity, haven't we. But Karran will be here, for a while at least, and you and she will be company for one another while I am in Paisley. I explained that I have my living to earn. We are not all heiresses.' He laughed with apparent lightness.

'Oh, but I said—'

'I know what you said. But there are unpleasant names associated with men who are drones, my dear, and I've no wish to be one of their number. You are well looked after and you know that I'll always come back, don't you? Don't you!'

'Yes.' Mary smiled, all at once the fey, enchanting creature Gideon had described. It was obvious that she had sulked in her room because her beloved brother had, first of all, bidden her to stay behind instead of meeting him as she'd anticipated, then arrived with a strange young woman and a baby, who seemed to have no place in her isolated life. Plainly, she'd been jealous.

It was no more Mary's fault than it was Gideon's, Karran decided, and was sorry for them both.

They sat down at table, Mrs Grace having provided a high chair that had been stored in the attic for no good reason, since there'd been no child so young in this house for half a century.

Hanna, intrigued by the dark oak chair, behaved very well, allowing herself to be fed without making the mess Karran had feared. The room was expensively furnished with its rich carpet, French clock, silver and silvergilt, Irish glass chandelier and fine, bees-waxed furniture. A picture above the mantel dominated the scene. A Collister face if ever there was one, Karran thought, the lavender-blue eyes spoked with black, the dark good looks. Yet there was something in those eyes that was not in Gideon's or Hanna's, something secret and disturbing, almost – vicious.

Karran turned to Gideon to mention the portrait, but he forestalled her by putting his finger to his lips and jerking his head slightly in the direction of Mary. His sister was absorbed in the sight of Hanna stretching out baby arms towards a porcelain cockerel on the sideboard and voicing her frustration at not being able to grab hold of it.

It was Aunt Madeline's face that looked down at them, the faintly derisive lips mocking the two whose lives had been spoiled and retarded because of her hatred for Gideon and possessive love for his sister. It was no wonder that Gideon had behaved as he had in refusing to admit that Mary was no longer normal. That he'd chosen to remain here. Karran began to understand the necessity for such strong persons as the Graces to be in charge of the household. Thwarted children were hard enough to control.

A sick feeling attacked Karran. Would the taint that had touched at least two of the women in Gideon's family visit his own child? She tried to tell herself that it was nonsense to imagine it and that Hanna always seemed perfectly rational. Then she was angry that Gideon had overruled her own misgivings in the way he'd always overcome her objections. But she needn't stay! She hadn't committed herself to anything irrevocable. How she wished that Mary wouldn't stare so unnervingly at the child.

Mrs Grace and Nettie served the meal and took away the dishes after each course. The conversation at table reminded Karran of the sort of chatter between Bart and Rosemary. Mary's fluctuations between extreme youth and her own real age both irritated and saddened her. Mary reminded her of a sullen sky occasionally illuminated by rainbows. Her horizons seemed dominated by herself and Gideon.

Karran was still haunted by that conviction that she'd already seen Mary Collister. But that was impossible. She herself had never until now been out of Man and Gideon's sister had been little further than the loch, the birch woods and infrequent trips to Paisley since she was a small girl. All that had so far been said pointed to that fact.

The long day had tired both Karran and Hanna so much that Karran asked if they might go to their room after supper. She would be perfectly all right after a good night's sleep in a proper bed.

Mary did not demur. It was obvious that she looked forward to having Gideon to herself. Did she still go to Gideon's room when she couldn't sleep, Karran wondered? And did he still tell her stories? Hold her in the unfriendly dark?

Mrs Grace went up with Karran to make sure that all

was as it should be. A small cot had been set up in the corner of the bedroom and Hanna was asleep before her head touched the lavender-scented pillow. 'Belonged to Macdonald's daughter,' the housekeeper said.

'Macdonald?'

'The gardener, Ma'am.'

'How kind of them to lend it.'

'You'll be tired, Ma'am. I've put the warming-pan between the sheets.'

'Thank you.'

Mrs Grace hesitated as though she meant to say something else, then changed her mind and took herself off with a good-night.

Karran let her clothes fall where they would and climbed into bed. Sleep pressed down on her insistently, but it was inevitable that Mary should return to her thoughts. The girl's face swam towards her, so familiar, so – expected, reminding Karran in some odd way of O'Ferrall. Why should she connect the two? There was a hazy memory of O'Ferrall's first visit to Ravensdowne, of her own weariness, burdened as she'd been with an as yet unborn Hanna, of a feeling of faintness, an impression that she saw the figure of a young woman who'd resembled Gideon. It had all passed over so quickly. Had she, influenced by the imminence of the child's birth, conjured up an image of her daughter of the future, or had it been Mary she'd glimpsed?

How foolish her thoughts were! Karran thought of pinching herself but leaned over instead, snuffed out the candle and allowed herself to drop into a deep dark well where unseen water whispered a sly warning.

She woke to sunlight flooding the room. Hanna had pulled herself up by the dark polished bars and was trying to catch a sunbeam. 'Mama!' she said as Karran sat up and pushed the rumpled hair from her face. Karran laughed.

Nettie, who must have been told to listen for sounds of wakefulness, knocked discreetly and brought a small pot of chocolate for Karran and milk and a rusk for Hanna.

They sat at the window, enjoying the view of the reedy lake and the autumn trees on the hill opposite. A horseman with dogs skirted the edge of the wood and a sparrowhawk hovered, then plunged earthwards.

Gideon came, resplendent in a crimson house-robe, and Hanna danced up and down on Karran's lap, her small face reflecting her evident pleasure.

If only it could always be like this, Karran thought, just the three of them. But that was only a dream. There was Mary, Bart with his difficult nature, the Graces with their strong bodies and ruthless hands. The peace ebbed away.

'What shall we do after breakfast?' Gideon asked, staring out of the window in a proprietorial way and dropping a kiss on Karran's neck.

'Won't you have to go to Paisley?'

'Not until Monday. We keep a very strict Sabbath up here in Scotland.'

'I couldn't remember what day it was!'

'That's what you'd enjoy so much, that timelessness.'

'Gideon—'

'You're frowning. A serpent in Eden? Already?' Gideon looked defensive. The beginnings of anger spoiled his mouth. Yet he must recognize that Mary was not like other persons of that age.

It would do no good to give voice to her doubts. Not yet. 'It's nothing,' she said.

'Get dressed then. I was despatched to tell you that breakfast will be ready in a quarter of an hour.'

'Despatched?' Her eyebrows rose.

'You've caught me out. I was a volunteer. A very willing volunteer.' He kissed her full on the mouth. 'I missed you last night. I did look in later but you were both too deep in sleep to have heard the last trump.'

Karran's stomach muscles tightened. If Gideon had been able to come into the bedchamber unheard, then so could Mary. The thought was unpleasant.

'Gideon—' she began again.

'Quarter of an hour, Mrs Orr said,' Gideon reminded her firmly.

'So soon!'

He went out laughing and Karran was forced to rush through her toilet, with Nettie looking in to help her fasten her gown and to take Hanna to the dining-room so that Karran could do up her hair.

Mary, Gideon and Hanna were in a close group when she entered the room. The baby was in the high chair over which Mary hung like a schoolgirl in the white gown, her brown hair tied at the back with a blue ribbon. She recited a children's rhyme in that little-girl voice that went so ill with her actual years.

Karran was thankful when the food was brought in and Mary was again at a safe distance. But all the time she ate she was aware of Madeline Collister's face looking down at them all with an expression of secret satisfaction. If Mary were *not* part of this household, how pleasant life might be. But she was there, an unknown quantity. She might be perfectly harmless. Yet, there were the Graces, undeniably more like jailors than typical servants. Last night, Mrs Grace had seemed on the verge of confiding in Karran. Perhaps she might be persuaded to finish what she had almost begun? She would know whether Mary's displeasures could become violent rages.

They went for a walk in the small, deep glen beside the house after the leisurely meal was ended. Gideon carried Hanna who much enjoyed being held so firmly in strong, loving arms. Mary walked close beside him, her expression sulky, as though she resented someone else taking up her brother's attention, then he spoke to her and her face lit up as though she'd seen the Holy Grail. She clung to his arm.

Karran began to feel that she was walking a tight-rope. Part of her mind delighted in the sight of the silver birches against a turquoise sky, the distant glitter of the lochan, but the rest remained in a silent conflict to which she thought there could be no end except in her departure.

They emerged from the embrace of the tight-packed

wood, on to a rough road that bordered the lochan. A cloud hung over it now and it looked sullen and unfriendly, then the sun burst through, making the waters sparkle. There was a boathouse halfway along the nearest bank, its red paint vying with the autumn leaves and its reflection shivering on the silver surface.

'How pretty it looks.'

'Many's the fine hour's fishing it's given me, though it's inclined to coarseness. Perch pike and roach mostly, though there's trout if you're lucky. Have you ever fished, my dear?'

Karran admitted that she hadn't.

'We could take a picnic before the weather precludes such outings. Next Sunday perhaps, if it's fine. I'll teach you how to make a cast. Mrs Orr has a light hand with pasties. They'd make your mouth water.'

'Hanna—'

'The boat will easily take four. She can feed the ducks, bless her little heart.'

Karran fell silent as Mary exclaimed how pleasant it would be, how much Hanna would enjoy the excursion, her mother, too, she added as an afterthought, realizing that Karran might feel excluded. Mary was not always childish and other-worldly. At times there could be a certain shrewdness.

They played cards in the afternoon while Hanna had her usual sleep, and Karran was reminded of Nick O'Ferrall and that unexpected but somehow heart-warming glimpse of him on the waterfront at Douglas. He'd imagine he'd seen the last of her as Karran Howard and would have gone in search of that fair-haired woman of his. Perhaps he'd marry her. He'd seemed lonely since Tom Allen was drowned.

Mary enjoyed the card games so long as she won.

'You can't always expect to win,' Gideon told her a little astringently. 'You must learn to grow up, my dear.'

Her eyes filled with tears.

'There now, don't be such a goose,' he said more kindly,

patting her hand. 'Why don't you and Karran come with me in the morning and do some shopping? Mrs Grace would look after Hanna. She'd be quite safe with her. I'd be able to meet you both later. Karran might find out that Paisley is more interesting than she imagines.'

'I'd like that so long as I'm not alone. So long as I feel safe.' But her tone was grudging, suggesting that it didn't matter who was her protector.

Somehow it was all arranged. At least, Karran thought, if Mary is with me I'll know that my baby is not in any danger. We might even get to know one another better. A trusting Mary would be infinitely more comfortable company than one filled with suspicion and resentment.

Much later, when all the household was asleep, Gideon got into bed beside Karran and stayed for an hour.

'You are going to marry me, aren't you,' he whispered afterwards.

'I said I'd tell you later,' she said carefully. 'It's a big step. Not to be rushed.' And she smiled.

'I'll find some way of keeping you here,' he threatened, only half-amused, then went away quietly, leaving her wide awake.

Next morning, Karran had difficulty in shaking off the notion that the entire household was aware of Gideon's early morning visit. It seemed to her that Mrs Grace never looked at her directly and that even Nettie's glance was evasive. She tried to tell herself that it was imagination, but the thought brought no real conviction.

Breakfast was spoiled by her feelings of guilt. Mary was high-spirited and infected with an excitement that brought the colour to her cheeks and a sparkle to her pretty eyes. In her youthful gown and the blue velvet bonnet and cape she looked like a charming eighteen-year-old. Vivacity suited her. How tragic that her nature had been so repressed.

Karran, who had slept little after Gideon's surreptitious sliding between the sheets, was a little pale and disinclined to make an effort, but it would have been cruel to disappoint Mary who was by now almost dancing with impatience to leave.

Hanna was quiet and docile, showing no sign of misbehaving. There was no excuse to be had in that quarter.

But, with the sun shining, the dog-cart bouncing along the pot-holed road, and Gideon in charming good-humour, Karran began to look forward to seeing something of the town that might provide a better impression than the one received on her previous visit.

The wind, blowing in a different direction, left the air sweeter as they came down towards the weavers' cottages. Recent rain had washed the tortuous wynds and left the cobbles shining. Mary clapped her hands at the sight of the sweet-shop and made Gideon stop so that she might by a poke of humbugs.

Gideon purchased copies of the *Tickler* and the *Paisley Magazine*. Karran who had written to both Bart and Mrs Quinn, and to Charlotte, took her letters to the tiny post-office-cum-stationery shop in Moss Street and reflected that the postmaster earned every farthing of his annual salary of sixty pounds, so busy was he in premises quite inadequate to cope with such floods of customers.

The solicitors' offices were within view of the impressive abbey and the River Cart. Gideon took both women upstairs with him to be introduced to old Mr Gilmour and young Mr Blackwell, and arranged for the dog-cart to be put in the yard behind the building, the cob being attended to by a small, hungry-looking youth whose face lighted up at the sight of the sturdy horse.

Karran could not help noticing how Mr Blackwell brightened on first seeing Mary looking pleased and girlish in her velvet bonnet and dainty boots, the packet of humbugs thrust carelessly into the blue reticule. Obviously, he thought her little more than a schoolgirl, her face lit as it was from within, her pretty mouth curved in a smile that he could not know was for Gideon alone.

Mr Gilmour put himself out to be charming to Karran,

telling her, in answer to her questions, that after Edinburgh and Glasgow there was no town in Scotland as large as this, and that there were in the region of thirty thousand people living and working in this warren of streets and lanes. The enormity of this figure oppressed her. She was used to the comfortable smallness of Port St Mary, the seclusion of Ravensdowne and Black Rocks. But this was to be Gideon's world and he would do his utmost to ensure that she and Hanna were made part of it.

She came out of her reverie to find that Mr Gilmour was telling her that the Mures of Caldwell, whose house was near the crossroads above the lochan and birch woods they'd walked beside yesterday, had always sent their children to the local grammar school. A very well established family. He'd gone to the school himself. There'd been an interesting custom on Candlemas Day. Each pupil walked by the master's desk to pay their contribution to the augmentation of the dominie's stipend. There was no reaction to the offerings of the poor but if the master said 'Vivat', that meant he was reasonably pleased. Two merks occasioned a 'Floreat!' and ten a 'Gloriat!' The largest contribution brought with it the privilege of becoming the school's Victor.

'I couldn't agree to my son attending such a school,' Karran said firmly.

'No?' Mr Gilmour looked surprised. He had been Victor in his day.

'How unpleasant to have been one of the poor. How – humiliating! A Victor should earn his place another way. By his efforts.'

'There have always been poor and those better off.' Mr Gilmour decided he'd say nothing about the cock-fighting at Easter. The beautiful Mrs Howard seemed a woman of strong principles and he felt that her sympathies would have been with the cocks.

'I should like to have been Victor,' Mary decided and offered her bag of humbugs which were accepted though it was much too soon after breakfast. 'I would have given

214

thirty merks. I have a good deal of money, haven't I, Gideon.'

'Yes, my dear, but it doesn't do to boast too much about such matters.' Gideon had not been unaware of the faintly avaricious flicker in the junior partner's eyes, but Mary's disarming candour had had the pleasing effect of taking attention away from Karran's disapproval of the ethics of Candlemas offerings. It wouldn't do to antagonize old Gilmour quite so early in their acquaintanceship.

'In any case, there is work to be done, so off you go and enjoy yourselves. The Cock-a-leekie Inn is as good as any for luncheon and you can come back at around four, which is when we close on a Monday.'

Karran, aware of the edge of Gideon's displeasure, smiled at Mr Gilmour to show that she considered him in no way to blame for his old school's less attractive practices, then ushered Mary out of the door and into the busy street.

'Take great care to hold tightly on to your reticule,' she warned Mary. 'It could quite easily be stolen where it is so crowded, and to anyone poor, it must be a temptation.'

Mary seemed glad to comply. It seemed she had a possessive streak. Away from Gideon she lost her pretty self-assurance and stayed close beside Karran as though afraid of being separated, even from a woman she did not particularly like. Alone in the midst of this vociferous, bustling humanity she'd have been a lamb among wolves. How she fluctated between high spirits and low.

It was not her fault, Karran kept reminding herself. With a normal upbringing, Mary might have been a very different person. Was it so unexpected that Gideon would long ago have realized Mary's failings and wish permanently to protect her? He'd had an idealized image of the little girl that once she was, a child like Hanna, and it might be difficult for him to see beyond it. To see that she was spoiled and unstable.

They left the congestion to walk across the bridge to view the abbey in its green fields. Something in its tall, grey isolation calmed the tumult in Karran's heart. It made her think of sanctuary and, in some disturbing way, of Nick O'Ferrall. That was what he'd offered her. But it was better not to think of that.

Mary tugged at her arm. 'Haven't you looked at the abbey for long enough? I want to buy things! Gideon said I might, I'm allowed to come so very rarely.'

'Of course. But it couldn't have been so convenient when Gideon was in Glasgow. Now that he's so close, I'm sure your visits could become more frequent.'

'You mean, if *you* are here to chaperone me.' Her voice changed.

'Haven't you any friends of your own age?'

'No. Aunt Madeline didn't like young people. Any people, really.'

'Don't you think that was – selfish?' Karran suggested, looking over the bridge into the brown depths of the river.

'What do you know about it? She loved me.'

'But she did leave you alone in the end.'

'I suppose she did. Only I have Gideon now. He's never going away.'

'What if – if he should want to marry? Wouldn't he want his own home?'

Mary's face turned very white. 'Marry? He won't. He wouldn't—'

Disturbed by her sick pallor, Karran asked, 'What did you want to buy?'

'Buy? A shawl, I thought. Yes, a shawl.' Diverted, Mary began to look less strained.

'Well, that shouldn't present too much difficulty,' Karran told her. 'Paisley shawls are famous. Look there, in the water! Fish.'

Mary stared. 'You can't see the ones in the loch. It's rather weedy. The weeds hide things. Tangle things. A boy drowned last spring.'

'Poor boy.'

Karran began to walk back purposefully. At least she knew now how Mary would react to Gideon taking a wife.

Obviously he had not mentioned the possibility.

They found a shop that sold shawls close to a shiversome place called Gallowgreen, on which suspected witches and warlocks had been throttled and burned in the past. There still remained the rotted stumps of those parts of the stakes' timbers that had been under the level of the ground. No one, apparently, had wanted the responsibility of digging them out after they'd been in contact with the Devil.

Karran, aware of certain obligations as Mary's guest, insisted upon making a gift of the shawl that Mary coveted. Gideon's sister did not demur, only drew the garment around slim shoulders and admired the reflection of its blues, creams and indigo in the cheval mirror in the corner of the shop.

Mindful of the good service of Mary's staff, Karran bought a few smaller presents, a pipe and tobacco for Grace who smoked, though not in the house, and another for the gardener, handkerchiefs for Mrs Grace and Sunday gloves for Nettie, the ever-willing. Karran had considered gloves for Mrs Grace, then remembering how large and mannish her hands were, decided that the cook should have them instead.

After lunch an enjoyable hour was spent at the Market Cross around which was arranged a profusion of stalls, mostly of garden produce, spun thread, ribbons, laces, hair-combs, gilded gingerbread figures and sweetmeats, the sight of which made Mary forget about the packet of humbugs and rush forward as eagerly as a child to purchase more delights. More than one pair of masculine eyes followed her ecstatic progress.

What if Mary should attract a would-be husband? There was the inducement of her comfortable circumstances as well as the attraction she sometimes displayed. But, long before wedding-bells were likely to be sounded, any prospective groom must be made aware of her strangeness. In any case, she'd probably turn hysterical at the thought of a marriage-bed.

Mary's spirits flagged after the excitements of her shopping and the discovery that her money was spent. She waited listlessly as Karran browsed through a collection of volumes of poems by what seemed an alarming array of local poets, many of whom appeared besotted by the Gleniffer braes, over which she, Mary and Gideon would shortly make their homeward way.

Poor Alexander Wilson, Karran thought, her eyes skimming the lines. With a penniless father, he could not have been Victor at the grammar school. Then there was Francis Sempil, who, though better connected, could not write as well as Tannahill, the weaver, who ended up, distraught after implied criticism of his work, caught in the reeds of the Caudren Burn.

'Oh, do come away!' Mary demanded pettishly. 'I find myself weary and long to go back to Gideon and the trap. Surely it must be time?'

'Not quite. Would you like a cup of chocolate or coffee, and some shortbread? That might help to take away the tiredness.'

Crestfallen, Mary reminded Karran of her lack of funds. 'Ridiculous, isn't it, that I, who have so much, am without a penny? Gideon will only allow me to take so much.' It was her first criticism of her brother.

'But a young girl like yourself could so easily fall prey to thieves. They can't all be honest men in so large a town. He is thinking only of your welfare.'

Mary smiled triumphantly. 'Yes. All of his life he will have me in his mind. Always.'

'I will pay for the treat. A guest should show her appreciation.' Karran's heart was heavy.

'How long do you intend to stay?'

'I – I'm not sure. Here's a pleasant-looking place. A coffee-shop.'

By the time they'd sat down, Mary had forgotten her boredom and listlessness and said no more of the prospective length of Karran's stay. Refreshed, they had just time to return to the premises of Gilmour, Collister and Blackwell before the clock struck the hour of four.

Mr Gilmour had already gone but young Mr Blackwell was so assiduous in his attentions towards Mary that Karran couldn't help but observe Gideon's irritation. It was plain that he couldn't envisage Mary with a beau, however suitable, and was aware only of the fact that he was being delayed.

'How was she?' Gideon murmured in an aside while Mary was otherwise diverted.

'Up and down.'

'More up, I hope?'

'Yes. But she asked me, very directly, how long I meant to stay.'

'I see. Well, don't worry about it. I'll speak to her.'

'Be careful, though,' Karran whispered, remembering Mary's reaction to any mention of a wife for her brother.

Mr Blackwell, obviously influenced by a look from Gideon, took reluctant leave of them. Gideon, with a last glance round the comfortable rooms, locked the door behind him.

Karran, sorry for the skinny lad who led out the cob, slipped a sixpence into his hand and laid a finger on her lips. Incredulous eyes thanked her. She thought of that innocent, hero-worshipping look as they rattled and shook over the crude cobblestones, Mary clinging to her brother's arm and recounting her day's doings, Karran's presence forgotten.

The following days passed pleasantly enough. Macdonald, spurred on by gratitude for his unexpected gift from Karran, produced a small painted cart used in the transport of his grandchildren. A harness, fastened by buckles to loops of leather, kept Hanna sitting safely, her body protected by cushions enclosed within fresh pillow-cases smelling pleasantly of lavender.

Karran kept every detail of its construction in her mind. She'd have one made when she got home. So long as the weather remained fine, she could push her child for respectable distances, a pleasure enhanced by the fact that Mary had caught a cold, which, though not serious, had the effect of keeping her in bed for most of the week.

Karran, while suspecting that Mary could have been up and about much sooner was nevertheless, delighted by her unexpected freedom, especially as the sun continued to shine with unseasonable warmth. It was joy to walk through the network of lanes, the crisp leaves crackling underfoot.

Hanna stretched out her hands towards everything she saw, flowers, branches, birds and the shining lochan on which Gideon was still determined to row on Sunday. He'd looked out all the fishing tackle, unsnagged lines, produced lead sinkers, cleaned the slim, supple poles, and unearthed the large picnic-basket, long unused, for Mrs Grace or Nettie to prepare.

Mrs Grace had not resumed her attempt to speak to Karran about anything other than the necessary running of the house and of mutual arrangements for mealtimes while Gideon was out and Mary confined to her room. But it was obvious that she and the rest of Mary's staff were pleased with their visitor's thoughtful presents.

Hanna quickly became a great favourite, a fact that could not fail to be noticed by Mary, and probably contributed to her prolonged stay in bed where she herself must feel cossetted and protected.

By Friday Karran knew every corner of the woods, each farm and cottage and the location of Caldwell House which looked grey and grand. As she noted the sun glinting on the large windows she wondered wryly if one of the Mures could be the present Victor in Paisley. Gideon had been cross about her outspokenness and had stressed the need for keeping Mr Gilmour in as good a mood as possible. It was he who'd feel the backwash of any resentment, he'd pointed out. New brooms must not always sweep clean too ostentatiously.

'You've been too much in Charlotte Kerruish's company,' he'd accused.

'I'm very fond of Charlotte! Anyway, when did I have such a choice of real friends! I certainly don't intend to give up those I have!'

'Does that include O'Ferrall?'

She'd given him a white, angry look and he hadn't repeated the question. But Karran knew that she must have forfeited Nick's good will. He'd told her she must choose between them, and had ridden to assure himself that she and Gideon had indeed left together on the *Robert Bruce*. Philly must be delighted that Nick remained free. Damn Philly!

Mary returned to normality on Friday evening, coming down for the evening meal and making a great fuss of Gideon. She'd gone to the spinet afterwards and played haunting little pieces that tormented Karran's senses with their poignancy and evocativeness. There seemed to be a piece for everyone for whom she'd ever had any feelings.

She was reminded of Clemence, her mother, and remembered that she hadn't visited her grave since Hanna was born. The omission grieved her, underlined by her realization of the distances between that time-worn stone and the place in which she now found herself. The minute she got home, she'd go to Croggan and put flowers on the grave. She must talk to Gideon and tell him that she meant to go back. Soon—

Later she lay awake, willing him to come, but he did not. Karran waited, tormented by the need to speak. An hour passed, then another. She would have to go to him.

Pulling on her house-robe, she tiptoed from her room and moved silently in the direction of Gideon's. There was a thin line of light under the door, so he too must be awake. She hesitated, her hand on the knob, then froze into immobility as she heard Gideon say quite loudly, 'But I *have* to marry her!'

'Why? Why must you!' Mary's voice was sharp, the little-girl quality missing.

'Don't pretend! You *know* why.'

There was a silence broken by Mary. 'I don't understand. Tell me again.'

'You do! Because of the child.'

'Hanna?'

'Yes. She's mine. You *must* accept the fact. But in order to claim her I must be married to her mother.'

'No – No, Gideon!' she protested violently, sobbing.

'Be quiet,' Gideon told her brusquely. 'You'll rouse the household.'

So Mary did still visit Gideon when she was sleepless or troubled. Karran knew she should not stay but was powerless to move.

'That's why you brought Mrs Howard. She'll take you away! Then I'll have no one.' She sounded desolate.

'No one is going to take me *anywhere*. I'll still be here. I promised to take care of you and so I shall. The only reason I must think of marriage is to be able to have my own child with me. It would be like turning you away if I allowed Hanna to go back to the island. She'd become a stranger to me.'

'And if Hanna had not been there?' Mary's voice had lost all expression.

'Matters would have been different. There'd have been no need to think of such a step. But you do see the necessity, don't you, my dear? Nothing need change too radically. Do you want to stay for a while? You like being here with me, don't you. Nothing will change.'

'Oh, Gideon.'

There was a pause. 'There, that's better, isn't it. Do you remember the stories? The secrets?'

'Yes. Yes—'

Karran could bear to hear no more. She felt cold and lost.

Stumbling, she returned to bed but there was no comfort.

She lay shivering, listening to the night noises and Hanna's quiet breathing. It was a long time before she fell asleep, to dream of Bart going up to a desk where Mr Gilmour sat, his gaze fixed upon a pile of coins beside his outstretched hand. Unseen boys' voices chanted 'Vivat, Floreat, Gloriat!' Bart laid a piece of gold beside the rest. It shrivelled into leathery blackness.

'Victor! Victor!' The cries rang in her ears and Karran started up. It was daylight and Hanna was shouting for her breakfast.

It was difficult to pretend that she had not overheard the conversation between Gideon and his sister. Karran wanted very much to get Gideon to herself for a few minutes to tell him what she knew, but no opportunity presented itself. Mary did not allow them to be together. She prattled incessantly about tomorrow's excursion and Karran's silence went unnoticed.

'Macdonald wants to see you, Mr Collister,' Mrs Grace told Gideon, 'about them rose bushes. It'll soon be time to plant, he says.'

'I should have decided on the ones I wanted sooner. I'll go and see to it.'

After he'd gone out to the garden Karran said, 'I'll take Hanna out for a walk.'

'I – I won't come. In case my cold gets worse,' Mary told her quickly.

'Are you wise to go out on the loch tomorrow, in that case?'

Mary's eyes flickered, and, just for a second, looked like the eyes in Madeline's portrait. 'Oh, I'll be all right tomorrow, never fear. That's why I'm staying in today.'

'Very well.'

Hanna was pleased to be strapped into the little cart. Karran went towards the woodland path where she knew no one was likely to go in the morning. They'd be even less likely to be there tomorrow. They'd be too afraid of the minister's wrath. She suspected that Scots religion would be of the hell-fire variety.

The changing colours of the foliage held her attention only briefly. Gideon had been using her. She'd suspected it in the beginning but he was certainly a persuasive lover.

223

He'd managed to convince her that he still loved her. That he wanted her as much as he did Hanna. It wasn't true and the realization hurt profoundly.

The stream glittered as it pursued its rocky course towards the lochan. Hanna chattered excitedly as a rabbit bounded across the path, its white scut shining as it vanished into the dense undergrowth. Wood pigeons crooned sadly, accenting Karran's mood.

Someone was coming after them. Leaves rustled and sticks cracked. 'Wait! Karran! Wait for me.' It was Gideon's voice.

Karran was minded to go on but Hanna wanted to wait. 'Gid-Gid,' she said quite plainly and gladly. 'Gid-Gid!'

'She knows my name, or a version of it,' Gideon panted, catching them up. 'Why didn't you wait for me? You must have known I'd want to come.'

'Must I?'

'What's that supposed to mean? Said in that cold little voice.'

'I came to your room last night.'

Conflicting emotions showed themselves in Gideon's eyes. 'I suppose you heard Mary.'

'Yes.'

'You mustn't pay too much attention to what Mary says. You must realize that she was the reason I didn't write to you a second time. When the pleasure of our reunion had worn off a little I realized that I was in a trap. A snare. Unable to let myself damage her any further by leaving.'

Karran's mouth twisted. 'You told her you had to marry me in order to gain possession of your child, after having assured me that it wasn't so.'

'It was – expedient.'

'And is our present conversation also expedient?'

'Karran! You know how I feel about you.'

'I don't. Truly, I don't,' she whispered. 'You said that if Hanna hadn't existed there'd have been no need—'

'I *had* to say that. If Mary knows I'm mad in love—'

'Finish it. What would Mary do?'

He laughed uncertainly. 'Scratch out your eyes, probably. Yes, you're right, she'd be jealous as sin.'

'So, if we were married we'd never be able to show our affection in public?'

He stood silent.

'You'd expect me to behave like a stranger, and me your wife?'

'Oh, it wouldn't be as bad as that!'

'Yes, it would. It could be worse. Would you still welcome her into your bedroom? Our bedroom?'

'She'd have to realize that would no longer be proper.'

'I couldn't Gideon. That's what I came to tell you last night. It would be better if I went back home. I've done what I promised. Spied out the lie of the land—'

'You've not given it long enough. A few days – I won't give you up, either of you. I can't.'

Somehow, Karran was in his arms, his violent kisses raining on her face and neck. She wanted to respond but the echo of his words came back to her. 'But in order to claim Hanna I must be married to her mother.' They'd sounded cold enough last night. The remembrance of them in the autumn sunlight was doubly chilling. Never again could she be entirely sure of him. She would pretend to be convinced but after he'd gone to Paisley on Monday she'd ask Grace to find some way to take her to Glasgow. She'd get a coach quite easily from there or there was the canal. She could try that. The Graces wouldn't be surprised that she wanted to leave. All she had to do was to act as normally as possible until Gideon went to his office. Mary wouldn't care that she and Hanna wanted to go. She'd be glad to see the back of them.

'Tell me you'll stay for a bit longer. Please?'

Held tightly against his breast, she whispered, 'Very well.'

'You won't regret it. I'll make you happy if it's the last thing I do. My lovely love.'

It was a long time since he'd called her that. The memories of last year came flooding back, sharp and bitter-sweet. It was not altogether pretence when she kissed him back and let him hold her for long enough for Hanna to become impatient and rock herself dangerously in the confines of the cart.

'Little wretch!' Gideon told Hanna fondly. 'Little monster. *You* won't desert me, will you.'

Karran forced herself to smile.

Sunday dawned dull and grey. Karran wondered how she would get through the day if they were forced to stay indoors. But luck was with her: it wasn't long before the clouds shifted and the sun made a tawny brilliance of the fells under an eggshell-blue dome. The skies had never looked as high as they did here, so thickly studded with stars at night. But how she missed the sound of the sea.

Gideon was good-humoured as he went about his preparations. He enjoyed having his own way as much as Mary. As much as Hanna most probably would. The last thought gave Karran no pleasure.

She wrapped the child well in two lots of clothing as Gideon said it was always colder on stretches of water, and put on an extra red flannel petticoat. Mary, subdued, submitted to being shrouded in a dark plaid cape, her neck swaddled in a red wool muffler.

'You've just got out of bed!' Mrs Grace said firmly as though speaking to a ten-year-old, her thick fingers knotting the scarf so that it would be difficult to remove. With the matching tam o' shanter perched on top of her thick hair, and her pale, small-featured face, Mary looked wistful and appealing.

Nettie closed the lid on the picnic-hamper and fastened the polished straps. Grace was to take them down to the boat in the dog-cart.

Once on the way, Karran enjoyed the feel of the air on her face. Hanna was full of joie de vivre, dancing energetically inside the circle of her arms. She was becoming quite pretty, Karran thought, now that she was rounding out, and her hair showed more than a sign of waves and curls.

Inside the boathouse there was a shadowy greenness. The name on the hull was *Madeline*. Suddenly, Karran knew she didn't want to commit herself to a boat of that name.

'Come on!' Gideon ordered with a touch of asperity, having settled Mary and the hamper at the bows and seen the rods stowed in the bottom, out of harm's way.

Grace steadied Karran while Gideon held the boat against the wooden jetty. She stepped aboard reluctantly and was helped into her own seat. Gideon, in the centre, put the oars into the water and propelled them into daylight. He pulled strongly, the shining drops spraying from the oars to fall back into the lochan. She watched the ripples widen.

'We sang when last we came here,' Mary said unexpectedly. 'Do you remember, Gideon?'

'I remember.

"Oh they rode on, and on they rode,
And a' by the light of the moon,
Until they came to yon wan water,
And there they lighted down."

That was it, wasn't it?'

'Yes. All about Lord William and Lady Margaret Douglas.'

Mary began to sing and her voice was like the music she evoked from the jangling keys of the spinet, pure as a boy's and haunting.

'"Hold up, hold up, Lord William" she says,
"For I fear that you are slain!"
"T'is nothing but the shadow of my scarlet cloak
That shines in the water so plain."'

227

Gideon joined in and the two voices combined eerily, echoing over the silent loch,

> '"Lord William was buried at St Marie's Kirk,
> Lady Margaret in Marie's quire;
> Out o' the lady's grave grew a bonny red rose,
> And out o' the Knight's a briar.
>
> But bye and rode the Black Douglas
> And wow but he was rough!
> For he pulled up the bonny briar
> And flung it in St Mary's Loch."'

The lingering notes hung on the air and died away.

There was something red in the depths of the lochan. The strong colours of Mary's scarf and tam o' shanter and the dark red of her plaid. Like blood running from an unseen wound, spreading as far as the reeds that grew thickly from the banks for quite a distance.

Karran held Hanna closer. There was something in the old ballad that curdled the marrow in her bones.

Mary and Gideon were not yet finished with tragedy. They sang 'Lord Randal' and the 'Lament of the Border Widow' before Karran protested.

'Something more cheerful?' Gideon repeated, straight-faced. 'How about the Bonny Earl of Murray?'

Mary laughed with more than a touch of hysteria. 'Yes. That's a happy one.'

The joke went over Karran's head until they began to sing again. She'd never heard these sombre ballads and this last one was by far the most terrible. The dirge worked on her senses like the icy wastes of winter.

'Oh, I'm so cold,' she said, shivering until Gideon, laughing, passed her his flask. 'I haven't the stomach for horrors!' She saw Mary smile.

The brandy was deliciously warming. Karran returned the flask and Gideon drank from it himself. She noticed that he did not offer it to Mary.

He dropped the anchor and the picnic was begun. Mrs Orr had gone to a good deal of trouble over small pots of delicious mashed food for Hanna.

'Here, let me feed her the rest,' Gideon said, sated with pasties and drumsticks and wine. 'You've eaten hardly anything, Karran.'

Mary's face changed as he held the child on his lap and took up the spoon. She looked away, staring at the distant woods and the smoke from the farm behind the glen. The knuckles were white on her clasped hands.

'Gid-Gid,' Hanna said, looking into Gideon's face. 'Gid-Gid-Gid.'

Karran, seeing the encarmined water where Mary now hung over the boat's side, dabbling her fingers in the loch, was not hungry, but she nibbled one of the pasties rather than hurt Mrs Orr's feelings. She'd be sure to ask what Mrs Howard thought of them. A chicken wing and a glass of wine finished the savoury course. There was fruit, cheese and plumcake but only Mary indulged herself with the rich dark cake.

Cumulous clouds had built up around the horizon, like mushrooms and castles and huge hunched gods, the billowing sails of three-masted schooners. Had George Seyler and Barney Kerruish begun O'Ferrall's yacht yet?

At the thought of Nick O'Ferrall, Karran closed her eyes. She was back at Ravensdowne with the shags preening and the gulls swooping past the window. Caldwell and the lochan receded into a far distance. The present had no reality, only the past and her longing to return to what was sweet and familiar.

'And now, my dear Karran,' Gideon said lazily, 'I am going to teach you how to make a cast. You must sing for your supper.'

Mary laughed.

Karran sat up quickly. Gideon was standing up, his feet firmly planted to stabilize the boat, steadying the rod. 'You were nearly asleep, weren't you.'

'Hanna—'

'Is perfectly safe on Mary's lap. It's time she got used to her aunt. You see? She's playing with the buttons on her cape.'

Karran stared. Hanna did seem all right and Mary looked pleased with her burden, yet a worm of disquiet uncoiled in Karran's stomach.

'Why don't you let Mary have a turn? I'm quite happy to remain a spectator. Hanna can be quite a handful.'

'They are making friends,' Gideon said in a way that allowed for no argument. 'Stand up in the centre. Whatever you do, don't step to either side. That's fine.'

Karran staring ahead uncertainly, could see only Gideon. The bulk of his body hid the others. There was only that glimmer of red in the water—

'Stand sideways, still keeping on a level with myself. Look across to the opposite bank. Now, put your hands on the rod, just where mine are.' Their fingers touched, both cold. Karran shivered.

Mary gave a little giggle. There was something in the quality of that sound that made the hair prick on Karran's neck.

There was a scream and a splash. For a moment something lay in the middle of that rust-coloured reflection, then, struggling, was swallowed up, leaving the water full of widening ripples.

Gideon whirled, shouting. Karran had a glimpse of Mary cowering white-faced, hands flashing upwards to cover her open mouth.

'Hanna? Where's Hanna?' Karran cried out, disbelieving.

'It was – an accident,' Mary whimpered.

'Christ! Christ in all the heavens!' Savagely, Gideon flung off his coat, sprang to the side of the *Madeline*, setting the boat lurching dangerously to one side, then plunged into the water.

'You let her go!' Karran screamed. 'You let my child drown!' She fell to her knees and crawled towards Mary. 'Gideon should have known better. But this was your plan, wasn't it! He was never to marry me and Hanna stood in the way.'

The full enormity of what had happened overcame Karran like a thunder-clap. She tasted the air, heard the greedy sucking of the water under the boat, Mary's hurried breathing, saw Mary smile. She wanted to reach out and destroy that smile but there was still Gideon to think of, struggling and splashing close by, the lochan so cold and the reeds so predatory. They had half-forgotten Gideon.

Karran saw his face turned towards her, white and set, the hair plastered to his head, arms searching, searching, then he dived under the surface again, leaving a great gout of water to fill the gap where, only a moment ago, he had been.

Mary, suddenly and terribly aware of Gideon's danger, leaned sideways, crying out his name. Her voice stabbed the air like gulls' cries. 'Save yourself! Yourself! Yourself!'

Gideon's head broke the surface, his mouth open, features contorted with pain. His skin was a strange bluish-grey. He gasped, brought up a great mouthful of water and raised his arms towards Karran. Sobbing, she recognized the colour of Hanna's coat, glimpsed the small blind face under the strands of wet hair.

Then she was hanging over the gunwale almost to the waterline and the soaked bundle was thrust into her own arms. She fell backwards, conscious only of being wet through to the skin, of the boat swinging upwards again, bringing a gush of loch water with it to foam and eddy around her.

Hanna was motionless. Karran knelt, sick and chilled, and turned the little body upside down, shaking Hanna until the water stopped running from her mouth. Then she opened her coat and thrust the infant into the warmest place, against her breast. Hanna was ominously still. So still, so icy.

It was then that Karran's dazed eyes returned to the loch's troubled face. There was no sign now of Gideon or

231

of any movement near the yawning boat.

Mary stood up, her voice still cutting shocking wounds in the surrounding quiet.

'You've killed him,' Karran said dully. 'You. Your fault – You murderess. Murderess—'

For a moment she saw Mary silhouetted against the sky, then the slim figure hurtled forward and hit the water with a violence that sent up a fountain of spray. The spreading redness was dragged below, leaving the water grey and lifeless.

Faintly, Karran was aware of distant shouting and the renewed thrashing sound that must be Mary struggling close by. Her senses spun. Then, for a long time, there was nothing.

The day of the wedding dawned cold but sparkling. There was frost on the leaves and rimed mirrors between the cobbles. The castle was like a fortress in a fairy tale.

Charlotte, who had wakened preposterously early and couldn't bear to lie abed any longer, got up quietly, wrapped herself in a warm cloak and let herself out of the house. The sun was just inching above the edge of the horizon, the colour of a blood orange.

Karran would have taken that as a bad omen. Her poor Karran! She'd promised to be back in time to see Charlotte wed, but there was, as yet, no sign of her. Bart had been sent over yesterday, as requested, to be present at the ceremony, more for Rosemary's benefit than for anyone else's. He must miss his mother.

The deserted waterfront was stained with watery redness. Empty windows glinted with a hint of fire. The sun, pushing itself higher, spilled a trail of yellow that lapped across the arctic sea and ran up all the ships' masts, shining on the brass rails, door-knockers, letter-boxes, filling in rectangles of glass so that the rooms behind them became illusionary infernos.

Charlotte hugged her happiness to her like a precious gift. She'd never quite convinced herself that she'd be allowed to marry George Seyler. Something must happen to prevent it. But nothing had! She couldn't believe her wonderful, miraculous luck. The golden light touched her face like a benison.

She laughed out loud. Erin would consider her mad, but who cared about Mama! George had bought a gem of a house so that they'd start their lives together properly. Tonight she'd sleep in her own bedchamber, under her own roof, away from her mother's curiosity and the shadow of Abel. But she wouldn't think of Abel, not on this special day. Yet, she had loved him once, with a never-to-be-forgotten intensity. Charlotte shivered.

The first cart rattled along the quayside, bound for the brewery. Its dark reflection moved sluggishly along the edge of the sea, like something drowned. Like the Collisters, livid, wrapped with treacherous weed, or Abel come back to claim her before it was too late.

Charlotte started backward, her eyes wide with a kind of horror. What ill thoughts for a wedding-morn! Her pulse slowed. It was not her business to mourn for the whole world, not today. She owed it to George to be happy, to make this an occasion that neither of them would forget, and so she would.

Retracing her steps, the huge sapphire shadow of Castle Rushen embracing her like some legendary lover of ice and stone, she found herself to be hungry. Letting herself in as quietly as she'd gone out, she surprised Erin, candle-stick in hand, at the foot of the stairs.

'You must be mad!' Erin exclaimed predictably. 'What if you'd met anyone, looking like a tramp, as you do? What if you'd met George?' Erin was even more superstitious than the Manx folk.

'I did,' Charlotte said meekly. 'We'd agreed we'd always be under a cloud.'

'You *what*!' The candle wavered perilously.

'Mama, it was a joke. I couldn't sleep. I wanted to taste the flavour of my wedding-day. What's wrong with that?'

'And what flavour was it?' Erin enquired sarcastically,

pulling her green peignoir closer with her free hand. It was chilly in the unheated hall.

'It tasted of – ice – blood oranges – fire, and the sea. Wonderful.'

They stared at one another in the candle-light, Erin uncomprehending, Charlotte's expression more like mother's than daughter's.

'Must you always talk in terms of poetry?' Erin enquired peevishly.

'It was reality. And a bit of magic,' Charlotte conceded. 'You go and put some clothes on and I'll make tea. Jenny will have lit the fire by now.' She watched her mother go upstairs.

The kitchen was warm and friendly. The maid had gone to see to the other fires so Charlotte sat, nursing the warm cup, thinking of the new garments up in the room she'd never need to use again. Mama had ordered her two boned-waisted corsets from London, made to Charlotte's measurements by the corset-maker to the Duchess of Kent. She'd discovered the woman on her visit to Boyce.

Charlotte couldn't resist a giggle. She'd wear one of them, of course. They were lightweight, pretty and reasonably comfortable. George might enjoy unlacing her later in the day. Swept by a wave of passion, she wished that it were already tonight.

There had been trouble over the dress. Mama had favoured a great, swollen-sleeved style with elaborate embroidery but Charlotte had insisted on something much simpler.

'You're back in the early twenties!' Erin told her, surveying the drawing Charlotte had made. But the finished garment with its close-fitting bodice, round neck and long tight sleeves was graceful and suited Charlotte admirably. The honey-coloured velvet both looked and felt soft and warm, as did the small matching bonnet and the little muff to which one white flower had been pinned.

Barney had backed Charlotte's taste staunchly. 'Who wants a fashion-plate?' And he'd given her a string of dark

234

amber and a ring with an amber stone to go with the outfit, that she'd treasure far more than cold, faceted jewels.

Charlotte had bought George a spy-glass, the better to view his beloved ships. The keel of O'Ferrall's yacht was growing day by day. George's plans had been well received, though O'Ferrall had gone to ground in the last few months. He was elusive as a will-o-the wisp. It was rumoured that even the doxy from Douglas had not been able to run him to earth. Others said that she'd moved into Ravensdowne altogether and that was why she no longer drove past Black Rocks and through the streets of Port St Mary.

Erin came back, tutting that Charlotte was sitting in the kitchen when it was more fitting that they all went to eat breakfast in the proper place. Barney and the children appeared, Bart silent and contained, Rosemary excited because she was to walk up the aisle behind her mother and take the muff for the duration of the ceremony. Virginia had not wished to be an attendant. No one was able to eat as much as usual, not even Charlotte who had thought she was hungry.

The morning-room was filled with presents and goodwill messages. The twins walked round them soberly, reading all the cards. Rosemary, who was far more interested in her own wedding finery, was driving poor Miss Philips mad in the bedroom she was still to occupy for two or three weeks while her Mama was having her honeymoon. She'd resented being excluded from this event but it was Bart who'd convinced her how stupid it was to imagine she could accompany a bride and groom. The thought was farcical! She'd be far better occupied coming over to Black Rocks whenever possible and riding along the frozen track to the spot where Ben was usually to be found.

No one mentioned Karran.

There was a great hubbub while everyone demanded hot water, spruced themselves and got into their finery. Charlotte turned pale as the flower in her muff, watching Erin, Miss Philips, Bart and the twins leave in the carriage that would soon return to take her, Barney and Rosemary to the church.

'What's this?' Barney demanded. 'You look more like a ghost than a woman who's bound for the best marriage she's ever likely to make. Aren't you happy?'

'Of course I am. I keep thinking of what might go wrong, that's all.'

'Nothing will go wrong. George worships you.'

'He's too good for me.'

'Nobody's that. You won't forget your old father once you've gone?'

Charlotte kissed him and found that his cheek was wet. 'Why, Papa! You soft-hearted old thing,' she whispered. They clung together briefly.

'The carriage!' Rosemary shouted from her position at the downstairs window. 'It's all decorated with bride-ribbons.'

As Barney emerged, Charlotte holding on to his arm, those neighbours who'd not already gone to the church pelted them with rice and dried rose-petals and oohed and aahed over the bride and the pink-gowned maid who was a miniature of her mother, right to the flower on her own muff.

They rattled the short distance, each foot of the way slowing the racing of Charlotte's heart. Everything would be all right. The future loomed ahead like an enchanted wood filled with treasures.

It was as she stepped out on to the pavement in front of the church that Charlotte became aware of another carriage that drew level with their own, that gave her a glimpse of a face she scarcely recognized.

'Karran,' she whispered, aghast at that fleeting sight of a profile carved and pale as a bleached bone in a great waste of black clothing and massed shadow. But why was she so surprised? Karran had said she would see Charlotte today and Karran always kept her promise.

The organ music swelled and Charlotte, turning, saw George waiting for her at the top of the aisle. The wheels of the carriage that carried Karran on her way clattered and grew fainter.

Charlotte, her heart swelling with a mixture of love and anguish, began her slow walk towards the man she loved.

THE END

ECHOING YESTERDAY by Alexandra Manners

As passionate as *Rogue Herries* – as evocative as *Poldark* – the story of the people of The Island . . .

Clemence was a child of the Island . . . fair, wild, with an ethereal beauty she seemed at one with the moors, the wind and the surging seas. It was inevitable that the near-pagan Luke Karran would be fascinated by her – drawn to her beauty – wanting to take her silvery fragile fairness and crush it as he would a butterfly . . .

As the people of the island – the farmers, the fishermen, the miners, who were her people also – watched the unfolding of their passionate courtship, a whole new saga was born – a story as tempestuous as the elements that raged around THE ISLAND : . .

0 552 12084 7   £1.50

KARRAN KINRADE by Alexandra Manners

She was made in the image of her father, the violent, untamed gypsy who had trapped her will-o-the-wisp mother into a wild and desolate love affair . . .

But the white-faced child with the cloud of dark hair had an elusive quality all her own – a quality that captivated John Howard, made him offer her a home at Ravensdowne, made him feel she was the child he had never had.

And so, while the Islanders watched and speculated, she began a new life in the house by the sea, a life of uneasy luxury, of tensions that were to spread outwards to encompass people of THE ISLAND . . .

Second volume in *The Island series*.

0 552 12206 8   £1.50

A SELECTED LISTS OF TITLES AVAILABLE FROM CORGI BOOKS

ORDER FORM

All these books are available at your book shop or newsagent, or can be ordered direct from the publisher. Just tick the titles you want and fill in the form below.

CORGI BOOKS, Cash Sales Department, P.O. Box 11, Falmouth, Cornwall.

Please send cheque or postal order, no currency.

Please allow cost of book(s) plus the following for postage and packing:

U.K. Customers—Allow 45p for the first book, 20p for the second book and 14p for for each additional book ordered, to a maximum charge of £1.63.

B.F.P.O. and Eire—Allow 45p for the first book, 20p for the second book plus 14p per copy for the next seven books, thereafter 8p per book.

Overseas Customers—Allow 75p for the first book and 21p per copy for each additional book.

NAME (Block Letters) ....

ADDRESS ....

....